Bestselling author ZANE is
"A legend among her fellow authors." —*Today's Black Woman*

**Praise for the *New York Times* bestseller**

THE HOT BOX   WITHDRAWN

"*The Hot Box* is an emotional thrill ride that will send you hurtling from tears and raucous laughter to fiery titillation. In a league of her own, Zane fuses smoldering sex, snappy dialogue, and social consciousness into a well-crafted tale that is written in her sassy signature style. Zaniacs be warned . . . you will not be able to put this hot book down."

—Allison Hobbs, author of *Stealing Candy*

**. . . AND FOR ZANE'S OTHER UNFORGETTABLE
EROTIC NOVELS**

"Arguably not since the emergence of Nancy Friday has American letters produced a purveyor of erotica with such mass-market appeal."

—*The New York Times*

"The woman does incredible, erotic things with words. Read with a lover nearby."

—Eric Jerome Dickey

"Sweaty, grab-the-back-of-his-head-and-make-him-scream sex."

—*Entertainment Weekly*

*The Hot Box* is also available from
Simon & Schuster Audio and as an eBook

# THE
# HOT BOX

## A NOVEL

## ZANE

**ATRIA** PAPERBACK

New York  London  Toronto  Sydney  New Delhi

**ATRIA** PAPERBACK
A Division of Simon & Schuster, Inc.
1230 Avenue of the Americas
New York, NY 10020

First Atria Paperback edition August 2011

**ATRIA** PAPERBACK and colophon are trademarks of Simon & Schuster, Inc.

For information about special discounts for bulk purchases, please contact Simon & Schuster Special Sales at 1-866-506-1949 or business@simonandschuster.com.

The Simon & Schuster Speakers Bureau can bring authors to your live event. For more information or to book an event contact the Simon & Schuster Speakers Bureau at 1-866-248-3049 or visit our website at www.simonspeakers.com.

Manufactured in the United States of America

10   9

The Library of Congress has cataloged the hardcover edition as follows:

Zane.
    The hot box / by Zane.—1st Atria Books hardcover ed.
        p.   cm.
    1. Triangles (Interpersonal relations)—Fiction.   I. Title.
PS3626.A63H68   2010
813'.6—dc22

                                                        2010018602

ISBN 978-0-7434-9927-9
ISBN 978-0-7434-9928-6 (pbk)
ISBN 978-1-4165-1622-4 (ebook)

To my ninety-two-year-old Aunt Rose, my biggest fan. Thanks for making my years in Kannapolis, North Carolina, exciting, even if my only adventures were driving you to Walmart to buy housecoats and to Johnson's Superette to get the baked chicken, pinto beans, tossed salad, and ingredients for your homemade sweet potato pies and cornbread, which you would cook for twenty-five-plus people every Tuesday for more than twenty years.

In my spare time, which was plentiful in the small country setting, I was finally inspired (bored) enough to begin my writing career. So while I was born in Washington, D.C., Kannapolis, North Carolina, was the birthplace of Zane, beginning with *The Sex Chronicles: Shattering the Myth* and *Addicted*.

Here is another one to add to your collection beside your rocking chair, one side piled up with Bibles and the other piled up with my books.

"Hot Box" is a baseball drill that can be played with three or more players and two to four bases. The players take turns being fielders and runners, ultimately trying to tag the rest of the players out. People often practice this drill in real life, but instead of tossing around baseballs, they toss around hearts and emotions. Once a person becomes damaged, he or she begins to damage other people; trying to beat the other party to the punch and often orchestrating the demise of his or her relationships in order to hasten what he or she perceives as the inevitable.

More and more people have stopped believing in "lifelong" and "unconditional" love, choosing instead to live in the moment and satisfy their urges and desires by sleeping with "friends with benefits." No matter how much people try to convince themselves that casual sex is enough, no matter how much they attempt to adapt to their environment, there is still nothing purer and more satisfying than "true" love. It may not come when we want it to, or in the form that we want it to, but it does exist. Things happen when they are supposed to happen. Remember, if God doesn't give you what you want, that's because it's not what you need.

# CONTENTS

# CONTENTS

# PART ONE

# CURVEBALLS

# Lydia

DON'T know how I got so lucky. Phil and Glenn working two different shifts at the Freightliner factory was like celebrating Christmas and New Year's every fucking day. And every day was a "fucking day."

Okay, let me break it down for you. Glenn and I were in a committed relationship for three years, and everything was copacetic. He was fine, sweet, romantic, and he had a scrumptious dick. Glenn was the man . . . my man. But here's the thing. No matter how terrific he was, I still needed a little variety and extra spice/dick in my life.

When I was younger, I believed in the fairy-tale kind of love. One woman per man and vice versa. Then, by the time I was in the tenth grade, I realized that shit like that really only did happen in fairy tales. Men were dogs—straight up pit bulls, Rottweilers, and Doberman pinschers. Either they were a new breed, different from previous generations, or people swept a ton of shit underneath the rug back then. Personally, I assumed it was a combination of the two. Surely, women stayed and endured a lot of drama, cheating, and abuse because they were scared, destitute, or ashamed to have to admit to a failed relationship. A ton of women still did that, but a lot of chicks decided to stay single.

I was single—meaning unmarried—by choice. I was so sick of all the articles, blogs, and news stories preaching and whining about how the majority of African-American women would never get married. And? What was the point of getting married? If a man was going to fuck around on you, disrespect you, and possibly bring some incurable shit home to your ass, you were better off running a game on him while he thought he was running one on you. It is going to get to the point when women will have to ask themselves the question, what man would you prefer to die for because he cannot keep his dick in his pants?

The only exception was if the brother was paid—*majorly* paid. Men with money could always get it. Women of all ages, races, and walks of life were willing to drop their drawers and spread them for the right amount of money and prestige. All except for my best friend, Milena. She was on some unrealistic, mind-bending shit.

She had it all in the palm of her hand and ruined it. Well, I kind of facilitated the drama—truth be told. I didn't have a choice. If I'd kept a secret like that from her and she'd found out later on that I'd been privy to it, our friendship would've been history. Milena was not the forgiving, or forgetting, type. Those two words were simply not in her vocabulary. So I told her, and the proverbial shit hit the fan.

It was a new day though. Jacour Bryant was back in Kannapolis and Milena needed to wake the fuck up and smell the coffee. She needed to hook back up with him before some other chick pussy whipped him. Jacour was a pro-baller who had suffered a knee injury that had ended his career but not his bankroll. He'd decided to move back to the area, and the town council was having a big shindig for him the next night. I hadn't seen him yet, but the hoochie grapevine had alerted me that he was finer than ever.

All of us had seen photos of him throughout the years, and I'd even watched several Yankees games to see what had been up with him. He'd dated all of the top celebrity divas; he'd run through them like they'd been bases on a diamond. It had seemed like he'd been tied to a different woman every other month. That hadn't really surprised me. All of that pussy had been thrown at him, but Jacour wouldn't have settled down with anyone but Milena. Too bad she didn't get that memo.

Those were the very thoughts running through my mind as Phil was sucking the lining out of my pussy—my juicy, delectable pussy. My pussy was like sunshine on a rainy day. Like fireworks in the middle of a snowstorm. Like flowers in the middle of the desert. Like . . . never mind. I'm sure you get the picture. My pussy was off the fucking chain.

"Hmm, your pussy is off the chain," Phil said, reading my mind and coming up for air. "I can't get enough of these cookies."

"You're not done eating the cookies until you drink your milk along with it." I loved talking dirty. "Until I bust in your mouth, you're still on the clock."

"Hell yeah! I'll put in the work!"

Phil went back to "servicing" me and I glanced at the clock. It was a little past noon. Glenn got off at three, the same time that Phil started his shift. I was playing a dangerous game, but it felt so . . . damn . . . good. Did I mention that Phil was one of Glenn's best friends? Oops, guess not. Glenn, Phil, and Jacour were like the Three Black Musketeers. They could literally fit right into their footprints, even though the novel was written in French nearly 160 years ago and the setting was way back in the seventeenth century.

Phil was definitely Athos. Even though he was the same age as

Glenn and Jacour, he acted a lot older than them . . . and looked it. He hit the whiskey hard, a side effect of living in a small town without shit else to do. Phil was handsome but very secretive and drowned his sorrows in liquor, exactly like Athos. I was glad that he used liquor to cope with his shit. I did not have to listen to his problems; just fuck him.

Glenn was damn near Porthos's twin. He was a bit extroverted, extremely honest, and slightly gullible. He could also eat a sister out of house and home, like Porthos. But instead of being a bit chunky, he worked out religiously to get rid of the excessive calories he inhaled. He never actually ate; he would inhale that shit . . . real talk.

That meant Jacour was Aramis Jr. In the novel, Aramis was portrayed as ambitious and unsatisfied. He was arrogant and loved intrigue and women. If that wasn't Jacour, my name wasn't Lydia Sterling.

I had this way of allowing my mind to wander to the strangest places while I was fucking. Somehow, imagining the Three Musketeers, along with their sidekick, d'Artagnan, fucking me in a barn back in the seventeenth century made me climax all over Phil's face. Athos had me bent down on my knees, slobbering all over his dick as he lay in the hay, while Porthos was hitting it doggie-style and slapping my ass like a true swashbuckler. Aramis was standing over us, jerking off and shooting a load on my back, and d'Artagnan was stroking an elephantine dick, moaning and waiting on his turn to ram his billy club up my ass.

"Oh shit!" I screamed out as I exploded. My thighs were shaking with the aftershocks as Phil lapped up all of my juices like a good little doggie.

"Can I pound you with this big cock now?" he asked when he was through.

"A cock is a chicken," I said. "Only dicks can enter my temple of immense sexual pleasure."

"Cock. Dick. Zipper Ripper. My Ramburglar. Whatever you want to call it, I'm 'bout to blow your back out with it."

"Damn, make it bounce, Daddy!"

The nasty talk was really what turned me on the most about Phil. Glenn would not even send me a sexy text message, much less say that kind of stuff to me in person. Plus, even though Glenn could definitely put a pounding on my pussy, he always wanted to be on top. Fuck that! I loved to ride.

I pushed Phil over onto his back and climbed on my saddle. "Hee haw!" I exclaimed as I started riding him cowgirl fashion.

I didn't give a damn what anyone said. I could cum the hardest when I was on top. A man hitting it from the back could give it a lot of depth, but unless his dick was shaped like a candy cane, he was *not* hitting the G-spot. Sometimes I could get close to the G-spot in the reverse cowgirl position, but I recognized what it felt like when that part of me was touched, and it wasn't happening with a dick.

Now, when I was on top, it was all good. All the right ingredients were there. I was in complete control and, nine times out of ten, he could last longer on his back. Besides, I didn't want dude sweating all over me; hell to the triple no. If anyone was going to drip sweat that day, it was going to be me. It was bad enough that I had to put up with that from Glenn.

A lot of women think that you're supposed to pounce up and down on a dick. Not! That's not riding. Men might be feeling it, but that breaks the continuity with the stimulation on my clit. Rocking my hips did the trick every time. I'd imagine myself riding an actual horse bareback, its massive body moving below mine, bouncing me gently as it trots, my clit rubbing up against it. The heartbeat of the horse between my legs was the same as the throbbing of a dick while I was riding one. Yes! There wasn't anything like it.

Phil became that horse and took me for a smooth ride. "Um, hell yeah!"

"Work this dick, baby." Phil grabbed my ass and started pounding on my cheeks like an African drum. "Take all this dick."

My cut came on the radio: "My Body's Hungry" by Teena Marie. My body was hungry as hell, too.

"I wonder if I'm a sex addict," I said to Phil, who couldn't have cared less if I was as long as he was getting pussy on the regular. "You think I am?"

"Wha . . . what?" he replied breathlessly.

"Do you think I'm a sex addict?" I asked as I started gyrating my hips like a professional belly dancer . . . or stripper.

"I *think* you're fucking fine, and I *know* your pussy's the best in town."

"How you know all that?" I slapped him playfully on the face. "You done fucked every woman in town?"

"No." He paused to catch his breath, then grinned. "Only half of them."

That motherfucker was lying. I had him so pussy whipped that he couldn't even see straight.

"Yeah? Well, I bet they didn't get it in with you like this."

That's when I fucked that fool into submission. He curled up in the fetal position by the time I finished with his Ramburglar, or whatever shit he was poppin'.

"It's after one," I informed Phil a little while later. "You need to bounce."

"I've got two hours left. Let me hit the shower first."

"You know I don't play that."

"How come you don't ever let me take a shower after we fuck? You let me do it before."

"That's because no funky-ass bodies—or balls—hit my sheets. You're not coming up in here after working an eight-hour factory shift, smelling like a muskrat, and touching me. You can take an after-fucking shower at your own crib."

"You're a trip, Lydia."

"So are you, *Phil*. We're both doing the wrong thing when it comes to Glenn. Don't front like it's only me."

"That's not what I meant. It's not about Glenn. It's about how cold and callous you can be at times."

I propped myself up on my elbow and stared into his eyes. "Look, you're my jump-off and I'm yours. It's as simple as that."

"Jump-offs don't last as long as we have and—"

I pulled the pillow from under his head. "You're getting too damn comfortable. Get going; I still have to change the bedding and air this place out before Glenn gets home."

Oops, I forgot to mention that Glenn and I were actually shacking. Yeah, I was lowdown, but Phil had a roommate and there was no way we were getting it in at his place. Briscoe was the biggest gossiper in town; fuck what you heard about women putting business out in the streets. He was the TMZ of Kannapolis.

Phil reluctantly got up and started putting on his clothes. "You want me to come through in the morning?"

"Nope. I got something to do in the morning."

"I don't have to stay long."

"Five minutes would be too long." I paused and wiggled my nose. My bedroom smelled like stone-cold fucking. I was going to have to open up all the windows and spray an entire can of Indian Money up in that bitch before Glenn got home.

"Whatever, Lydia. Like I said, you're a trip."

"Have you seen Jacour since he got back?"

"Yeah, we all hung out last night after I got off work. Glenn didn't tell you?"

"No, but that's cool. I was wondering where he was."

"Humph, you've got a lot of nerve, clocking Glenn's moves."

"Is he cheating on me, Phil?"

Phil looked at me and laughed. "You don't really expect me to respond, do you?"

"Hell yes, I do."

Phil shrugged. "Hell if I know. Maybe, maybe not."

"Well, if I ever find out who the bitch is, I'm cutting her."

Phil smirked. "I'm out of here." He turned to leave. "Call me if you need anything. I'll be home by midnight, as usual."

"Wait, one more question," I said, sitting up in the bed and letting the comforter fall off my bare chest.

"What?" Phil crossed his arms with much attitude.

"It's not about Glenn. What do you think about when we're fucking?"

He shrugged. "I think about us fucking."

"You don't fantasize about other women, or worry about busting a nut too quick, or keeping it up?"

"No, no, and no. I think about how good your pussy feels. I've got to go."

"Oh, now you're in a rush?"

"Damn right. I can't shower here and I have to be at work on time. Plus, you need to do what's good to get this place straight before my boy gets home."

Phil left, and a moment later I heard his car leaving the driveway. The good part about where Glenn and I lived was that it was down a dirt road and no one could spot people coming or going. Otherwise, Phil and I would have been busted ages ago.

Glenn got home about four and I had dinner ready for him by five. Lasagna, garlic bread, and salad: his favorite meal. We put in some overtime that night in bed. He must've felt guilty about being out late the night before and not telling me where he'd been. I waited for him to bring it up. Like I said earlier, Glenn was like Porthos; honest.

After I'd sucked him off real slow and lovely, he filled me in on everything that was going on with Jacour, who hadn't been home in years. Glenn had spoken to him on the phone about once a week, but now that Jacour was back, I was hoping they wouldn't be running the streets every night, hitting the bar scene in Charlotte. That was all I fucking needed; my man hanging out with a famous athlete around a bunch of money-hungry hoes. Shit, most of the chicks would fall over a man if he bought them a few drinks. Jacour in a Charlotte nightclub would damn near cause a stampede. My baby wasn't going to be riding shotgun with Jacour when that shit went down. If he brought home even one photo of Jacour and him standing in front of a spray-painted backdrop with a bunch of sluts hanging all over them, I was pulling out my box cutter. There was one surefire way to make sure that wouldn't happen.

"Does Jacour still have the hots for Milena?" I asked Glenn as we were falling asleep in each other's arms.

"Jacour still *loves* Milena, but I told him that's a wrap."

I sat up and stared at him. "Why'd you tell him that?"

"Oh, she still feeling him?"

I sighed and lay back down. "She hasn't said that *exactly*, but once they see each other, you never know what might happen."

"I'm gonna call him first thing in the morning and tell him to ask her to his party. You think she'll go?"

I shrugged. "He has a good shot."

"Cool," Glenn said and then turned over. I hated when he did that, but he preferred to sleep on his right side and I had this attachment to the left side of the bed.

I stared at the ceiling. Milena couldn't stand Jacour, but I needed her to come to her senses.

# Milena

ALWAYS realized that letting myself go would eventually catch up with me. Looking like a cave witch, with my hair strewn all over the place, wearing baggy overalls practically every day, and gaining more than thirty pounds over my ideal body weight were all mechanisms to prevent men from paying me any attention. If men never noticed me, they could never hurt me. It sounds ridiculous, but it actually made sense to me at the time—eight years ago—when my heart was broken for the first, and last, time.

The long-suffering winds of August in Kannapolis, North Carolina, would make anyone want to scream. We'd been enduring a heat wave of ninety degrees minimum for the past week. It didn't help matters any that I spent half of my day outside, keeping up the health of animals and trying to save those that were sick. Ever since I was a child, I wanted to be a veterinarian. In the third grade, I found a dead bird on my way home from school. It was raining that day, and the poor little thing was lying in the middle of a dirt road, sopping wet and as dead as a doornail. I put it in my tin lunch pail and brought it home.

My mother thought it was cute when I said, "It's one of God's creatures!"

My father looked like he wanted to scream.

I put it in a black plastic box and placed it out by our fence, determined to bring it back to life. After a few days, when I raced outside one morning to check on my patient, both the bird and the box had disappeared. My father told me that my love and affection had worked and that the bird had been reincarnated. He tried to convince me that it had spread its wings and left to find its family. Being eight years old, I might've believed it except for one thing; the box was also gone.

"Daddy, what happened to the box?" I remember asking.

He sat there at the kitchen table, stirring his coffee and looking dumbfounded for a few seconds. "Uh . . . the bird took it with him. So he can sleep in it."

I let the spoon topple into my bowl of oatmeal and stared at him. "But how could he carry the box?"

He tried to come up with something right quick but decided it was useless. "I saw that the bird was gone when I came in from the factory last night. I threw the box away, hoping you wouldn't notice."

My mother was standing by the stove and cleared her throat before wiping her hands on the bottom of her apron. "Milena, you need to get cleaned up. The school bus will be here in a couple of minutes."

I slowly got up from the table and went to the bathroom to brush my teeth. When I came back out to the kitchen, my parents were whispering in hushed tones. By that time, I realized that Daddy had thrown the bird away . . . inside the box. I was eight; not retarded.

That was the beginning of my fascination with animals. A fascination that flourished into a career. Milena Clark, D.V.M. Most veterinarians deal with pet medicine and work predominantly on dogs, cats, birds, and other household pets. I was knowledgeable in treating all of those, but I specialized in production medicine. I worked on dairy cattle, beef cattle, sheep, swine, and poultry. I also was qualified to do equine medicine and worked on all types of horses.

It was simply my bad luck that I was outside, chasing Mr. Slater's prize-winning pig, Bessie, through the mud when Jacour pulled up in a brand-new Phantom Rolls-Royce. My best friend, Lydia, was sitting beside him in the front. I wanted to wring her neck.

Mr. Slater shielded his eyes with his right hand as they pulled down my gravel driveway. "Isn't that Jacour Bryant?"

"I suppose so," I said with disdain.

As Jacour put his luxury vehicle in park and cut the engine, I finally tackled Bessie and got a chain around her so I could tie her to a post to examine her. I was a hot mess, with mud all over my overalls, and my hair was frizzy and wild from the heat.

Lydia jumped out of the car with a shit grin on her face. "Hey, sis! Look who I found in town!"

Mr. Slater started chuckling. "Didn't you and that fella used to be an item?"

There was no way I was going to respond to that. "Mr. Slater, why don't you come back in the morning to get Bessie? I'm sure you need to get back to your farm."

"Well, I guess that'll be all right." He spit out some chewing tobacco, and it made my stomach turn. For the life of me, I couldn't comprehend how a woman could kiss a man who chewed tobacco and spit it out. "Be here around seven."

"Okay."

I watched Jacour climb out of the driver's side, looking like a black Adonis. Six-two, flawless cappuccino skin, almost zero body fat, and curly black hair. I was sick!

Mr. Slater spoke for a brief moment to Jacour as they crossed paths. Lydia had rushed up to me so she could whisper.

"Aw, sookie sookie now. Your man is back."

"He's not my man, and I knew he was coming back. That's all everyone in this small-ass town has been talking about," I stated sarcastically. "The return of the hometown hero."

"Be nice to him," Lydia warned. "I ran into him at the gas station and he asked me to show him where you live."

"And your dumb ass showed him? Great!"

"Pull the fangs in, Milena. Give the man a chance."

I leered at her. "Do you see what I look like?"

Lydia looked me up and down. "You look the same way you look every day."

I rubbed some mud on her white T-shirt. "Now we're twins."

She jumped back a step. "Why'd you do that?"

"Because you should've warned me that you were bringing him over here."

"You should've known Jacour was going to blaze a trail to your ass the second he came back here. I ran into him and he wanted to see you. Consider me security, in case something gets set off, like you shoving an electric cow prodder up his ass."

Lydia thought that shit was humorous; I didn't. The idea sounded good to me.

"There's no way that I—" I stopped in midsentence. Mr. Slater was pulling off in his pickup and Jacour was less than five feet from us.

"Milena!" He flashed his charming smile at me and I practically melted. "What's up, baby?"

Sure, showing Jacour basic human kindness would've been the right thing to do, but I wasn't about to pretend like nothing had ever happened.

"You're trespassing!" I blurted out as he tried to reach his arms around me for a hug and, heaven forbid, a kiss. "No one invited you here."

Jacour looked from me to Lydia and then back at me. "Are you for real?"

"I've always been real. You're the phony-ass piece of shit."

"Milena, it's been eight years. Can't we put that past us?"

"Yeah, can't we?" Lydia interjected. Then she leaned in to whisper in my ear. "Look at his fine ass!"

Jacour grinned, obviously overhearing her comment. "I've missed you . . . *so much.*"

"Yeah, that's obvious from all the text messages, emails, and birthday cards you've sent me."

"So your parents did give you my cards, huh?"

Before I could respond with something smart, Lydia said, "She keeps them in a scrapbook."

"No, I don't! Don't tell that lie!"

Bessie started making rank noises and then farted. Dirty little bitch lit up the entire sky.

Jacour twitched his nose and Lydia coughed. What a Kodak moment!

I glared at Lydia and then looked at Jacour. "I do *not* have the cards in a scrapbook. In fact, I have no idea where they are. I guess they're still around here someplace."

"As long as you received them and realized that I was constantly thinking of you, that's all that matters." Jacour gestured toward my house. "Nice place. Aren't you going to invite us in? For a glass of water or something?"

"Actually, I need to—"

"I'm definitely parched. Did you make any of that bomb-ass lemonade today?" Lydia was halfway to the front door before she had finished talking. She disappeared inside.

"Come on in," I said reluctantly. When I turned to go toward the door, I could sense Jacour's eyes boring a hole in my ass. "But you can't stay long. I have a lot of animals to attend to."

"So your animal hospital is out back?"

"Yes. The pig took off, so that's why we were out in the front yard. I'll move her later."

I couldn't believe that we were talking about a pig after eight years of being incommunicado. Granted, Jacour had tried his best to contact me, but any interaction between us would've been pointless. They say that pain never lasts always, but I was as pissed as I had been on my wedding day.

# Milena

THERE was no way that it was real. It had to be some sort of
sick joke—a prank that one of Jacour's friends had come up
with during a drunken stupor.

Lydia was standing behind me, rubbing my left shoulder gently,
as if that was going to lessen the blow. "I feel bad about being the
bearer of such devastation, but there were no options." She sighed,
her minty breath tickling my ear. "A true friend won't allow you to
make one of the biggest mistakes of your life."

I took my eyes off the laptop screen for a few seconds and stared
at Kayla and Donita, both of them rendered speechless by the unexpected turn of events.

I glanced back at the screen and could barely stand to watch. "It
can't be him. It just can't," I whispered. "Someone doctored this
shit."

"Milena, don't curse in church!" Donita exclaimed, finally finding her tongue. "God don't like ugly!"

"Donita, that's the least fucking problem," Lydia said, lashing
out at her. "This is Milena's big day and—"

"This *was* my big day." I swatted at the laptop with my grand-mother's handkerchief—my something old—and faced all three of them. "Now it's the worst day of my entire life."

Kayla walked over to me and gave me a tender hug. "It's going to be okay. We're here for you."

"I know," I replied, and then kissed her on the cheek. "All of you are always here for me."

"Are you mad at me?" Lydia asked.

"No, I'm not mad at you." I hugged her. "You did the right thing. I would've done the same for you."

"So are you going to go through with it?" Donita stared at me like she was serious.

"Are you insane?" Lydia asked her and damn near slapped her. "Of course she's not going through with it."

Donita shrugged. "All I'm saying is that everyone makes mis-takes. After all, last night *was* his last night of freedom. From what I hear, all men get laid at their bachelor parties."

"That's a good point," Kayla interjected. "It's not the same thing as cheating. He was simply having a good time. Remember, we also had a good time last night."

Lydia placed both of her hands on her hips, a clear indication that she was about to lose it. "We had a good night, but the night didn't culminate with Milena spreading her legs or sucking dicks. Did it?" Kayla and Donita both stared at each other but didn't respond. "Did it? Did either of you hookers see Milena fucking some other dude last night? If you did, I must've missed it. We got drunk, had a couple of male strippers give us a little teaser, but Milena's drawers *never* left her ass."

"Ease up on them," I told Lydia. "They're only trying to be helpful."

There was a lot going on in the dressing area of The First Calvary Baptist Church that afternoon. Lydia didn't feel that Kayla and Donita should be standing there in the beautiful cherry red bridesmaid gowns that I had spent months picking out. She'd accused both of them of being backstabbers, unworthy of standing by my side as I exchanged vows to commit the rest of my life to Jacour Bryant. Both of them, at some point in time throughout our youth, had tried to date him—or simply fuck him—but neither had succeeded. But that was all child's play. We were kids in a small-ass town and Jacour was the finest thing walking. The only thing that mattered to me was that he hadn't done it. They were still my friends and had covered my back more than they'd stabbed me in it since elementary school. Still, Lydia wasn't feeling either of them, and that had served as the basis for much drama during the planning stages for the wedding of the century. I had heard that jealousy among friends and relatives could practically destroy a wedding; now I realized it firsthand.

Jacour had recently been drafted by the New York Yankees. A four-year, eighty-five-million-dollar contract would've been a big deal anywhere, but in Kannapolis, North Carolina, land area of 29.9 square miles, population of 42,581, with a median household income of $35,532, and only 12 percent of the residents obtaining a degree past a high school diploma, it was a *huge fucking* deal.

I'd been in love with Jacour since junior high and we'd attended undergrad together at Duke University. Now we were on top of the world. I was headed to veterinarian school, and he was about to become the biggest star player in Major League Baseball. I'd been planning to attend the North Carolina State University College of Veterinary Medicine, but after Jacour had been drafted by the Yankees, I'd applied and been accepted to the College of Veterinary Medicine at Cornell University. We were planning to set up house in Ithaca, New York, and maintain a lavish apartment in New York City. Eighty-five million dollars could provide a lot of lavish, after all.

Jacour was going to do the majority of the commuting while school was in session for me. In the summer and on the weekends and during school breaks, I would be in New York City. It was a great plan. We were in love, and we trusted each other, until I saw him fucking some sluts at his bachelor party.

"Okay, fine; I'll *ease up*," Lydia said sarcastically, breaking me from my train of thought. "But you can't walk out there and marry Jacour."

Donita took an aggressive step toward Lydia. "You're not her mother! You can't tell her what to do!"

It was like we had conjured my mother up. Before Lydia could respond to Donita, there was a tap at the door and Momma opened it without waiting for a reply.

"Mrs. Clark!" Kayla exclaimed as Donita tried to shield the laptop screen, where some tramp was slobbering all over Jacour's dick. "How's it going?"

Lydia slammed the laptop closed before Momma could make out Jacour whispering, "Oh shit! Work it, baby!" Thank goodness the volume wasn't turned up too high.

Momma looked stunning in her red and ivory gown. My being her only child, she had been waiting for the moment to strut her stuff with pride on my big day. Everyone always knew that Jacour and I would end up married; our parents, our friends, and us. Now it was never to be, and I had to be the one to break my mother's heart, as mine had been broken.

"You young ladies look fabulous!" Momma exclaimed, a smile like a beacon spread across her face. "The sanctuary is packed." She looked at Donita. "You did an incredible job with the decorations, Donita."

"Thanks, Mrs. Clark." Donita cleared her throat and stared at all of us. "So, what now?"

I stood up and sighed. "Do you all mind leaving Momma and me alone for a few moments? I need to speak with her in private."

Kayla and Donita looked relieved and made a bumrush for the door, almost knocking each other down and tripping over their gowns. Lydia stood frozen in place.

"Lydia, you too. Please."

"You sure? I can stay and help you out with this, if you want."

I patted her on the arm. "I'll be fine."

"Are you mad at me?" she asked.

"No, I'm *grateful* for you."

Lydia tried to force a smile and then walked out. Momma stared at her as she passed. There is one thing about mothers that can never be denied: they possess a bullshit detection radar that's out of this world.

Lydia closed the door behind her as she left, leaving Momma and me standing there face-to-face.

"Were those girls in here fighting?" she asked. "They better not be showing out on your special day."

"No, nothing like that."

"Why'd Lydia ask if you were angry with her?"

"Lydia's my best friend and she only has my best interest in mind—*always*."

Momma seemed prepared to drop it and started fixing a strand of hair that was dangling in front of my left eye. "You look stunning, Milena! This is going to be the perfect wedding, leading up to the perfect marriage!"

My hands started shaking. "Momma, you might need to take a seat."

"Don't scare me like this." She sat down and stared up at me. "What's wrong?"

I took a seat beside her on the embroidered antique chaise. "Something happened last night." I took her hand, more in an attempt to calm my nerves than anything else. "Something with Jacour."

Momma giggled. "Who filled your head with such foolishness? Jacour's fine; I just saw him."

*I bet he is fine,* I thought, *after having his dick sucked and ridden half the damn night!*

"He looks great, smells great, and he can't wait to marry you. I don't think I've ever seen him so excited, even when he landed that huge contract."

The sad thing about the entire scenario was that what Momma was saying was probably true. I did believe that Jacour loved me, but he obviously didn't appreciate me and he damn sure didn't respect me . . . or his damn self.

"Momma, how would you feel if I decided to go to North Carolina State for veterinary school after all?"

"But why would you do that?" she asked, stunned. "Cornell is one of the best schools in the world, and it's a closer commute to New York City from there."

I took a deep breath. "Jacour will be moving to New York . . . without me."

I sat there and watched the meaning behind my statement sink into Momma's head.

"Why would you do this? *Today?*" she asked sternly. "What could the boy have possibly done?"

"Take one guess!"

Momma glared at me. "And you would throw all of this away, your future, because Jacour slept with another woman?"

*She caught on quick.* "He slept with more than one woman, at his bachelor party."

I couldn't believe the words that left Momma's mouth next. "All men have sex at their bachelor parties. Even I know that, but that's not considered cheating."

I pulled my hand away from hers in dismay. "Why isn't it considered cheating? To me, having sex with someone else the night before our wedding is the most disrespectful act of all. And then to do it when all of his friends were around. Hell, one of them even taped it. Lydia ended up with the tape, Momma."

Momma grew irate. "And that idiot showed it to you?"

"She's not an idiot. She's my friend, and she did the right thing."

I stood up and straightened out my expensive lace wedding gown—the wedding gown that I'd always dreamed of. I stared at the eight-carat diamond ring on my finger and somehow felt even more disrespected. How could he present me with something so exquisite and then fuck some common whores?

"I can't walk out there in front of all those people and put on pretenses," I continued. "Half of them know about what happened."

"Half of them don't know shit!" Momma said. I'm not sure who was more shocked that she had cursed; her or me. I'd never heard her curse in my entire twenty-two years on earth. "You're making too big of a deal out of this! That man loves you! We have hundreds of people waiting out there, and you *will not* embarrass your father and me by not going through with this wedding!"

"Momma, I can't marry Jacour!"

"You can, and you will!"

"I would rather be embarrassed now than a few months down the road when we go through an ugly divorce!"

"There will be no divorce!" Momma started fanning herself

with a program from the wedding that was never going to happen. She calmed down a little and lowered her voice. "You've lost
your senses, and you need to get them back within the next"—she
glanced at her watch—"fifteen minutes. Jacour is worth nearly a
hundred million dollars, and you'll never find another man like
him. *Never*. Think about what you're doing, Milena."

"I don't care how much money Jacour's contract is worth. I
stuck by him for over a decade when he didn't have a dime. Playing
professional baseball doesn't give him a pass on trampling over my
feelings."

Momma was quiet for a few seconds. I could see her mind
switching gears, trying to find a weak spot. Then her brain cells
landed on Daddy. "What about your father? This will kill him."

"No, it won't," I stated sarcastically. "Daddy's as healthy as
an ox."

"It will. You're his baby, his only baby. If you don't marry Jacour, he'll never be able to give you away."

"What are you implying?" I asked, getting her hint. "Are you
trying to say that if I don't marry Jacour, I'll never find another
man to marry me?"

"No, Milena, I'm not. What I *am* saying is that you'll never find
another man with an eighty-five-million-dollar baseball contract to
marry. Not in this hick town."

"You want me to marry for money?"

"I want you to marry for love . . . and money. Jesus, you act like
I'm encouraging you to marry some man you picked up in a bar
last week. You and Jacour have been together since you were kids.
You can't throw him underneath the bus because he made one
mistake."

"Oh yeah? Watch me!"

I stormed out of the dressing room before Momma could get

up off the chaise, and I damn near toppled down the steps to the church vestibule, where about a dozen people were still entering and getting programs. They were startled to see me and quickly eked out "congratulations" and "you look beautiful" comments. I could hear Momma on the steps, calling out my name as she tried to get to me.

I stomped into the sanctuary with the veil on the top of my head instead of covering my face, and without my bouquet. Everyone looked shocked. My two flower girls, Jacour's younger cousins, tried to run out in front of me and sprinkle flowers as my aunt Susan started playing Mendelssohn's "Wedding March."

I held my palm up toward her, motioning for her to cut the music, and everyone froze in place. My father started walking toward me as all of the commotion started. Lydia, Donita, and Kayla appeared from the area to the left of the altar, and Jacour, along with his best man and brother, Jante, and his two best friends, Phil and Glenn, appeared from the right side.

"What's wrong, baby?" Daddy asked once he reached me.

Momma was right on my tail. "Sylvester, there's been a misunderstanding. You need to take Milena someplace and talk to her."

"Talk to her about what?" Daddy's eyes rotated back between Momma and me. "What's the matter?"

By that time, Jacour was standing beside Daddy. "Milena, what are you doing?"

I lost it. "What am I doing? What the fuck were you doing last night?"

My grandmother, Honey Bear, almost fainted in her seat as my grandfather, Papa Bear, tried to hold her up.

Mr. and Mrs. Bryant were the next to join the pile congregating in the middle of the pews. "Jacour, what's happening here?" Mr. Bryant demanded.

"Why don't you tell him?" I said to Jacour. "Tell them all about your bachelor party sex marathon."

"Oh my God!" Mrs. Bryant yelled out and then held her right hand over her chest. "Jacour! You didn't?"

Jacour tried to take my hand, but I yanked it away from him. "Milena, let's go outside and get some fresh air. We need to talk."

"Talk!" I started poking his chest with my index finger. "I don't ever want to talk to or see you again!"

Jacour tried to grab me and I lashed out at him, striking him with my engagement ring. It was an accident, and for a second, I felt horrible when a little blood started trickling down his cheek.

At the sight of a drop of blood, Honey Bear did faint in her seat then, for real.

"Milena, it's our wedding day!" Jacour exclaimed. "All of our friends and family are here . . . *watching us.*"

I glanced around the sanctuary at all of the shocked expressions. A few chicks were smirking; jealous tramps.

"Let's go through with the ceremony and then we can talk about this later," Jacour pleaded. "On our honeymoon. Italy is waiting for us. Haven't you always wanted to go there?"

I couldn't believe his trifling ass.

"Take those tramps from last night with you to Italy, and they can live with you in New York, too. I'm staying right here . . . in North Carolina, and going to State."

Mrs. Bryant started rubbing my back. I felt sorry for her. She and I had a genuine bond, and now Jacour had gone and fucked everything up.

"Milena, I'm sorry that my son has hurt you," she said. "But the two of you *can* work this out."

I turned to her. "He let them tape him . . . tape him having sex in front of all his friends. The same friends that planned to stand up beside him at the altar." I stared at the so-called groomsmen, who had all pretended to care about me, and sighed. "I love him," I said as I gazed into Jacour's eyes. "But I can never trust him. It's over."

I walked slowly out of the church, past everyone who would be gossiping about my misfortune until the end of time, got into the limousine that was supposed to have been taking my new husband and me to the Charlotte-Douglas airport, and instructed the driver to drop me off at my parents' house.

Part of me wanted to cry. The other part of me felt a sense of relief. Oftentimes God will step in right at the last moment to prevent you from making major mistakes. If Jacour was capable of doing something like that the night before he planned to promise to love, honor, and cherish me forever, he was capable of anything. At least I would still be close to my friends and family. That had to count for something.

# Lydia

MILENA was on the other side of through with me for bringing Jacour over to her crib. That was cool though; I was on a
mission. For eight long, stressful years I'd watched Milena embark
upon a path of self-destruction. Sure, she was successful in her
practice, but how do you go from being a chick that was supposed
to be married to a gatrillionaire and shopping on Park Avenue to
patching up nasty pigs and funky-ass horses?

Now I'll be the first to admit that I was the main cheerleader
when she broke off the wedding. The fact that Jacour would fuck
around on my girl like that at his bachelor party, allow Phil's ass
to tape it—who in turn gave it to me—and then be beaming at the
church like "Mr. Innocent" had pissed me off. How did I get the tape
so quickly? Even back then, I was fucking Phil down into the mat-
tress every chance I could get. There was something about "secret
fucking" that was a huge turn-on. Phil and I had been going at it
since our senior year in high school and, to that day, no one was
privy to it; not even Milena.

I suspected that Jacour knew, but then again, since I was in a committed relationship with Glenn, he couldn't have. He would've been happy as hell to spill my beans in reciprocity for telling his dirt. As the three of us sat in Milena's living room, sipping ice water because she was out of my favorite lemonade, you could've heard a mouse pissing on a cotton ball.

Jacour was staring at Milena, and she was boring a hole through me. I smirked and took another sip of my water.

"It was my luck to run into Lydia at the gas station," Jacour said, setting his glass down on the coffee table.

That was actually a lie. Glenn had called Jacour, as I had requested, and told him that Milena was still feeling him and that he should meet me at the gas station. I met him and rode out there to her house with him, to make the charade look good. Milena was no dummy, and I needed my car to be at the BP, in case she insisted on giving me a ride back to it.

He stared around Milena's cozy quarters. "Nice place. You were always such a wonderful decorator. Remember the furniture you picked out for the apartment in New York? I still have it."

Milena half-giggled and half-hissed. "So why are you telling me that?" She glared at Jacour. "What does that have to do with me?"

"I'm only trying to make conversation."

Milena guzzled down the rest of her water and slammed her glass down on an end table. "Why are you here?"

"The town council's having a welcome home party for Jacour tonight," I interjected. "Everyone's coming."

"I know about the party," Milena said. "How could I not? What I meant is why is he *here*? In my house?"

Jacour flashed that priceless grin of his. "I want you to accompany me to the party."

"You can't be serious!" Milena stood up and walked over to the window. Steam was coming out of her ears.

Jacour got up and walked up behind her, touching her on the shoulder. I watched the entire scene like a bargain matinee.

Milena jerked her shoulder away. "I'm not going to the party, and I'm *certainly* not going with you."

"Why not?" Jacour asked.

Milena turned to face him. "Why not? I'm not about to show up on your arm at a party in front of all the people you embarrassed me around eight years ago."

"I didn't embarrass you; you embarrassed *me*, Milena."

Milena's mouth flew open. "Oh, don't even go there." She pushed him out of her way and came and sat beside me on the sofa so she could pinch my leg.

"Ow!" I slapped her hand away. "Stop being violent!"

"I can't believe you!" Milena watched Jacour cross the room and stand in front of us. "You both need to leave and get ready for your party. I'm sure Mata Hari over here is planning to attend."

"Of course I'm going," I said. "Glenn's one of Jacour's best friends."

Maybe that was why I'd suddenly had a change of heart about Milena's predicament and was urging her to forgive Jacour. After all, I was fucking both of Jacour's best friends. Phil obviously knew about Glenn, but Glenn had no clue that I was giving up the cooch to Phil long before he'd ever gotten a whiff of it. I'd never told Milena and never planned to tell her. I envisioned the lectures, the judgment, and the never-ending "what the fuck are you thinking" comments.

Jacour stared at Milena. "Is there anything I can do to convince you? I heard you're still single . . . and so am I at the moment."

Men say the dumbest things. Jacour was doing fine until he added "at the moment," a reminder that he'd been ramming pussies the entire eight years he'd been gone. Milena was well aware of that already. He could've kept that comment to himself.

"Let's go together and dance the night away," he added. "We used to rip up the dance floor. Our parents would be so excited. Your parents already RSVP'd. It can be like old times."

That's when the biggest lie on earth came out of Milena's mouth. "I don't know what you *heard*, or where you heard it . . ." Milena paused and stared at me. "But I'm *not* single, and my man wouldn't take kindly to me going someplace with you or anyone else."

Jacour looked like he had been hit in the head with a baseball. "What man? Who is he?"

"That's none of your business."

*It must not be any of your business either,* I thought, *because you don't have a damn man.*

Jacour glared in my direction. "Why didn't you tell me that she was hooked up?"

"I . . . I . . . ," I stuttered.

"It's not Lydia's responsibility to spread my business. I prefer to keep the intimate details of my life private; she knows that."

Jacour burst out laughing and then waved his index finger in the air. "You're lying. I can always tell when you're lying. Your nose twitches a little bit to the left."

"I'm not lying," Milena protested. "You're so arrogant that you want to think I'm not telling the truth. While you were traipsing off with all the famous singers, movie stars, and spread all over the headlines, you certainly didn't expect me to be sitting here twiddling my thumbs."

"Don't forget that stripper," I found myself interjecting.

The *National Enquirer* had run this story about Jacour getting caught up with some stripper from Magic City in Atlanta. Men never learn. As soon as those hooker-types find out that a man doesn't plan to wife them, they spread their shit all over the press for a few bucks and fifteen minutes of fame. Now I was reminding Milena of shit. I guess men aren't the only ones who say the dumbest things, but I couldn't help myself with that one. That stripper was a straight-up skeezer.

"Yeah, the stripper," Milena repeated. "She was some piece of work."

Jacour seemed to be trying to come up with a swift "Plan B" to schmooze Milena over. "You look nice," he said. "Very nice. I like that little bit of new weight on you."

*That is the last fuckin' thing you should've said, dufus,* I thought. Milena was very self-conscious about her appearance.

"So does my man," Milena stated with disdain.

"Does your man have a name, or do you just call him 'my man'?"

"Of course he has a name."

Jacour and I both waited with baited breath for Milena to reveal the name of her imaginary boyfriend. When she didn't, Jacour asked, "So, are you going to tell me?"

"What for? You don't know him."

"I might. I know a lot of people. Does he live in Kannapolis?"

"No, he lives in Charlotte," Milena replied.

Now I realized for sure she was making all this shit up. Milena never ventured to Charlotte unless it was a die-hard emergency. Even though it was less than forty miles away, it might as well have been four hundred. Over the years, I'd tried to get her to go clubbing or to concerts or plays. Shit, I couldn't even get her to go to a museum in Charlotte. And since she never went there, neither did I. Glenn's middle name should've been "Homebody."

"I know a lot of people in Charlotte, too," Jacour insisted. "What's dude's name?"

Milena paused and then smirked. "His name is Randolph. Randolph William Henderson the third."

"Wow, that's a big-ass name!" Jacour chuckled. "How long have you been seeing him?"

Milena sighed. "Long enough to be madly in love with him . . . and him with me."

Jacour glanced at me. "You know Randolph, Lydia?"

I could feel Milena's eyes warning me to make some shit up, or else. "Yeah, I know Randolph. He's cool; a good guy."

"What does he do?"

"He does him," Milena said. "Stop asking so many questions. Shouldn't you be getting ready for your party?"

"The party's not for nine more hours, Milena." Jacour stared at her for a few seconds. "I have an idea. Why don't you bring Randolph to the party? Unless, of course, you're ashamed of him."

"The only person that I'm ashamed I ever dated is you." Milena stood up and walked toward the door. "I'm afraid the two of you have to leave. I have several animals that need to be attended to out back."

"So are you bringing your fantasy man to the party?" Jacour asked, his voice dripping with sarcasm. "I'm sure *everyone* would like to meet him."

That's when Milena did the stupidest thing ever. "Sure, why not? We'll stop through."

Jacour walked to the door and I got up to follow him. Milena was staring at me while Jacour's back was turned. I mouthed the words "What the hell?"

Milena frowned. "I'll see you guys tonight." She turned to Jacour, who seemed dumbfounded. "I'm sure a gazillion women would love to be your date for tonight. After all, you *are* Jacour Bryant; injured or not." That statement struck a chord. Milena must've felt bad about it. "I really am sorry about what happened to your knee."

Jacour shrugged. "I had eight solid years in the league. A lot of dudes don't even get that long. I've managed my money well."

"I'm surprised you've decided to move back here."

"My family's here . . . and you're here," Jacour said.

When Milena didn't respond to that, Jacour walked dejectedly out the door.

"What were you thinking?" I whispered to Milena as he went toward his car.

"I wasn't thinking, Lydia. What were you thinking when you brought him over here?"

"You need to let what happened eight years ago go. That shit is far in the past. That man didn't move back here to be closer to his parents. He's still in love with you; he practically said as much."

"Well, he should've thought about that before."

"You're going to die a miserable old woman, Milena. Every man is entitled to one mistake."

"What about all the women he's been with since?" Milena asked.

"He was only with them because you dumped him. He was going to marry you and take care of you, but no, you had to prove a point. It's been proven. Now take Jacour back and start making some babies instead of delivering little porkers."

"Just leave." She giggled. "I'll see you tonight."

"You're not actually coming." I was stunned. "If you show up without a man, Jacour will never let you live that down."

"I have no intention of showing up without a man. Randolph and I will be there . . . on time."

That was it! Milena had lost her freaking mind. I shook my head and walked out the door. I had no clue what or how things were going to go down later on that night, but one thing was for certain: I damn sure was going to have a front-row seat for the festivities.

# Milena

AFTER Jacour and Lydia left, I felt like I was in a stupor for a good hour. I sat on my sofa, staring out into space, weighing my options—what few options there were. There were exactly three: I could not show up at all and fabricate an excuse, like a horse going into labor or a sick puppy. I could show up alone and feel ridiculed while Jacour flooded me with questions about what happened to Randolph. Or I could show up . . . with Randolph.

It was a damn shame that I didn't have a single brother I could call upon for a date. I'd avoided men altogether, and now, when I needed one, just one, to do me a solid, there was nobody.

Then a lightbulb went off in my head. I had eight hours to locate a man—a fine-ass man—and talk him into being my date for Jacour's welcome home party. I know, I know. I should've kept it simple and stayed at home, but by that point, I had something to prove. Jacour had heard that I was single, and dick-less, and there was no way that I wanted him to realize that I'd spent eight years pining over his cheating ass.

I got up and went into my walk-in closet in my bedroom, trying to pick out something sexy to wear on my hunting expedition.

Most of my clothes were straight out of Walmart or Target, and none of them were even remotely exotic.

"Fuck it!" I pulled a red sundress out and some sandals with cork heels and headed into my bathroom to take a shower.

Thirty minutes after that I was in my Dodge Ram pickup headed to Charlotte. Searching in the Kannapolis, Landis, China Grove area was out of the question. I had already said that Randolph was from Charlotte, and, besides, I knew all the men around there and none of them would work. The few attractive ones were married or on lockdown and everyone else knew them, too. So, no, none of them could pretend to be Randolph William Henderson III.

I pulled into the parking lot of Harris Teeter on Central Avenue. Like every other grocery store on Saturdays, the parking lot was packed. One woman was getting out of a minivan with five kids in tow that looked to be between two and ten. I had to admit to myself that I was envious of her. If Jacour hadn't showed his ass, that could've been me. Maybe not five kids over the eight years that were wasted, but at least two or three. A fresh wave of anger shivered up my spine, making me even more determined to find a date for that night.

Pickings were slim in the parking lot. While I waited for a spot, I checked out the men walking in and out as I sat patiently behind a senior couple who were putting their groceries in their trunk and returning the cart. Now, if I had already been in a space and out of the truck, I would've offered to assist them. Both were slightly bent over and moving slow. Yet, a bunch of men walked right past them without blinking an eye, much less lifting a hand to help. Chivalry seemed damn near nonexistent. Once, when I had to fly to Los Angeles for a conference, I was amazed at the number of men who wouldn't give up their seats on the Hertz Rent-a-Car shuttle bus. It was cool if they didn't move for me, but there were a bunch of women standing who were old enough to be their mothers. One woman almost fell down when the bus turned a corner. I shook my head and glared at the lowlife pieces of shit sitting there listening to their iPods or chatting on their cell phones.

The couple finally got it together and pulled out. Out of nowhere, this chick tried to take *my* space. That wasn't going to happen. I cut off her tiny compact and laughed. She blew her horn, paused for a few seconds like she was going to wait for me to get out, and then moved on.

"You need to move on, bitch!" I yelled out loud. "Not the day to try me!"

When I walked into Harris Teeter, I immediately noticed a pattern. Either there was a woman by herself, a woman with kids, or a woman with her man and their kids. There were only a few individual men scattered about. I grabbed a cart and headed toward the produce section. I'd always heard rumors about people hooking up while they were grabbing for the same grapefruit or cellophane-wrapped tomatoes.

Ah-ha! I spotted a brother who could easily pass for a Randolph. He was digging through a bin of green beans, meticulously rummaging through them to make sure all the ones he placed in his produce bag were fresh. That meant that he was going to be there for a moment. I pushed my cart toward him; he was even better-looking up close. He was about five-eleven, dark-skinned, and had short dreads.

"Excuse me. Can you hand me a bag, please?" I asked, not wanting to be rude and reach over him. He was blocking the elevated bag holder.

"Sure."

He ripped one off and handed it to me. The way he tore that bag off the roller made me wonder if he could yank my panties off with the same amount of strength.

"Thank you."

"No problem."

He smiled at me; I smiled back. I started picking through the beans as well.

"I've never been good at picking out produce," I said, lying. "Besides the obvious, them being green, is there something else I should be on the lookout for? You seem to be an expert."

"I'm extremely careful about what I put in my body. My career dictates that."

"Cool." I wondered if I should ask him what that career was, but I didn't want to come on too strong. "Well, whatever you're doing sure works."

He smiled again; I smiled back.

"The best ones are, like you said, green. But you also want ones that have a smooth feel. Ones that don't have any brown spots or bruises."

"Wow, you *are* an expert." I giggled, trying to do it seductively. "Thanks for the tip."

We both started digging through the beans again. He held one up and examined it, then snapped it in two.

"They also should *snap* when they're broken. No mushy stuff."

"Uh-huh," I replied, trying to get up the nerve to ask him his name, his marital status, and whether or not he owned a nice suit to wear to the party. I picked up the one he had snapped from the pile and tossed it in my bag. He stared at me and I shrugged. "At least I know that one is good."

He chuckled and then put a plastic tie around the top of his bag.

*Do it now, Milena. Just ask.*

"Looks like my time is up. Nice chatting with you," he said.

*Don't let him walk away!*

"So what's your career?" I asked as he started pushing his cart toward the deli section.

"My career?"

"Yeah. You said earlier that you have to be careful about what you put in your body . . . because of your career."

He blushed. "That I did. I have to try to stay in shape because I'm a dancer." He raised an eyebrow to see if I understood. "A male dancer . . . at a club."

Now I was the one blushing. That must've meant he had a decent-sized dick. No matter how cut a brother was, he had to be swinging low to make any money as a dancer. I hadn't been to a strip club since my bachelorette party, but even I realized that much.

*Damn, this entire thing might actually turn into a blessing in disguise.*

Even though I hadn't been with a man since bandanas with rhinestones were popular, the man was making my pussy wet.

"Which club? Maybe I can check you out sometime."

*Ask him about tonight! Ask him about tonight!*

*Give me a damn second!*

He cleared his throat. That made me nervous.

"Just a club."

I threw a few more green beans in my bag and closed it. "Never mind. It's not a big deal."

"I'm not ashamed of it or anything," he stated defensively. "I work at the Sweathouse."

I tried to suppress a laugh. I smiled; he didn't.

"I've heard all about the Sweathouse."

"What does that mean?"

I shrugged. "It means that I've heard of it."

The fact of the matter was, he was definitely ashamed. The Sweathouse was known to be dirty, smelly, and sticky. I shuddered to think of where the "stickiness" all over the seats came from, but I had heard the rumors. Lydia had tried to convince me to go there once, as well as a lot of other places, but I rarely left Kannapolis outside of business-related jaunts into the city.

It was "rumored" that the male dancers in there were all super freaks that were ready to fuck, suck or be sucked, and act a fool for small amounts of cash. The place hadn't been renovated since the sixties, yet desperate women flocked there in droves. Lydia had been with Glenn for a few years, so she was tripping for even suggesting that we go there. Three years with one man for Lydia was like three hundred years to other women. She'd never been the one-man type, but I was proud of her for sticking it out with Glenn.

"You should come through some time. I'll buy you a drink," he said.

"Maybe I'll do that."

There was no way that I could take this fool and pass him off as Randolph. Knowing that he was a stripper at the Sweathouse killed that notion. Most of the chicks in Kannapolis would probably recognize him on sight at the party.

I tossed my bag of green beans in my cart and started walking in the opposite direction from where he was headed, trying to get away from him as soon as possible.

"Hey!" he yelled after me. "You never told me your name."

*And I'm not about to now.*

I turned to face him. "I'm Lydia. Um . . . Lydia Scott." I used

Lydia's first name but caught myself before I went hard and used her last one, too.

"Lydia, it's nice to meet you. My name is Gary . . . but my stage name is Back Banger."

I fell out laughing. "I get it, because you bang out backs?"

"Yeah, something like that." He grinned. "Let me get your number, Lydia."

I started to give him Lydia's number; it would've served her ass right. If she hadn't brought Jacour over to my house, I wouldn't have been out there searching for a date. I could've been working on Bessie and eating my triple chocolate ice cream in front of a rotating fan on my front porch.

"Um, why don't you give me yours, Gary?"

"Because I know it'll be a waste of time. You won't call."

He stood there, eyeing me up and down like I was a big piece of sirloin.

"But if you did call," he continued, "I'd make it worth your while, if you know what I'm saying."

I smirked. "I guess you're saying that you'd bang my back out."

He moved closer to me, and I had to admit, he had some fresh-smelling breath. "Not before I eat your pussy for a couple of hours."

"A couple of hours?"

He lowered his voice and looked around to make sure no one else was within earshot. "I have this game I like to play."

I'm not sure why I was still standing there, but my curiosity got the best of me. "What kind of game?"

"I like to bring a broad over to my crib, put in a DVD, and eat her ass out from the beginning credits to the ending credits." He licked his lips. "So, you down for that?"

"Wow, is this what the world has come to?"

The shit grin disappeared from his face. "What does that mean?"

"It's been a minute since I've been out and about on the dating scene. I didn't realize that men actually offer to eat women out after they meet them in the grocery store."

"I'm not just any man," he stated arrogantly.

*God, I hope not!* I thought. Granted, men had been doggish forever, but I couldn't imagine that women were so casual with their pussies, unless they were strippers or hookers. Then I remembered that Gary was a stripper, so it kind of made sense. Maybe there was some hope that people in general were not simply fucking everything that moved.

"Let me go ahead and knock those cobwebs off that pussy," Gary said. "Now that you said you've been off the scene for a while, that makes my dick even harder."

I sighed. "Look, Gary, I'll be honest. If you give me your number, I'm not going to call. I don't want you to eat me out with those lips that probably should've fallen off by now because they've been locked between so many thighs. I want to take my green beans to the register and bounce."

Surprisingly, Gary smiled. "You're a good girl. I like that." He started pushing his cart away, then paused and turned. "Keep playing it safe out here. You don't know how close you just came to catching something you can't get rid of."

He gave me this sly grin, winked, and then headed toward the deli section. I was stunned. What the hell!

*I need to get the hell out of here!*

A few minutes later, I was sitting in my car with my green beans beside me, panting heavily and going through a laundry list of what-ifs.

*What if I'd hooked up with him and fucked him!*

*What if I'd let him fuck me raw dog!*

*What if I'd ended up being taken out of this world over a piece of dick!*

"I should swallow the bullet and go to the party alone," I said out loud, glancing at myself in the mirror. "Why is it so important to you to prove something to Jacour?"

I turned on the engine, and "Incomplete" by SisQó was on the radio. Talk about huge, blinking signs. That was the same song that Jacour used to sing to me all the time. In fact, he sang it to me the night he proposed marriage, *asshole!*

No, I wasn't going to show up at that party alone. I was going to find a date or die trying.

A few hours later, I was feeling so dejected and stressed completely the fuck out. I had walked the entire SouthPark Mall, not window-shopping but man-shopping, only to come up empty-handed, with the exception of a cute pair of shoes that I couldn't resist from Neiman Marcus. I'd met a few men, but none of them would've worked. One man had been standing in Montblanc, trying on expensive watches. I peeped him out while I pretended to be checking out fountain pens. He had a nice ass and a bald head, two things that I found appealing.

I inched closer to him to get ready to speak but he spoke to me first . . . in a deep, sexy voice.

"You smell great!"

"Thanks," I replied, smiling at him.

"What's the name of your perfume?"

"It's not really a perfume. It's a body spray."

"Well, whatever it is, it's working. You're like a magnet. Of course, that has a lot to do with you being pretty."

I blushed. "Thanks for the compliment."

"So, what's it called?"

"Oh . . . uh . . . it's called Midnight."

"I can see why. That smell will have someone beating on your door at midnight, trying to knock a hole in something."

*Great! Another freak!*

I was going to go for it anyway; ask him to go to the party with me and pretend to be a dude named Randolph. But, during the midnight hour, he wasn't going to be knocking a hole in a damn thing; not in my bed.

"Listen, I was wondering if—"

"I'll take this one," he told the clerk. Then he turned to me. "Sorry, what were you saying?"

"I was wondering if you'd—"

"Hey, baby, sorry I'm late," I heard a man say from behind me.

The one that I'd been chatting with smiled, and his eyes lit up.

*Damn, is he blushing?*

"It's okay, Booty Pie," he replied as a taller man appeared and threw his arms around him in a loving embrace.

They shared a brief kiss. The new one spotted me standing there, probably looking astonished because I was, and decided to put on a PDA performance.

He grabbed his man tighter and started tonguing him down.

I quickly put the pen that I had been holding down and started high-tailing it out of there. I could hear the man's lover laugh at my back.

"Baby, we need to get some Midnight. That stuff is off the hook."

That's when I headed to my truck.

• • •

Now I was sitting there, practically in tears. How could I be such a failure? With millions and millions of men in the world, why couldn't I find *just one* to take me on a date?

I pulled out of the parking lot and moments later I was on I-85 North headed back toward Kannapolis, the one place where I didn't have a chance in hell of finding a man that I could pass off as Randolph.

At the last second, I swerved into the right lane and took the exit for Concord Mills. I had to give it one more shot. There was a NASCAR race that day, so traffic was thick. The mall was always packed, but whenever there was a race, it was crazy around that area. Recreational vehicles were strewn all over the place, people were grilling out in the August heat, and vendors were peddling everything from T-shirts to beer steins.

I was stuck at a stoplight down near the Charlotte Motor Speedway when it happened. The tears started falling and I couldn't stop them. Many of the other motorists were angry and blowing their horns at no one in particular. It wasn't like any of us were going anywhere quickly. People killed me with that. They'd know someplace was going to be crowded before they got there and then would have zero patience when they couldn't maneuver like they wanted to. Impatience is really a condition for people with control issues; people become impatient, and angry, when they find themselves in any situation beyond their control. You could have two people in a doctor's waiting room. One would flip through magazines and enjoy catching up on interesting articles and the other one would sit there huffing and puffing, damn near hyperventilating, when it wasn't going to get them into an exam room any faster. I would've been the one reading, and Lydia would have been the one getting on everyone else's nerves by complaining and being overdramatic.

Even though I realized they were all foolish, I started banging on my horn, too. It had nothing to do with the traffic, or control issues; I was pissed. Pissed at myself for not being able to handle such a simple task. Pissed at myself for wasting eight years being angry with Jacour instead of living my life to the fullest. Pissed at myself for watching him parade a bunch of women through the media while I was sitting on my sofa eating buttered popcorn sprinkled with chili powder and buffalo wings. Pissed at myself for feeling like I had something to prove to a man who had hurt me so badly. Pissed period.

The traffic wasn't moving at all, so I put my truck in park and laid my head on the steering wheel. "Like a Star" by Corinne Bailey Rae was playing on the radio when my life was changed forever. As I sat there wondering when the man who would be by my side forever would show up, I heard a light rap at my window. At first I didn't look up, but the rap came again, a little louder.

I looked to my left, only to see a homeless man holding a tin can and a small sign that read, HOMELESS. PLEASE HELP.

I'd always wondered how people with no money and no home found all the gear they needed to beg for money. He had on tattered clothing and his hair was nappy. He had a knotted beard and dirty fingernails. He smiled at me, shrugging as if to say, "You gonna help a brotha out or not?"

I rolled down my window at the same time that I was reaching into my purse.

*What the hell?* I thought. *A couple of dollars won't hurt.*

I handed him the money.

"Thank you, young lady. You will be blessed for this."

He had this voice that only dreams could be made of; deep, sensual, and smooth. He smiled again, and I realized that the man had a perfect set of teeth; a bit dingy, but as straight as an arrow.

*Milena, you're tripping. Now this vagrant is even looking good to you.*

"Are you okay?" he asked me.

I realized that he must've known that I'd been crying. I wiped my face with my sleeve. "I'm fine. Just fine."

The traffic was still at a standstill. "Thanks again for the money. Have a pleasant day."

He backed away from the truck and I realized how tall he was; at least six-five.

"You have a pleasant day, too."

He stood there on the curb, staring at me, and holding his sign down on one side and his tin cup down on the other. I would've thought he'd move on to the next vehicle, but he remained in place, making eye contact with me. He had the softest brown eyes. His skin was the color of the deep-dish fudge brownies that I would often bake on Sundays to take to my parents' house after church service.

Something about those eyes drew me to him like a magnet.

*Milena, this is absurd!*

It was absurd, but I was contemplating it anyway.

*What if I could clean him up in the next few hours!*

*What if he could pull it off!*

*What if he gets the wrong idea!*

*What if he has voices in his head!*

*What if he's a fucking serial killer!*

Most serial killers throughout history were unattractive, but there were a couple that were attractive and charming, which aided them in luring their victims. Case in point, Ted Bundy. A lot of African-Americans assumed that the average serial killer was

white and male, but I knew better. Everyone bleeds red, and being
cuckoo has never been race specific.

The traffic moved a couple of feet but I remained in park. I
never understood the reasoning of moving up if you're not even
making it a car length. I kept staring at the man and him back
at me.

*You've had way too much time on your hands,* I thought to myself as
flashbacks of television shows like *Forensic Files* flooded my head. I
started running a list of African-American serial killers through
my head. There was Jake Bird from Tacoma, Washington, who
started offing people in the forties and killed at least forty-four people nationwide. There was Vaughn Greenwood, who killed eleven
people in Los Angeles and, of course, John Allen Muhammad and
Lee Boyd Malvo, who had people crouching down beside their
cars while they pumped gas in the Washington, D.C./Maryland/
Virginia area so they wouldn't end up with a bullet in their heads.

"Shit, this is Concord, North Carolina!" I yelled to myself.

I forgot that my window was still down. Before I realized it,
he'd left the curb and was walking back up to my window.

"Did you say something?" he asked once he was standing beside
my truck again.

"Oh, no, I was talking to myself." I had to fix that one, even
though it was true. "I mean, I was thinking aloud."

"Is there a difference between talking to yourself and thinking
aloud?"

We both laughed.

"I guess not," I replied and bit my bottom lip, a habit of mine
when I was nervous. "If you don't mind me asking, what's your
name?"

"My name is Yosef. Yosef Sampson. And yours?"

*Damn! Powerful name!*

"Milena Clark."

He reached out his hand to shake mine. I was reluctant but reciprocated. He had a hard grip, but I could tell that he was trying to be gentle with my hand. I liked that.

It was foolish, what I was about to do, but necessity is the mother of all inventions.

"So, Yosef, do you have plans for this evening?"

He frowned, and I wondered if I'd said something wrong. Then I thought about it. If he was truly homeless—and I presumed that he was—what the hell would he have to do that night other than crawl up on a bench or in an old refrigerator box and go to sleep?

"I mean . . . I meant . . ." Wouldn't you know it? The moment I got up the nerve to start a conversation, the traffic started moving. The car ahead of me was at least forty feet away, and the man behind me was irate that I wasn't following suit.

"Move it, lady!" he yelled out of the window of his Toyota. "I don't want to miss the race!"

I wanted to tell the man behind me to shut the hell up, but I kept my cool. I was on a mission, after all.

"Yosef, this might sound crazy, but can I buy you a cup of coffee?"

Yosef stood there for a few seconds, probably wondering what the hell was wrong with me. A woman in a pickup asking a homeless man to share some java.

The man started blowing again and the other people behind him joined suit. Some were about to wreck their cars, trying to merge into the next lane to get around me. The man behind me revved his engine like he was going to hit my pickup.

*Yeah, right!*

"Never mind, Yosef," I said. "Have a nice day."

I put my gear in drive and started to pull away.

"No, wait!" Yosef yelled after me. "I'd love some coffee!"

I hit the brakes and the man behind me had to squeal his tires to keep from hitting me. All of a sudden, getting into a rear-end collision was a concern. *Idiot!*

"Get in," I said, reaching over and pushing the passenger-side door open.

When Yosef got in, I almost fainted from the smell.

*Oh, hell no! What were you thinking!*

It is amazing how people can become immune to the worst scents, especially if they come from them.

I kept driving though. He must've sensed that his body odor was offensive.

"I apologize for my lack of hygiene. I haven't had the opportunity to wash up in a few days."

"That's okay," I lied, realizing that bird baths were probably like heaven to him, when I adored basking in my bubble baths for hours on end. "I understand."

Less than ten minutes later, we were sitting inside the closest Starbucks with all sorts of people staring at us, mostly rednecks who were in town for the race. Yosef obviously felt uncomfortable and embarrassed. I should have, but instead, I found myself growing irritated. Granted, on any other day, if I'd been sitting inside an establishment and someone had been funking up the joint, I would've been pissed as well. But we'd paid for our coffee and asiago cheese bagels and we were going to sit there and enjoy them. But not for too long . . . time was wasting away, and I had less than three hours before Jacour's party was scheduled to begin.

"This is very kind of you," Yosef said as he took a sip of his coffee. "Thank you so much."

"You don't need to keep thanking me." That was the fifth or sixth one so far. "I appreciate the company."

*This man must think I'm the most desperate woman on the planet! Shit! Right now, I am!*

"Milena, why don't you tell me about yourself?"

Damn, he was really going to play this out like it was a chance encounter of two equally meshed singles trying to make a hookup. It was time for me to cut to the chase.

"I'll give you an abbreviated version. Cool?"

He smiled at me with those arrow-straight teeth. "Cool with me."

"You must think something's wrong with me right about now, but I promise you, I'm perfectly sane. I just needed to find a man before eight o'clock tonight."

*Could you sound any more fucking stupid!*

Yosef raised a brow. "What happens at eight o'clock tonight? Does your stagecoach turn into a pumpkin?"

"That's funny." I frowned. "No, it's nothing like that. I'm supposed to be attending an event tonight, and I need a date."

Yosef looked around Starbucks, and then back at me. "And you think I'm an appropriate choice for a date?" He sat back in his chair. "Is something wrong with you?"

I glared at him and reared back. "No, there's nothing wrong with me. It's just . . ." I wrapped both of my hands around my cup and sighed. "Okay, here it is . . . in a nutshell. For the past eight years or so, I haven't been that sociable. I haven't been out on a date; I barely go off my property. I have this boring-ass life where I treat cows, pigs, and horses, and I—"

"You're a veterinarian? How cute!"

"Trust me, Yosef. There's absolutely nothing remotely cute

about being a veterinarian, but, yes, I am one. Now, here's the issue. My ex-fiancé, who you've probably heard of because he's kind of a celebrity, came back to town and they're throwing him this big shindig tonight. He asked me to go with him and I lied and told him that I was hooked up with this dude named Randolph William Henderson. He's a third, on top of that, and he doesn't freaking exist." I was rambling, but I didn't care. "So when you saw me crying in my truck, it was because I've been out searching for a date to no avail. I went to Harris Teeter and tried to pick up a man in the produce section, but he was the Back Banger, or something like that, and I couldn't show up with a stripper and—"

"But you can show up with a homeless person?" He chuckled. "This is quite interesting."

"Well, no, you can't be homeless. People can't *know* you're homeless. I'm at my wit's end. I left Harris Teeter and went to a mall and thought that I'd found a dude to take me, but then his male lover walks in, he calls him 'Booty Pie,' and starts tonguing him down in the middle of the store." I paused and glared at Yosef. "You're not gay, are you? Not that it matters. We won't be having sex, or touching, or anything, but I need to make sure you won't go in there trying to pick up men. I'd die if you did that."

He crossed his arms in front of him and chuckled. "No, I'm not gay."

"Whew! That's a relief, because that would've been a hot mess and—"

"Excuse me, Milena. What makes you presume that I'd agree to pretend to be this Randolph person?"

"Randolph William Henderson the third."

"Okay, Randolph William Henderson . . . the third. Why would I do such a thing?"

"Money, of course!" I exclaimed. "You're obviously hard up for days. Marrying dudes locked up in prison for twenty years"—she pointed at us—"and now this."

Her friends laughed, and Yosef looked ashamed.

"Your hair weave is unbelievable," I lashed out at her. "But it's not half as nasty as your attitude."

She stopped and turned to me. "Who the hell you think you're talking to?"

Her two friends, both fake divas in their own right, started laughing.

I stood up. "I'm talking to you; the woman with sixty-four teeth instead of thirty-two. I guess God was showing off when He made you, huh?"

I had the bitch there. She had more teeth than a set of triplets.

"Those bad boys are double-parked up in your grill."

Her friends tried to suppress their laughter, since she was now on the receiving end, but they couldn't.

"Damn, she said double-parked," one of them said as she giggled.

I could hear Yosef chuckling at the table behind me.

"Look, tramp, you're chilling up in here with Magilla Gorilla, and you've got the audacity to come at me? Hooker, please!"

"At least I have a man," I heard myself say, much to my own surprise. "And he's a good man. Where's yours?"

Her friends waited for her response. Then one of them said, "Yeah, Keisha, where's yours?"

They both fell out laughing. Apparently I had struck a nerve. Not that I actually had a man, and I was sure she'd had one in the past eight years—she walked like she'd had a hundred dicks in her anus—but I was going to front anyway.

I turned, grabbed Yosef by the hand, and pulled him up from

money. Look at that tin can and sign sitting beside you. I car[
you out with that. At least going out on a date with me is a [
up from begging on the street." He glared at me and made [
feel silly. "It would be a step up, right? I'm not that unattracti[
am I?"

Yosef laughed. "You're beautiful, Milena. That's why all [
this is so intriguing. You are a *very* intriguing woman, Milen[
Clark."

There was something about the way he said my name that
made me want to climb underneath the table and suck his dick.

*Girl, get your thoughts together!* I thought to myself. *That must be
the sweatiest, funkiest dick in America right now, and you haven't sucked
a dick in eight years!*

"Am I intriguing enough for you to do it?"

He touched the lapel of his tattered jacket. "I can't accompany
you to an engagement dressed like this."

"You talk mighty intelligent for a homeless man."

"I haven't always been this way, Milena."

I felt horrible for talking down to him like that. Of course the
man could speak. He wasn't from another planet.

"I apologize for that comment, Yosef. I'm a little stressed out
right now." I paused. "If you agree to accompany me to the . . .
*engagement*, we need to high-tail it to Concord Mills to pick out
a suit and a pair of shoes, and we'd have to hit a barbershop, and
you'd need to bathe, of course."

"Of course." He started giving me that stare again; the one he'd
given me when he'd been standing on the curb. "Sure, why not? I'll
do it. It's not like I have anything else requiring my presence."

"Good, so let's—"

"This is unbelievable," some chick said as she walked past our
table with two of her friends. "Sisters are seriously pressed these

the table. Then I wrapped my arm around his elbow. "If you'll excuse us, we're late for an . . . *engagement*."

"Girl, you're a damn fool!" Keisha a.k.a. Bitch yelled after us. "Before I'd resort to dating a man like that, I'd slit my own fuckin' throat!"

Everyone in Starbucks was looking as Yosef and I walked out to my truck, arm in arm. I had this huge, forced smile on my face. I was scared to breathe, or I might've passed the hell out!

# Lydia

I WAS trying to call Milena all day—both her home number and her cell. She was avoiding me; I knew it. The party was only a couple of hours away, and she was nowhere to be found. I even made Glenn drop by her crib to see if she was there. He said that he didn't get an answer at the front door, and when he went around back, all he heard was animal sounds coming from her kennel.

I rushed into the house from my part-time cashier job at Food Lion; the thrill of my life. Times were hard in Kannapolis, and jobs were damn near nonexistent. Luckily, my uncle Joe was the assistant manager at Food Lion, and he'd hooked me up. There had to be a better life for me out there; I needed to find it and quick.

As soon as I walked in, Glenn pounced on me. He pressed me up against the doorframe and started feeling my tits with one hand and grabbing my ass with the other.

I pushed him off of me. "Stop!"

"What's wrong, baby?"

"What's wrong? Glenn, you know good and damn well I'm not going to come in here from Food Lion and drop my drawers. I'm not clean."

"Then let's go fuck in the shower," he suggested.

"We have to get ready for Jacour's party. I don't want to be late."

Glenn chuckled. "You mean when Milena shows up with her imaginary man?"

"Who told you that?" I hadn't mentioned the situation to him when I'd asked him to go find her.

"Jacour told me that she turned him down for tonight and *claimed* she had a man."

*Here I go with the cover-up!*

"Milena does have a man."

Glenn stared into my eyes for a few seconds and then laughed even harder. "Bullshit! You're always talking about how Milena needs a good dick down."

"You haven't heard me say that in a while." I walked past him. "She's good to go, and I'm very happy for her."

Glenn followed me toward the bathroom. "Who is he and where'd she meet him?"

"His name's Randolph and everyone will get to meet him tonight."

"Including you?"

"No, not including me, smart-ass. I've met Randy . . . Randolph a few times."

Glenn regarded me with suspicion. "Describe him then."

"Why you want me to describe a dude to you? You're not trying to date him!"

Glenn smirked at me. "You've never met this Randolph; his ass doesn't exist."

"Whatever, Glenn. We'll see about that in a few."

"Yeah, we *will* see."

I started taking off my ugly-ass uniform and turned on the shower so the water could warm up. "I keep telling you that you need to check the water heater. It shouldn't take so long for the water to get hot."

"I'll check it tomorrow."

"You've been checking it for a hundred tomorrows, Glenn. What good are you if you can't get basic shit running around here?"

"I'll tell you what good I am. I pay the bills while you sit on your ass all day."

"I've got a job. You know, the one I just got home from."

"That part-time shit don't count. I'm pulling down sixty grand a year at that factory. If it weren't for me, you'd be below the poverty line."

"Don't brag, Glenn. The way factories are shutting down around here right and left, you might be in the same boat as me by the end of the year. Last year, this time, I was making more than you at the towel factory. It's not my fault they shut down because of the economy."

"I'm sorry, baby. You're right."

He was only apologizing because I was butt-ass naked by then. He couldn't fool me. He realized that there was zero chance that he'd get some pussy if he made me angry. Some people get off on "make-up sex." Not me. If a man came at me the wrong way, my thighs might as well have been clamped shut.

Glenn came up behind me as I stood staring in the mirror, trying to decide how I wanted to wear my black, shoulder-length hair that evening. I was too *phat* and *fione* to be stuck in Kannapolis, North Carolina. I belonged on Broadway, singing under the bright lights like Fantasia had done in *The Color Purple*. I couldn't sing a lick, but in my mind, that didn't matter. My looks could carry me wherever I needed to be. I was five-two, a hundred and thirty pounds of *phatness*, and red. Every brother loved a red chick, whether they cared to admit it or not. My red ass had provided for me my entire life, but I was sick of merely *surviving*; I needed to be *thriving*.

Glenn reached around me and started feeling my breasts. "You're so fine, baby."

"Don't I know it," I replied.

He stared at my reflection and winced. Sure, I was conceited, but he'd realized that before he hooked up with me. I'd never tried to hide it.

"Wouldn't you like to relax for an hour or so before we get ready for the party? There's time."

"In other words, you're demanding that I fuck you, or suck you, before we can leave?"

He let go of me. "No, I'm not saying that. Damn, Lydia, you're my girlfriend, and I'm only trying to be romantic. I realize you had a hard day at work, and since I have the weekends free, it's the only time that I can really contribute to anything around here. That's why I did the laundry and washed the dishes while you were gone."

He announced that shit like it was a given that it was my responsibility to do the laundry and wash dishes. I wasn't feeling that. I wasn't feeling that garble at all.

"Glenn, I realize that you're on this 'me man, you woman' caveman tip, but that's not the way I roll. After three years, you should know that."

"I was only saying that—"

"I know *exactly* what you were saying. That you deserve some brownie points for handling some of my womanly duties." I reached into the shower to see if the water was hot yet. It was lukewarm; I still couldn't get in. "Meanwhile, you put fucking eighteen-wheelers together and can't get the hot water working."

Glenn stared at me for a moment and then walked out of the bathroom. He'd already had his shower, the bastard, and now I had to wait for more hot water.

I sat down on the toilet and tinkled while I perused the latest issue of *Ebony*. All the beautiful sisters, living life, dating or married to successful men; it made me sick to my stomach.

The shower finally heated up enough for me to get by. I hopped in, knowing that I had about a ten-minute window to wash everything that needed attention. Of course, I started with my coochie—the most important part. There was no way I was going out in public smelling tart down there. Some women didn't get it when men made fish comments. It was very likely, highly probable even, that if a woman didn't wash her pussy good, she could end up smelling like "katfish" with a K.

After I was showered and smelling all good from three different types of body wash, I found Glenn sitting on the sofa, staring at a blank television screen.

I sat down beside him with a towel wrapped around my waist, ta-tas hanging. "So how's the movie?" I asked with dripping sarcasm.

"Lydia, don't talk to me right now. I'm trying to stay in a good mood for the party."

I had to give it to Glenn. I could treat him any old kind of way and he would never truly go off on me like most men would have. His mild temperament was one of the main reasons why I kept him around; that and his big dick. Between the constant pounding that Glenn and Phil put on my body, it was a miracle that my pussy wasn't as big as the Arabian Sea. Thank goodness that I'd always done my Kegel exercises. Believe it or not, my mother had schooled me about pussy exercises way back in high school. She must've known that I had a fast ass, and she hadn't wanted to see me end up with a loose pussy by the time I was twenty-five.

In case Milena didn't come to her senses in regards to Jacour, I had already devised a backup plan.

Glenn was wearing a pair of basketball shorts and a wifebeater to stay cool until it was time to get ready for the party. He had a stand fan on blast, since the air-conditioning system was another thing constantly malfunctioning in our house. I opted not to bring that up.

I reached over and grabbed his knee. "I'm sorry about earlier. I was tired after work. Ms. Bart came in there today, trying to make a scene."

That got a rise out of Glenn. He chuckled and took my hand. "Ms. Bart is always trying to make a scene. That old broad needs to get some dick."

Ms. Bart was the typical God-fearing, country senior citizen. She sat out on her front porch the majority of the day, gossiping with her cohorts about who was doing what, who was doing who, and spreading rumors like wildfire. They'd sit there, gumming buttered ears of corn with their dentures sitting on the arms of rocking chairs, waving to people in passing cars and then talking smack about them before they could drive around the bend.

"So what'd she do today?" Glenn asked, in a much better mood. He always liked talking about Ms. Bart, or anyone else. Like I said earlier, men are worse than women when it comes to spreading rumors.

"She was upset because they had a misprint in the sales paper for ham hocks. She tried to pull a fast one and claim that she'd gotten some earlier in the week for the same price. I told her that the ham hocks actually go on sale tomorrow and that they'll be listed in the Sunday paper."

I lifted his hand to my lips and kissed his knuckles.

"Then she demanded to see Uncle Joe, like he was going to make me sell her some shit at a discount. It ain't his store no more than it's mine."

"She don't care about that. She needs some dick. I keep telling you that."

"It's like she doesn't have anything else to do. I've never seen someone in the grocery store so fucking much."

"That's her entire life. Church, Food Lion, and her crusty fingers in her pussy."

"Ew, don't give me that visual," I said, and then laughed. "Can you imagine that chick with her legs propped up, digging in her wrinkled pussy?"

"Now that's some snatch that even a blind man would turn down."

We both laughed.

I reached for the remote on the coffee table and turned on the television. I searched for *Spartacus: Blood and Sand* On Demand and then started the episode called "Whore." I had no idea where they found so many fine-ass men to put in one series, but they were all hot; every last one of them.

"The sex on this show is off the hook," Glenn said.

"Why you think I tune in every week?" I unwrapped the towel from around my waist and spread my legs. "The sex in this house is off the hook, too."

Glenn's eyes locked on my freshly shaven pussy. "I thought you said you didn't want to do nothing before the party."

I started fingering my pussy with my left hand and used my

right hand to dig his dick out of his shorts. "That was before I got horny. Besides, I need to make amends for the way I came at you earlier. You know you're my baby."

Someone was fucking on *Spartacus*, and that made me horny—real talk. I grabbed a toss pillow off the sofa, threw it on the floor, and got down on my knees.

"I skipped lunch today. I'm starving. You going to feed me, baby?" I licked the head of his dick. "You going to feed me some of your big . . . hard . . . juicy dick? Hmm? Can I have some?"

As usual, Glenn didn't say shit when I started talking dirty to him. Phil was the one who liked to get it in with some verbal stimulation. That was cool, though. I wanted to appease Glenn so he would be feeling the topic that I planned to bring up after I finished waxing his dick. I wasn't going to fuck him before Jacour's party. That was out. He could wash his dick off with a cold washcloth, but I wasn't dirtying up my pussy and heading out smelling like tilapia.

There is something extremely empowering about giving head if you know what the hell you're doing. Some chicks think it's all about plopping the dick in their mouth and sucking. A true dick-sucking master like me knows that it's a combination of licking and sucking. Men love it when you show a lot of enthusiasm; when you gaze into their eyes and make it seem like their dick is the best thing you've ever tasted in your entire life.

I drew as much of his dick into my mouth as I could handle without gagging, moaned, and wiggled my mouth on it. I slowly lifted my head as I locked eyes with Glenn and made a "pop" sound as I released it from my suctioned jaws.

"Damn, Glenn, every time I suck your dick, it seems bigger. You been lifting weights with this dick?"

"No," he replied and grinned like a Cheshire cat. "You crazy, baby."

"Crazy about you." I started pulling at his shorts like a hungry lion and pulled them down around his ankles. "I want to get at those doorknobs of yours. Have I ever told you how much I love sucking on your balls?"

Glenn went back to his code of silence. I bobbed his testicles on the tip of my tongue, moaning and groaning while I worked the shaft of his dick with my hand.

"Let me go ahead and give you a good wax job. You need to relax," I said and then swallowed his dick once again.

I sucked and licked all over Glenn's dick, balls, and even dabbled in his asshole with a finger for the next twenty minutes or so until he couldn't take it anymore and shot a geyser down my throat.

I made a true performance out of guzzling and licking every last drop and acting like I was hungry for more. I was never one to toot my own horn, but when it came to sucking a dick, TOOT MOTHERFUCKING TOOT!

"Damn, your semen tastes so good, baby. Must be something you ate." I dipped the tip of my manicured index finger into the slit in his dick and rubbed around for any excess cum. Glenn knew that shit turned him on; that's why his ass wasn't going *nowhere*. "Whatever you had for lunch, you need to eat some more of it." I used the tip of my tongue and took one last, long lick from the bottom of his balls and took it to the head. "Umm, now I'm going to be floating on air for the rest of the night."

"We might have to skip the party. I'm worn out now."

I stood up and looked down at Glenn on the sofa. "Now you've got jokes. We're not skipping Jacour's party. It's the biggest thing that's hit Kannapolis since Martha Stewart rolled through waving at people to celebrate the opening of that research center where no one around here is qualified to work." Glenn's eyelids were fluttering. That's what I got for sucking his dick so damn well. He was ready to fall off to sleep like a newborn baby. I nudged his left knee with my right one. "Glenn, wake the fuck up. We need to get dressed."

"Okay . . . baby. Give . . . me a few . . . minutes to—"

I straddled his lap and lifted his chin so he had to look at me. "Glenn, don't play. It's time to get ready to go. I want to get there before Milena shows up."

That got his attention. He chuckled. "Oh yeah, I don't want to miss that either. I can't wait to see what she has to say when she shows up solo."

"She's not showing up solo," I said, not really knowing whether she was or not. One thing was for sure; if she did show up with a man, his real name damn sure wasn't going to be Randolph.

I pulled Glenn up off the sofa and led him to the bedroom so we could get dressed.

"Wait 'til you see my dress, baby. I'm going to look so good on your arm tonight."

"You always look good, Lydia."

"Don't I know it!"

# Milena

THAT particular Saturday had to be the longest day of my entire life, and it wasn't over yet. After we left Starbucks, we went to Brooks Brothers at Concord Mills and tried on a bunch of suits. The shoppers in the mall and the salesmen all seemed disgusted by Yosef's appearance. It reminded me of that scene from *Pretty Woman* when Julia Roberts's character, Vivian, was mistreated when she went into a clothing store on Rodeo Drive to find an outfit for her date with Richard Gere. That was one of my all-time favorite movies and the situation was so similar that I had to laugh. Except I wasn't a multimillionaire businessman, and Yosef wasn't a streetwalker. Well, not in the technical sense.

We finally settled on a black, pin-striped, double-breasted suit, a black-and-silver tie, a crisp white shirt, a pair of gold-plated cuff links, and a pair of smooth, black leather shoes. Oh, and we definitely snatched up a pair of clean tidy whities and some socks. I couldn't even begin to imagine what his drawers must've been like, and I didn't want to imagine it.

The next stop was Fresh Cuts, a barbershop in Concord. There was no way that I could take him to one of the shops in Kannapolis. Either I knew everybody or, worse, I was related to them. The men in the barbershop were ruthless with their comments, but Yosef brushed them off his broad shoulders. By the time the barber named Tito had finished cutting Yosef's hair and giving him a clean shave, most of them were jealous.

My breath caught in my chest as I whispered, "Damn!"

Yosef Sampson looked like he had stepped out of *GQ* magazine. Well, except for the raggedy and stinky clothes that he was still wearing. That odor could've made dogs drop dead in the streets. George Clooney and that movie *The Men Who Stare at Goats* didn't have anything on him.

Still, Yosef was quickly turning into "Hot Chocolate." I got excited; I was about to pull off the plan of the century, even though I'd only conceptualized it out of necessity that morning.

After we left the barbershop, I told Yosef to sink down into the passenger seat of my pickup. It was time for us to make our way through Kannapolis to my house and I didn't want to risk anyone seeing him before the party. Ms. Bart and her friends were always on her porch, but as we passed her house on North Main Street, her porch was empty. It dawned on me that everyone in town was either getting ready for Jacour's party or already there early, sitting around working their gums and eating fried whiting and cole slaw.

When we got to my house, I told Yosef flat out that he couldn't go inside through the front door. If I'd allowed that scent to infiltrate my crib, I never would've gotten it out. He was not walking on my carpet, sitting on my sofa, or anything else of the sort.

"I hope you won't hate me for this, but would you mind washing off with the hose in my kennel before you come inside?"

"What did you just say to me?" he responded indignantly. "If you said what I think you said, drop me off at the nearest public place."

I sat there in the pickup, thinking.

*You've come too far to blow it, Milena! Work this shit out!*

"Okay, how about this? You can take your clothes off on the porch. I'll give you a towel to wrap around you, and then you can shower in my bathroom."

Yosef glared at me for a moment. Then he took a whiff of his shirt and cringed. "I smell that bad, huh?"

"I'm sure it's mostly your clothes. Will what I said be acceptable?"

"Sure, why not," he replied. "Will you at least wash my clothes for me so I'll have something clean to wear later on . . . after the party?"

"I'd be happy to."

There was no way those clothes were going into my personal washer and dryer. I had a stackable set in the kennel to wash the towels and blankets for the animals. His clothes were going right in that bad boy, but he didn't need to know all of that.

Yosef waited out on the porch while I went inside to get him a towel. Instead, I grabbed a raggedy bathrobe that was at least four sizes too big for me. I had this thing about wearing oversized clothes that made all of my friends wonder about me. Again, I didn't want men looking at my body; that might've led to them wanting to date me, and that was a no-no.

I handed Yosef the bathrobe and a trash bag for his clothes. "This should fit. You can put your clothes in the bag. I'll go start the shower."

"Thank you, Milena," he said in that sexy-ass voice of his.

A few moments later, I heard a light tap on the front door. I had been in my bedroom trying to decide what to wear to the party. What a fool. I'd been to two malls that day and hadn't bought a dress. At least I did have that cute pair of shoes from Neiman Marcus. But what the hell was I going to wear with them? Yosef was going to have on a bad-ass Brooks Brothers suit and I was going to have on some outdated nonsense.

I rushed to the door to let Yosef in and my breath caught in my throat once again. With each step in the process, the man kept getting more and more attractive. Even with my tattered bathrobe clutched around him, I could see that he was built like a god.

"Um . . . come on in." I stood aside so that he could enter. "I'll take that," I said as I reached for the trash bag containing his clothes.

*Remember that once this party is over tonight, this man is going right back out on the streets, Milena!*

"Thanks." Yosef came inside and looked around. "Interesting posters."

"Thanks, I collect them."

Yosef was staring at the movie posters from old African-American films that I had on my walls. Being a recluse had also made me an eBay junkie, and movie posters had become my bidding preference. I had posters from *Gone Harlem*, *Carmen Jones*, *Cabin in the Sky*, *The Joe Louis Story*, *The Exile*, *Porgy and Bess*, *Native Son*, *Underworld*, and *Stormy Weather*, to name a few.

Then he spotted my massive DVD collection. Really, it was more like a DVD wall.

"Wow, you're some movie buff!"

"There's not much to do here in Kannapolis," I told him. "So, yeah, I like movies. I like them a lot, so I try to get the new ones when they're released on Tuesdays."

Part of me wondered if this was a good idea after all. He could've been a crackhead for all I knew. What if he tied me up and took all of my shit to pawn?

I pointed down the hall. "The bathroom's that way. The shower should be nice and steamy by now."

He grinned at me. "I like steamy stuff."

*Oh shit!*

"I'll be out in a few. Where would you like me to get dressed? After I shower?"

"I put the suit and everything in the guest bedroom. It's directly across from the bathroom."

"Great."

"I'm going to get dressed as well."

"Okay, see you . . . once we're both dressed," Yosef said and padded down the hallway in his bare feet. Even his feet were pretty. Damn!

I went into my bedroom and locked the door, something I hadn't done since I'd first purchased the home six years earlier and had been too scared to stay there alone for the first few months.

I slipped out of my dress and headed into the master bathroom to shower. As I stood up under the steam, I started talking to myself again . . . or thinking aloud. Like Yosef had said, there really wasn't a difference. Talking to yourself is talking to your damn self.

"This is by far the stupidest thing you've ever done!"

"I hope you can pull this shit off!"

"He is fine; that's the good part! All the chicks in town will be creaming in their panties!"

"Not if they knew you picked his ass up begging for change near the Charlotte Motor Speedway!"

"What if someone recognizes him?"

"No, hell no. The difference between the Yosef from this afternoon and the clean-shaven Yosef is like water and oil."

"You've been too long without a man! You're actually thinking about fucking him!"

"No, I'm not," I responded to myself. "I'm not going to fuck that man. I only want to make Jacour realize that he's not the only fish in the pond."

"Sure, like Jacour's going to be jealous of a man with a tin cup when he's worth a hundred million!"

I realized that time was wasting away and ceased the conversation that I was having between me and myself, and got out of the shower.

Miraculously, I found one dress that I could get by with for the party. It was black, slinky, and didn't cling to my body tight enough to show the kangaroo pouch that I'd developed over the years. I stared into the full-length mirror in my walk-in closet and hissed as I remembered the comment that Jacour had made earlier that day about my weight gain; that it looked good on me. He was lying his ass off. I'd seen the kaleidoscope of waif-thin women he'd paraded around with while he'd been playing for the Yankees.

After slathering on half a bottle of moisturizing lotion, I put on the dress and my new shoes. I pulled my hair up into a bun, spent about five minutes putting on makeup, and was ready to get the entire ordeal over with.

Yosef was waiting in the living room. I almost fainted when I saw him. God, he looked like a movie star!

He was holding a small bunch of dogwood, the state flower. "I hope you don't mind. I went outside and canvassed your yard for these. Ordinarily, I would never pick up a lady for a date without a bunch of roses. Due to my current circumstances, these will have to make do." He shrugged. "Like they say, it's the thought that counts."

I was trying to find my voice. Yosef was standing in my living room looking like the words F-U-C-K M-E T-O D-E-A-T-H spelled out.

"You look stunning," he continued. "That's a lovely dress. It becomes you." He glanced down at my manicured feet; the one thing I did try to keep up with. "So do the shoes. You have beautiful feet."

"So do you," I heard myself say. He blushed. "I mean . . . um . . . never mind." I walked toward the front door. "You ready to go? We shouldn't be too late."

"Don't we need to talk about this first?" he asked.

"Talk about what?" I wondered what he meant. "Oh, you're right. We never discussed your payment for tonight. I can't afford that much, but—"

"No, that's not what I meant, Milena. Shouldn't we get our stories together before we show up at some engagement together? I haven't a clue who I'm supposed to be, with the exception of a name: Randolph Henderson."

"Randolph William Henderson the third."

"Yes, whatever. Who am I? Where did I come from? How did we meet? What do I do for a living?"

I sighed and plopped down on the sofa. "What was I thinking? You're right. We'll never be able to pull this off."

"Don't give up so quickly." He sat down beside me. "I'm beginning to enjoy this little charade. I haven't had this much fun in years."

I glanced at him. "So where do you come from?"

"Originally, I'm from Barbados, but that's back when I was a child."

"Oh, I was about to say. You don't have an accent."

"I got rid of it early on in life. My parents immigrated here and we lived in Boston."

"Boston? How'd you end up in North Carolina?"

"That's a long story and one we don't have time to discuss right now. We need to figure out who this Randolph person is . . . quickly."

I sighed and stood up. "We'll talk about it on the way. Either this is going to work or it isn't. The consequences of not showing up with you are worse than a blunder or two. Let's roll."

"Yes, let's roll." Yosef grinned and followed me out the door.

We pulled up to the Cabarrus Elk Lodge about twenty minutes later. Much to my surprise, more like my dismay, it seemed like everyone in Kannapolis was already at the party. I spotted my father's champagne Lexus in the parking lot and almost shrieked.

"What's wrong?" Yosef asked. "You knew it would be this crowded, right?"

"I suspected it, but suspecting it and witnessing it are two totally different things."

Yosef looked at the banner hanging over the entrance that read WELCOME HOME JACOUR BRYANT! "Jacour Bryant? The pitcher for the Yankees?"

"Ex-pitcher for the Yankees. He damaged his knee," I replied.

"I do recall that he was originally from North Carolina." Yosef paused for a moment. "He's your ex?"

"Yes, he is." I put the truck in park, removed my seat belt, and scooted in my bucket seat to face Yosef. "You really don't have to do this. I appreciate the effort, but even if I can pass you off to Jacour and my friends, my parents are in there and they'll know all of this is a façade."

"I'd love to meet your parents." Yosef chuckled. "After all, we've been dating for five months now, ever since we met at that veterinary conference in Los Angeles. I don't get this way to see you that often, so we shouldn't miss out on this opportunity for me to meet the family."

I giggled. "Damn, you're pretty good at this."

Yosef winked at me. "Wait until you see the stellar performance that I put on inside." He motioned toward the lodge with his right hand. "That's providing that we're actually going inside."

I took a series of deep breaths. It felt like my insides were being ripped apart.

"You really think we can get away with this?" I asked, full of worry.

"Milena Clark, I adore you. I always have, and now that we're in a serious, committed relationship, you need to stop hiding me."

"You're right, Randolph," I said, and then laughed. "My mother's going to flip. She has this thing for tall, attractive men."

"You think I'm attractive."

*You're fine as shit!*

"Yosef, I'm sure you realize that you're a handsome man. Down on your luck, but that doesn't take away from what God granted you naturally."

He turned his head away from me, trying to hide a blush. That's when I realized for the first time that he had dimples. Looking at him and not wanting to jump his bones was too much for a sexually repressed sister to handle.

"Let's go on inside, Milena," Yosef said.

"Okay, Yosef."

"Get into character. No more Yosef. Call me Randolph."

"Okay, Randolph. I hope this works."

We started to climb out of the truck. "As long as no one asks me how to spay or neuter a pet, we should be straight."

I laughed. "I hope no one will be bored enough to do that, but try not to talk too much."

"What would you consider too much?" I pondered his question while he took my hand in his and started walking. He smelled good, he looked good, he talked good; it was *all* good. "Am I not articulate enough for your friends?"

"Pu-leeze! Most of the people in here will be country bump-kins. You speak the King's English compared to most of them. I only meant, try not to get caught up in a deep conversation with a nosy person, especially Jacour or my best friend, Lydia. To be frank, everyone in here is going to be snooping when they get a load of you."

Yosef chuckled, and I forced a slight laugh. Truth be told, I was so nervous that I was shaking from my head to my toes.

# Lydia

Aт exactly 8:32 p.m. on Saturday, August 8, 2009, the town of Kannapolis, North Carolina, was hit by a nuclear bomb. Milena Clark, my best friend in the entire world, walked into the Cabarrus Elk Lodge *with a man*. Everyone froze in their tracks, whether they were dancing to the music, which seemed to freeze in time as well, or chowing down on fried fish and cole slaw. I'm telling you, I've never seen anything like it before in my entire life.

Not only did she show up to Jacour's welcome home bash with a man, she showed up with movie star material. He was dark, tall, creamy, sexy, muscular, and everything else you could think of. I wanted to fuck him on sight; I won't even make an attempt to tell a lie about that one.

I was about to back that thing up on Glenn to "Flashlight" by Parliament Funkadelic. Yeah, it's an old-ass song, but that's how they roll at Elks lodges in the country. Besides, it made sense to play that because George Clinton is about the only other person from Kannapolis who ever became famous; him and NASCAR legend Dale Earnhardt. When Milena walked in with "Randolph," I nearly knocked Glenn down on the floor.

After a few seconds of complete silence that felt more like a few minutes, Glenn said, "Aw, hell naw! She actually has a dude with her! Jacour's going to flip the fuck out!"

When he said that, I immediately searched the room for Jacour. I spotted him posted up beside Milena's parents, probably trying to get back into their good graces after messing up all of the wedding plans years earlier. Mrs. Clark always wanted Milena to forgive Jacour, but that shit was simply not happening. Mr. Clark seemed on the fence. He wanted Milena to be happy and recognized that money could purchase a whole lot of happiness, but he was also upset that Jacour had disrespected his baby girl. Rumor had it that Jacour had reimbursed the Clarks for all of the money they had shelled out for the wedding that had never taken place. I'd brought up the topic once with Milena; she'd rolled her eyes at me and smacked her lips, and that had been the end of that. I'd never mentioned it again. But her pops was rocking a Lexus.

Before I knew it, Jacour was making a beeline for Milena and Randolph. I pushed through the crowd to get to her first. I didn't want to miss a single word of what was about to go down. Glenn and Phil, who had been ogling me since I'd arrived, were right on my tail.

"Milena," I said, giving her a hug. "Don't you look great!"

"So do you." Milena was as nervous as a virgin about to star in a gang-bang porno. I was determined to have her back. As Jacour walked up, I made a show of it and flung my arms around Randolph. "Randolph, it's so nice to see you again. How are you?"

"I'm awesome, Lydia. How are you?" he replied.

*Damn, Milena must've really schooled him. He knew exactly who I was.*

"I'm good. I'm good. It's *all* good," I said, eyeing him up and down.

I didn't think it was possible, but up close, the man was even finer than he'd been from across the room. I wanted to hug him again and push up on him harder to see if he had a big dick. With that height, he must've been holding. My eyes dropped to his shoes. Yes, damn, he definitely had to be holding.

"Hello, I'm Jacour Bryant." Jacour held out his hand and gripped Randolph's tightly, looking like he was trying to snap it off. "I'm Milena's ex-fiancé."

"So I've heard," Randolph said. "It's nice to meet you. I'm Randolph William Henderson the third."

"Oh really now?" Jacour asked suspiciously.

"Yes, really." Randolph glanced around the crowded room; all eyes were on him. "They must really love you in this town. This is a great turnout. I'm glad Millie and I were able to make it."

"Did you call her Millie?" Jacour asked, irate.

"Yes, that's my pet name for her." Randolph winked at "Millie." "Sorry we're a tad bit late, but my plane landed from Los Angeles about ninety minutes ago."

"Los Angeles!" I heard Glenn exclaim behind me.

*Good one,* I thought. *Make him from out of town to cover the fact that nobody's met him.*

"Randolph, this is my boyfriend, Glenn," I said, pointing to him.

"Good to meet you, Glenn. I've heard so much about you," Randolph said, shaking Glenn's hand. He looked at Phil and reached for his hand. "You must be Phil. What's up, man?"

The expressions on all of their faces were priceless. I was pissed that I didn't have my camera phone out and ready. That would've been one of those photos to be passed around the internet. It could've been called "Jealous Ass Men."

Glenn proved that I was right by saying something stupid. "I'm not Lydia's *boyfriend*. I'm her *man*. There's a big difference."

Randolph laughed. "Yes, it does seem a bit immature for adults to reference their significant other as 'boyfriend' or 'girlfriend.' " He lifted Milena's hand and kissed it. "In our case, I always introduce Millie to my colleagues as 'the light of my life.' "

"Oh, brother," Phil said behind me. "This dude is a trip."

"I thought Milena said you were from Charlotte?" Jacour asked. "So now, all of a sudden, you're from the west coast?"

Milena and Randolph stared at each other for a few seconds.

I was thinking, *Uh-oh! They done gone and fucked up!*

"I said that because none of this is really any of your business and I wanted to get you out of my home, where you were trespassing, as quickly as possible," Milena said. "I like to be as sexy as possible when I pick Randolph up from the airport."

"You could be wearing a burlap sack and still be stunning to me," Randolph said as Milena blushed.

Jacour was staring at Randolph like he wanted to punch him. Thank goodness Milena's mother walked up to join the conversation.

"Momma, hey there," Milena said nervously. "I'd like you to meet Randolph William Henderson the third; the light of my life."

That's when I really had to prevent myself from cracking up laughing.

Mrs. Clark shook Randolph's hand and stared up at him. "Light of my daughter's life, huh? In that case, give me a hug." Randolph hugged Mrs. Clark, and she lingered in the embrace a little bit longer than was necessary. "Muscular and strong, I see." She looked at Milena. "Nice."

Milena blushed. "Yes, he's very nice, and very good to me."

"So when did all of this happen?" Mrs. Clark asked.

"Oh, I thought I'd mentioned it. I met Randolph when I attended the conference in Los Angeles earlier this year. We've been seeing each other ever since."

Mrs. Clark looked at Milena, and then at me. "Lydia, you knew about this?"

"Yes, of course," I replied. "Uh . . . Randolph's been flying into Charlotte just about every other weekend to see his Millie."

*Now I was getting all into the lies!*

"Millie?" Mrs. Clark said. "Interesting." She tapped Jacour lightly on the arm. "Well, looks like your plans aren't as clear-cut as you described earlier tonight."

"Plans? What plans?" Milena asked, obviously upset.

Jacour laughed nervously. "Nothing. I was talking to your parents this evening about my plans to start a business."

We could all tell by the look on Mrs. Clark's face that he was flat-out lying. He'd thought getting Milena back was going to be a breeze, and, quite honestly, so did I before she pulled the mother-fucking "rabbit out a hat" trick of the century.

From my peripheral vision, I saw Mr. Clark making his way toward us. He'd been talking to the Bryants over in the corner, all of them probably wondering who the man was with Milena. Everyone knew that Milena had been locked away at her house in misery for eight years. Now she'd shown up with a fine, sophisticated man on her arm who certainly was from nowhere around there.

Milena must've spotted her father; she grabbed Randolph by the hand. "Ooh, that's my song. Let's dance."

Randolph played along. "Remember we danced off of this the night we met, in Los Angeles, underneath the moonlight on the terrace."

"Of course I remember," Milena said. "You're so romantic; that's one of the things that turns me on about you the most."

"Pretty Wings" by Maxwell had only been released in July, the month earlier, and I was hoping no one else would pick up on what appeared to be the happy couple's first slipup of the evening. The entire thing was hilarious.

Mr. Clark arrived five seconds after Milena had pulled Randolph onto the dance floor. "Who's that, honey?" he asked his wife.

She shrugged. "That's our daughter's life lighter."

"Come again?"

"She's been seeing the young man for quite some time, apparently."

"How come we didn't know about him?"

Jacour was standing there looking dejected. "Because he's nothing to know about. Look at him; he has nothing on me."

*I don't know about all that! Most women would spread 'em!*

"Whoever this Randolph thinks he is, he'll never stop me from getting Milena back. She's mine and that's not ever going to change."

I didn't like the way Jacour made that statement. I didn't like it one bit. True, I felt like Milena would have to be a fool not to take his ass back, considering the dick drought that she'd experienced for the past decade, but he didn't need to sound threatening and shit.

Everyone watched Milena and Randolph gaze into each other's eyes on the dance floor. Glenn, who, I had almost forgotten, was standing beside me, grabbed my elbow. "Let's dance, baby. I want to get close to them so we can eavesdrop."

I yanked my elbow away. "We will do no such thing. Leave my girl and her man alone." I stared at them and Milena broke into a smile that I hadn't seen in ages. "Look at her. She seems so happy with him."

• • • •

About an hour later, I spotted Milena leaving the dance floor and heading toward the bathroom. I was sitting with Phil, making plans for our next fuckfest while Glenn was off consoling Jacour. All of the chicks in town had come dressed hoochified and prepared to surrender their pussies to Jacour, but he barely noticed any of them. He was too upset about Milena.

"I'll be back," I told Phil, standing up. "I need to go check on Milena."

Phil scanned the room for Randolph. He was standing by the punch bowl with a group of women in their thirties eyeing him like they were planning a dick-jacking. I couldn't hear what they were saying, but I'm sure they were bombarding him with questions and trying to flirt. Men like him didn't even drive through Kannapolis, much less come to the Cabarrus Elk Lodge.

"I'm going to go tell Jacour that dude's free!" Phil exclaimed.

I stopped and turned to look at him. "Free . . . for what?"

"I'm sure he wants to holler at him."

Before I could say something smart, I'll be damned if Jacour and Glenn were not making a rush toward him. I started to go over there and intervene but decided it was more important to go talk to Milena. I needed to find out where the hell that man came from and, more important, who the fuck he was.

Milena was coming out of a stall when I entered the bathroom. Donita and Kayla, *heifers*, were already in there waiting to pounce on her. The one good thing about Milena calling off the wedding was that those two hookers didn't get to be her bridesmaids . . . not officially.

Milena glanced at all of us as she pulled her dress down over her knees and giggled. "Damn, can't a sister take a leak without an audience?"

Donita was the first to get her two cents in. "Milena, that man is *too* fine. Where'd you find him?"

Kayla added, "He's sexy as all get out. Does he have a big dick?"

"Wow, you two are something else," Milena replied. "Can't I show up to one party with a date without being interrogated?"

"No, you can't," Kayla replied. "We need to know *everything!*" She looked at Donita. "Did you see the size of that man's feet?"

Kayla and Donita slapped each other a high five.

"You two chickens need to hit the bricks. Milena's not telling ya'll shit," I said. "I can't believe you; asking her about dick. Have some class. We never ask you about the dicks your men have."

Donita pouted. "That's because Timmy's dick ain't nothing to write home about."

Kayla punched Donita lightly on the arm. "Shame on you for talking about Timmy like that. You guys have been married for five years."

"Five long, miserable years," Donita sighed. "I'm thinking about getting me some dick action on the side."

"That's it." Milena finished washing her hands and was straightening out her hair. "The three of you can stay in here and talk about dicks. I'm getting back to my date."

Kayla glared at me. "Lydia, you know good and damn well you want to know everything, too."

"Yeah, but I don't want to know about his dick." I pointed to the door. "Now get out! Hit! The! Bricks!"

Donita grabbed Kayla's arm. "Let's go. It's obvious that we're not wanted here."

"Oh, it's not like that, Donita," Milena said.

"Oh, yes, it is like that." I held the door open for them. "See you two whores later."

As they were walking out, Kayla gave me the finger. "I've got your whore."

I slammed the door on them and walked over to the sink area, where Milena was refreshing her lipstick.

She looked at my reflection in the mirror. "I'm positive that you have a lot of questions, Lydia, but I need to get back out there. I can't leave Randolph alone for too long."

"Okay, then let's cut to the chase. Does he have a big dick?"

We both fell out laughing, crying laughing even, and we were still laughing when Ms. Bart came inching into the bathroom. She didn't take footsteps; she took "inchsteps." We tried to compose ourselves long enough to exchange pleasantries, and then waited patiently for her to use the bathroom and leave. Milena and I kept rolling our eyes. What usually takes a normal woman no more than a minute to do took Ms. Bart fifty fucking years. She was in the stall pulling and yanking at clothing. At one point, I tried to peek through the opening in the stall door to see what kind of drawers her decrepit ass was wearing. Milena pulled me back and chastised me for doing that.

"I'm just saying," I whispered. "What's taking so long? It's not like she's taking a dump."

"Thank goodness," Milena whispered back. "Can you imagine?"

We both covered our mouths to prevent our laughs from escaping, and Milena turned the sink on full blast.

*Finally* Ms. Bart came out of the stall, took another fifty fucking years to wash her hands, and then inched out.

"Good gracious, if she'd taken a shit, they would've had to lock her ass in the lodge overnight," I said. "Come let her out in the morning."

"It wasn't that bad." Milena laughed. "We shouldn't make fun of old people. Hopefully one day, we'll be even older."

"Well, I'm staying in shape, because I'm not ever going to stop fucking. I'll be riding dick until they toss my bones in my grave."

"You're sick, Lydia."

"Not as sick as you." I grabbed both of her wrists. "Who is that man out there and where on this earth did you find him?"

"He's Randolph," Milena lied. "Randolph William Henderson the third."

"Cut the bullshit! There is no Randolph William Henderson the third, and we both know it."

Milena tried to look serious and then cracked a smile. "Okay, okay. His name's not Randolph. It's Yosef."

"Yosef? What kind of name is that?"

"I think it sounds sexy . . . powerful . . . like a gladiator."

"Honestly, as fine as that man is, I wouldn't care if his name was Dorothy. I'd still want to fuck him."

Milena giggled. "Damn, Lydia. What about Glenn?"

"Glenn who?"

We both laughed.

"Where'd you meet *Yosef*?" When Milena seemed hesitant to answer, I added, "Milena, don't front. A little bit more than ten hours ago, you were standing in your house in your dingy overalls making up a man, and now you have the finest motherfucker in the world out there waiting for you. What gives?"

"He's a friend of a friend."

"A friend of what friend? You don't have any friends other than me and those two chickens that waddled out of here."

"Stop calling them chickens."

"Okay, chickenheads. Is that better?" Milena rolled her eyes. "So how'd you meet him? It wasn't through a friend."

"Damn, you're like Agatha Christie or something." Milena paused. "I met him near the Charlotte Motor Speedway. He was in town for the NASCAR race today."

"Sis, we've been living around these parts our entire lives and the only people that come to town for races are rednecks and hillbillies."

"What's the difference between rednecks and hillbillies?"

"Rednecks are usually farmers, or people who hunt squirrels, and their necks are red from being out in the damn heat. Hillbillies usually live in the mountains and shoot off guns and run moonshine stills." I smirked. "Don't fuck with me. I'm quick on the draw."

"You made that shit up," Milena said, and then laughed.

"Yeah, but it sounded good. Almost as good as the lies you and *Yosef* are telling out there."

"I need to get back out there."

"Not until you tell me everything."

"I'll tell you tomorrow."

I was about to protest, but when Milena opened the door, I'll be damned if Ms. Bart was not taking inchsteps back into the door.

"I give up!" I exclaimed.

Milena winked at me. "Tomorrow."

She walked out, leaving me with Ms. Bart, who stared at me suspiciously. "You still in here?" She whiffed the air. "You better not be in here smoking."

"Smoking what, Ms. Bart?" She was getting on my last nerve.

"You know what I'm talking about. Margigana, that's what I mean."

"I think you mean *marijuana* and no, I never touch the stuff."

That was a lie. I was the ciggaweed queen of Kannapolis, but I was strange. I preferred getting high alone, with few exceptions. I wanted to roll my own joints, and smoke my own shit. I even grew it out in the woods behind the house. Glenn didn't even know about my stash. He'd always ask me for the hookup, because my shit was primo. Both he and Phil thought I was paying for it and refusing to give up the 4-1-1. There was no way in hell that I was going to tell anyone about my spot. My plants would've disappeared quicker than I could blink.

Ms. Bart stared at me for another few seconds, then waved me off. "I need to do number two."

"Then I need to leave," I said. "I hope everything comes out all right."

She hissed at me and I giggled. As I left to see what was good with the horse-and-pony show that Milena and Yosef were putting on, I wondered if I should tell somebody to make sure Ms. Bart was off the toilet before they locked up.

# Milena

WE pulled it off!" I squealed as Yosef and I turned back into my driveway a little past midnight. I had become so comfortable with him that I'd allowed him to drive my truck. "Did you see how everyone acted?"

"Yes, I definitely saw that," he responded, cutting the engine and the lights. He turned to me. "Would you like for me to wait out here while you retrieve my things?"

There was this deep sadness in his eyes; I imagined that same sadness existed in mine. For me, it had become an actual date—at least in theory. A handsome and charming man, dancing the night away among my family and friends, holding hands and gazing into his eyes, having him cater to my every need and lavish me with attention. But Yosef was a vagrant I had picked up from the side of the road.

My heart started pounding so fast that I swore I could hear it. Yosef was awaiting my reply.

"You can come in for a few minutes, if you'd like."

"It's getting pretty late. Since you're going to drop me back off in Concord, we should probably get going."

"Yeah, we probably should," I whispered. I opened the passenger-side door and climbed out. "Be right back."

"I'll be here."

When I got to my front door, I paused and stared back at the truck. I could make out Yosef's massive frame and could tell that he was staring at me. I sighed, unlocked the door, and went inside.

A few moments later I was back with his clothes neatly folded, along with his tin can and sign. It felt so crazy, handing him the items, which he laid next to the gear shift between the bucket seats.

"You want me to drive?" he asked solemnly.

"If you don't mind."

"No problem."

He started the truck and we drove in silence. It would take us about twenty-five minutes to get back to where we'd met. I wanted to ask Yosef where he was going to go once he got out of my truck, but I couldn't find the words. I felt like such a bad person. I'd picked him up panhandling and had treated him to one evening of normalcy, and now I was about to toss him back like a fish that had been caught merely for entertainment. But what else could I do? Offer to make him some pancakes and sausage, or offer to suck his dick?

There were so many reasons why I couldn't do the things that started running through my mind. I hadn't been in a relationship in years. Scratch that! Let's not even go hard and discuss relationships. I hadn't been intimate with a man in eight years. I was like a recycled virgin or something. Sure, I was a masturbating queen, but fucking yourself and fucking somebody else were two totally different things. And while I didn't consider myself prudish, or expect a potential mate to be worth a hundred million dollars like Jacour, I did have some standards.

*The man is homeless, Milena! Get a grip on yourself!*

*But he's so sexy!*

*He wasn't sexy earlier today when he could've given a skunk a run for his money!*

*No, but he bathed!*

*One shower couldn't have possibly erased all of that funk!*

*He can take another shower! Shit, you can take it with him, and wash his balls yourself!*

*Now you're just being a skank, straight-up!*

*Maybe I want to be skank after all of these years! I wouldn't mind giving my pussy away!*

*Then give it to Jacour! At least you know he loves you! He's an asshole but he's rich and he adores you!*

*Adores? He cheated on me! Adores, my ass!*

There it was; the nail on the head. My real issue with Jacour, Yosef a.k.a. Randolph—or any other Tawando, DaQuan, or Henrico—was that I had trust issues with men. I didn't simply have a hard time trusting men. I didn't trust their testosterone-driven asses at all. I was brought up to believe that when God doesn't give you what you want, it's because it's not what you need. But I was also brought up to believe that people shouldn't be judged unfairly. I really knew little to nothing about Yosef, but his looks were *clearly* clouding my judgment.

Before I realized it, he pulled up to a dirt road near the Rock City Campground, less than a mile from the Charlotte Motor Speedway in Concord. I had spent the entire time arguing with myself in my head about what to do about Yosef.

He put the truck in park and stared at me. I was looking out of the passenger window, avoiding his eyes.

"I guess this is it." He paused. When I still didn't say anything, he opened the driver's-side door. "I had a wonderful time, Milena Clark. Maybe I'll see you around again sometime."

That's when I was able to speak again. I couldn't let him walk away from me without addressing him. "Wait!" I exclaimed. He had his left leg outside on the ground already. "I need to pay you." I started digging through my purse. "I only have about two hundred dollars on me, but if you want me to go to an ATM, I can."

I held out a small wad of bills for Yosef to take, but he stared at them and then at me. "It's okay, Milena. Tonight was my pleasure. It was the first time in a very, very long time that I felt like a man again."

His words hurt me to the core. "But you are a man, Yosef. You're a man every day."

"It's easy to say that, and sure, biologically I'm a man. But grown men are supposed to have certain things and handle certain responsibilities. One day, I'll be back on my feet, but for now . . ." He shrugged and picked up his pile of tattered clothing, cup, and sign. "For now, this is my world; much, much different than yours."

I looked around the area where we were parked. There were a bunch of RVs still parked there overnight, after the race. Some people were still lingering outside, talking, eating, and drinking beer. For the most part, however, since it was so late, most people had ventured inside for the night.

"Where will you sleep?" I asked Yosef, feeling heavyhearted.

"I have a spot out in the woods." He pointed to a patch of trees on the left side of the campground. "Some people that I've met over the past few months and I have constructed a little village. It's not that bad, actually. At least I have someone to talk to."

*A village? A few months? This was too much!*

*Force him to take the money, Milena!*

I tried to hand him the money again. "Please, I really need you to take this money. You've held up your end of the bargain; now let me hold up mine."

He waved the money off. "To take money from you would be a criminal act. I realize that you met me begging for pennies, but what you've given me today can't be equated to monetary value. You've made me feel special, and that means the world to me."

*Damn, he's so sexy!*

"Can you show me?" I heard myself say. I was seriously losing my mind. "Can you show me the village?"

Yosef shook his head adamantly. "No."

"Why not?"

"Why would I?"

"You said it's not that bad."

"Yes, it's not bad as far as places where homeless people could land. I still don't want you to see it. What you've already seen me doing has been degrading enough. I don't want you to see that place."

Yosef lowered his head in shame. Living such an existence had to be very hard on him.

"Don't they have shelters?"

"Yes, a few, but they're overcrowded, and unless you're there by a certain hour, you can't get a spot."

"Are you saying that going to that party with me tonight prevented you from staying in a shelter?" Yosef stared at me for a few seconds. "Did I do this?"

"No, it's not your fault. I float between shelters and the village. The village is actually probably safer. The people there look out for each other and have a familiarity. In shelters, anyone can show up and cause problems. A lot of drug addicts and schizophrenics end up destitute. Some of them can be rather dangerous."

"I can't even imagine." I wanted to reach out and touch his arm, but I hesitated.

"But don't get me wrong. I'm not saying that all homeless people are bad. Most are good people who've fallen on bad times."

I was dying to ask him why he was homeless, but I didn't want to make him feel any worse. I also wanted to kiss him.

*What the hell are you doing, Milena?*

*Showing basic human kindness!*

*You need to let him walk off into those woods and take your ass back to Kannapolis!*

*It's not that simple!*

"You should get going," Yosef said, interrupting my thoughts. He looked at the sky and a few raindrops trickling onto the hood of my truck. "Looks like a nasty storm is headed this way."

As if giving confirmation to his statement, a huge lightning bolt struck in the distance, followed by a roaring clap of thunder. In less than what seemed like ten seconds, a torrential rain started pouring down, out of nowhere. I could hear some people scream from the campground as all of them rushed inside their RVs.

"Close the door!" I instructed Yosef. "You can't go out in the woods in this weather!"

He pulled his leg back in and shut the driver's-side door. "I'm used to it. It's not a big deal; really."

"Yosef, I may not be a meteorologist, but I do know that trees are one of the last things you need to be around when there's lightning."

Another bolt of lightning struck, this time much closer than the last one. The thunder was so loud that it made me cringe. The thought of him going out into that terrible weather was unfathomable.

Yosef and I sat there in silence for a moment. He turned on the radio, I guess to calm my nerves a little. "Pretty Wings" by Maxwell was on. Recalling our first dance together earlier that evening made me smile.

"That's the song we danced to earlier tonight. Remember?" I asked.

"I'll never forget a single moment of tonight."

Yosef was saying all the right things; things that I longed to hear, despite having tried to convince myself over the years that being alone was better than trying to love again.

He reached over and took my hand. "If you're scared of the weather, I can stay until the rain stops."

"That would be nice," I replied, and that was an honest answer. As long as he was sitting in the truck with me, he couldn't be outside in that storm. "I'm in no hurry."

Yosef looked at me and smiled. "Neither am I."

As "Pretty Wings" went off and "Lost Without You" by Robin Thicke came on, Yosef and I sat in my truck, holding hands, and gazing into each other's eyes.

PART TWO

# BASES LOADED

# Lydia

SERIOUSLY had a problem. Sunday morning, the day after Jacour's party, I got up at seven and told Glenn that I was going to the eight o'clock church service. In all actuality, I was mad as hell that Glenn hadn't come home until after three. The dance had ended at midnight and he'd *claimed* that he was going to help console Jacour's devastated heart after Milena showed up with Randolph. While I was *extremely* confident that Glenn was wrapped around my pinkie finger, I didn't want him staying out that late. Now that Jacour was back, unless Milena got back with him, Glenn would be gone all the time and I wasn't having it. Worse yet, Phil would likely be right along with them. Not only would my man be missing in action, but my dick action, too? No fucking way!

I couldn't wait to get the rest of the dirt from Milena about this Yosef dude, but first, I had something else to attend to. While I was sitting on the toilet taking my morning dump, I sent Phil a text message. Yes, women take morning dumps, too. Any woman who denies it will also claim her shit doesn't stink. Memo: there is no such thing as sweet-smelling shit; real talk.

ME: MEET ME AT BAKER'S CREEK.

PHIL: RIGHT NOW?

ME: YES, RIGHT NOW.

PHIL: WHY? WHAT'S UP?

ME: YOU KNOW WHY.

PHIL: NO, TELL ME.

ME: GET YOUR ASS OVER THERE. 30 MINUTES.

PHIL: I'M STILL ASLEEP.

ME: 30 MINUTES. DON'T BE LATE.

PHIL: I'M GOING BACK TO SLEEP. HOLLA LATER.

As much shit as Phil talked, he would show up. He wasn't going to turn down pussy; not *my pussy*. I started to put something raunchy in the text message but wasn't about to be a fool. Text messages had gotten more people busted than used condoms in the wastebasket. Former Detroit mayor Kwame Kilpatrick had more than 14,000 of those bad boys leaked all over the internet after the powers that be decided to do his ass in. I wasn't a politician, but I still had shit to worry about. Glenn was covering the bills that I couldn't afford from my part-time job at Food Lion and I needed him to keep paying them. One day, I was going to get the hell out of that dismal town, but until then, I needed him to stay put. If he found out that I was fucking Phil, and had been fucking Phil even before I started fucking him, my life as I knew it would be history.

Now you would think that the possibility of not being able to pay bills would've been sufficient enough to encourage me to stop fucking Phil. But, like I said, I seriously had a problem, and it was entirely related to the need for dick.

•  •  •

Less than twenty-five minutes later, I was sitting in the parking lot at Baker's Creek Park. That's the beauty of small-town life. You could shower, get dressed—oh yeah, take a morning shit—and still be anyplace in town within a half hour.

There wasn't a soul out there that time of morning. It wasn't like Central Park or South Beach or the Santa Monica Pier or the other places they showed in movies. People weren't riding bikes, jogging in expensive spandex, or rollerblading at Baker's Creek. The only things getting exercise around there were the squirrels, possums, and raccoons. And shortly, my pussy was going to get a workout.

My clit started throbbing at the thought of it. I tried to decide what I was going to demand that Phil do to me first: suckle on my tits, eat my pussy, or lick my ass. Yes, my ass. I showered after my morning shit. Did you?

That was one thing I never played with; proper hygiene. I remember when Donita was dating Timmy, her now husband. Milena had forced me to have dinner with the chicken at the Golden Corral. You know it's a small town when the hottest meal ticket is the Golden Fucking Corral. Anyway, we were chowing down on the selections when Donita said something that almost made me barf up my salisbury steak and gravy.

"Timmy keeps leaving beads on my sheets," Donita said.

"Beads! What kind of beads?" Milena asked.

"Poop beads." Donita looked terribly uncomfortable as the words left her lips. "Should I say something?"

I placed my fork down on my plate, suddenly losing my appetite. "Please tell me that you're not talking about what I think you're talking about. Not while I'm trying to eat."

Milena giggled. "It's okay, Lydia. At least she's not getting graphic."

That's when Donita went and did it. She got graphic. "Every time we get finished fucking, there are these little pieces of shit all over my sheets. As soon as he leaves, I have to strip the bed and throw everything in the washer."

"Not graphic, huh?" I glared at Milena. "Little pieces of shit all over her sheets?" I turned my attention to Donita. "Donita, let me help you out here. Yes, the hell you need to tell that Negro to stop shitting in your bed."

"I don't think he's actually shitting in the bed. I'm saying, the beads are already there from when he did take a shit, and they end up on my sheets."

"In other words, Timmy's not wiping his ass when he takes a dump," Milena added. "A lot of men don't wipe properly."

"And how would you know that, Miss Never Fucked Another Man In My Life Besides Jacour? Did Jacour wipe his ass?"

"Of course he did," Milena replied.

"And all of my men have always wiped their asses," I said. "Furthermore, no funk occupies my space. I take a shower before I go to bed, and I'll be damned if any man that I'm fucking around with is lying with me with a musty dick."

There was an older couple sitting in the booth behind us. The man cleared his throat. I tried to see if I recognized them, but I didn't. While the blacks and whites in Kannapolis dealt with each other in some respects, the area was still very segregated as far as living space and communicating with one another. There was a ton of jungle fever going on though. My mother used to always say that future generations of black boys were going to be lost between the thighs of white women. I believed in to each his or her own, and I wasn't down with the swirl.

I didn't know the couple, but they needed to mind their business. If they didn't want to hear real talk, stay the fuck out of the real world.

I cleared my throat back, loudly, and then stared at Donita. "You nasty, Donita. Real, *real* nasty. The first time that man left a single bead in my bed, not that I *ever* would've allowed it, his ass would've been told. For you to even have to ask us if you should say something proves that you're hard the fuck up."

"Ease up, Lydia," Milena said, taking a sip of her lemonade. I couldn't see how she could still drink, much less eat, after Donita's "shit talk." "You shouldn't make fun of her. Obviously, this is really bothering her or she wouldn't have mentioned it."

"Well, she shouldn't have *mentioned* it when we weren't eating."

Donita seemed like she was on the brink of tears. "I'm sorry. You're right, Lydia. This was the wrong time to bring it up. It's just that I care about Timmy, *a lot,* and I don't want to say anything that might upset him or make him stop dating me."

Milena was about to say something, but I held my index finger up to hush her.

"Let me get this one," I said. Milena gave me a warning look. "Don't worry. I'm going to be nice about it." I looked at Donita, who was wiping her eyes with a napkin. "I can tell this is a serious matter."

I sat up straighter in the booth and noticed the man in the next one cropping his neck to try to listen. Now the old dirty bastard was all into it. He'd probably left his share of shit beads in the bed over the years his damn self.

"Donita, if you can't talk to Timmy without feeling like you have to walk on eggshells, then it's not a true relationship. When you're with someone intimately, you should be able to talk to them about anything. Ask the man—no, *tell him*—that he needs to bathe before you have sex. In fact, make it a sensual time. Suggest that you bathe together before you get it in. That way you can make sure that he's nice and clean all over: his ass, his dick, his balls. He'd probably get a kick out of being able to lather up your pussy and dig out the coochie with a washcloth. Hell, it might even lead to some freaky shit in the shower."

"Freaky shit like what?" Milena asked.

"One time," I whispered, sick of the man in the next booth being nosy, "I sucked Ph . . . a dude's dick in the shower with a bar of soap in my mouth."

Damn, I had almost fucked up and mentioned Phil. Even though Glenn and I were not together way back then when Donita was dating Timmy, I still didn't want anyone to know that I was fucking Phil.

"Damn, you do things like that?" Milena asked.

"That's hot!" Donita seemed excited and perked up. "I need to try that. Thanks, Lydia."

I glanced at Milena. "Yes, I do things like that. I never play when it comes to sex. If I'm going to fuck a man, I'm going to give him the fuck of his life. If I can't win a game, I don't want to play; real talk."

"You and all of your *real talk* is going to make you write a check one day that your ass can't cash," Milena said.

Sitting there at Baker's Creek, waiting for Phil to show up with his dick in tow, made me recall those words. I had certainly written the check. Hopefully, I'd never have to cash the damn thing.

Phil came speeding into the parking lot in his pimped-out metallic blue Ford Fusion with the vanity plate that read URideMe. *Nasty ass!*

He pulled up beside my white Honda Civic and rolled his window down. I did the same.

"You're late," I told him.

"No, I'm not. You said thirty minutes."

I glanced at the time on my dash. "And it's been thirty-two minutes."

"Whatever, Lydia. I couldn't be considered late anyway since I told you that I wasn't coming in the first place."

"Well, then, why are you here?" I asked, already knowing the answer.

"Shit, I'm not turning down your pussy."

I blushed as he rolled up his window, cut his engine, and got out. He climbed into my car.

"You want this dick in here or you want to fuck out in the woods with the animals?"

"Ooh, that's what I like about you."

He reached between my legs. I was dressed for church, where I would eventually end up late for the service, in order to cover my ass, but I hadn't bothered to put on panties. Phil started fingering my wet pussy and I laid my head back and closed my eyes.

"You've got that premium shit, Lydia. Men would go to war over this pussy. You know that?" He kept fingering me, setting my pussy on fire. "Sometimes, while I'm at work in that factory, all I can think about is your pussy. How lovely it smells. How wet and creamy it is. How good it tastes. How it drives me crazy when I'm deep inside of you."

"Damn, Phil, I love it when you do that sexy talk." I squirmed in the seat, gyrating my pussy on his fingers and holding onto his wrist, guiding the motion. "You're going to make me come already."

"No . . ." He tried to pull his fingers out but I continued to grasp his wrist and locked my thighs around his hand. "I don't want you to come all over that beautiful dress or your car seat.

Neither one of them will appreciate your juices as much as me. Let me lick that cat real good for you."

"I don't want to do it in the car." I changed course and pulled Phil's fingers out of me. "Let's go out in the woods like you said. I feel like doing something really freaky this morning."

"You've always been my little freak." Phil smiled as I sucked my own juice off of his fingers. "That shit with Glenn makes no damn sense. He'll never fuck you like me; that's why you won't stop."

"You won't stop either," I reminded him. "I've never forced myself on you."

"And as long as there is a breath in my body, you won't have to." Phil licked his fingers one by one to see if I'd left any juice for him. "No one turns me on more than you do, Lydia. We need to come out with it and tell Glenn the truth."

I slapped Phil across his face, damn near drawing blood. "Don't ever make that suggestion again, Phil. It's not going down like that."

Now the typical man would've either slapped my ass back, followed by a serious beatdown, or gotten out of my car and rolled out. Phil sat there, staring at me intently for a moment.

"I'm sorry that I hit you," I said. "I'm really hormonal right now; that's not an excuse though. But you know how I get when my period's about to start."

"Yeah, it is about that time. Couple more days or so."

See, that's the type of shit that Glenn should've been on top of, being that we lived together. Phil was more up on my bleeding calendar than my own man. Then again, he'd been digging my back out much longer.

"I bet you are horny, huh? You women start acting all crazy and shit when your Aunt Flo is headed to town."

"Yeah, we do." I grabbed Phil's chin, slipped my thick tongue into his mouth, and bit his bottom lip gently. "But you don't need to busy yourself worrying about any other woman. I take good care of you, don't I?"

"Sure you do." Phil sighed. "But sometimes I wish things were different. What are we really doing here . . . with each other? We fuck damn near every day. I've been seeing you longer than Glenn. Yet you want to keep it a secret . . . like you're ashamed of me or something."

"It's not like that, and you know it." It was exactly like that but I had to lie. "You've got a roommate. What do you expect from me? For me to move up in your crib with you and Briscoe? Don't forget that Glenn has brought me over there before. Briscoe can't even spell housekeeping, much less do any."

Phil looked extremely upset. I had to do something quick or he might've withheld the dick.

I started rubbing him through his jeans. He was already so hard, he could've split bricks. "Come on, Phil. Let's not start tripping. It's Sunday morning . . ." I looked around the park. "We're out here all alone. Last night, you looked so damn good at the party. All I could think about was sucking on your big dick."

That perked his ass up. "Really?"

"Ooh, yeah." I unzipped his pants and pulled his dick out. "Look at that. It's a thing of beauty. I was so horny for you last night that I went in the bathroom and played in my pussy until I came."

"Word?"

"Word." I ran the tip of my thumb back and forth across the head of his dick. "I was yearning for you, baby. I imagined your fingers all over my body, caressing my tits, my ass. I wanted you to split my pussy wide open with this piece of wood right here."

I was lying my ass off. There was no way that I would've masturbated at the Elks lodge, especially not in that same stall that Ms. Bart was pissing and shitting in half the night.

"You still want to go out in the woods?" Phil asked, grinning.

"Uh-huh, I want you to fuck me rough . . . hard . . . punish me with your dick."

"I'm going to fuck you so hard, you won't even be able to walk straight."

I giggled. "Now that's what I'm talking about." I reached down on the side of my seat and popped the trunk. "I've got a blanket in the trunk. Go get it so we can get it in."

Phil chuckled and got out of the car. I cut the engine and was about to get out when my phone rang. It was Glenn. I sent him a text message, letting him know that church had started and I would be home right after. Glenn never went to church, unless it was for a funeral or a wedding, so there was no chance of him showing up and seeing that I wasn't there. However, it was a small town, and I was running the chance that he might bring it up to someone in casual conversation. People in Kannapolis took great joy in busting someone's bubble. I couldn't blame them. Boredom could make people do all kinds of trifling shit, like what I was about to do with Phil.

All I can say is there was much to be said for fucking out in the bush. It had its pros and cons, but the idea of doing it someplace different did it for me. I could've done without the insects, both those on the ground and the ones flying by. I definitely could've done without the animals rustling through the woods and making it seem like a scene out of *Friday the 13th* when Jason would sneak up on a naked couple so busy getting their groove on that they didn't notice him about to whack one of their heads off. But what I did like was the breeze teasing my nipples and the hardness of the ground underneath the blanket as Phil plummeted his dick in and out of my pussy. There had been a terrible storm the night before and the ground was still fairly damp, another reason why the park was so deserted.

When we first got out there, I told him to put the blanket down. I lowered to my knees and gave him a serious dick-sucking. *TOOT MOTHERFUCKING TOOT!* I had him screaming out like a maniac by the time he came all down in my throat.

"Take your dress off," Phil said, dropping to the ground in front of me and groping at my clothes. "I want to see every inch of you."

As soon as it was visible, he grabbed my left tit and started milking it for dear life.

"Umm, that's it. I love breastfeeding you, baby."

"I want you so bad, Lydia."

I slipped the rest of my dress off but kept my heels on. "Then take me. Take me right here like a beast. Show me what a powerful fuck feels like. Drill a hole in my snatch."

I turned around and got down on all fours.

"Oh, you want it from the back, huh?" Phil asked.

"Damn straight. Take all this pussy."

Phil grabbed onto the sides of my ass and crouched down with his thighs on both sides of me, his knees still elevated and brushing against my sides. Then he laid it on me. I felt the tip of his dick enter me, and within seconds, he was all the way in. He fucked me with reckless abandon. That shit was off the chain and lasted for a good twenty minutes.

I came all over his dick and collapsed to the ground.

"You need to be careful what you ask for." Phil panted and tried to catch his breath. He lay beside me on the blanket. "I don't play when it comes to working pussy over."

"You don't have to tell me." I turned over onto my back and then threw my leg over his and started playing with the small hairs on his chest. I kissed the underside of his armpit gently, then laid my head on him. "You're the truth; real talk."

Phil was quiet for a moment, and I sensed something was wrong.

I looked up into his eyes. "What's wrong with you?"

"I was wondering, if I'm *the truth*, why are we out here fucking in the woods instead of setting up house together?"

I rolled my eyes to the sky. "Didn't we have this conversation back in the car?"

"No, not really. You spoke and I listened." He pushed me off of him and sat up on his elbows. "Now you're going to listen to me."

"Phil, can't you tell when you're beating a dead horse? I'm not going to change my mind. You and I function well . . . as fuck buddies. A relationship? That would never work."

"You don't know that. How can you even make an assumption like that? We've never tried to do the real thing. You were with me first, and instead of trying to make something serious work with me, you went out and made a commitment to my friend. *My best fucking friend*. Do you have any idea how much that hurts?"

I took a long breath and counted to ten in silence.

"Do you hear me, Lydia? This is really bothering me, and you don't seem to get it." I started to get up. Phil pulled me back down. "I'm sick of you running away from me. We're going to talk about this. You send me a text message early in the morning, expecting me to whip my dick out on demand, like some good little doggie."

*You are a good little doggie!*

"You leave Glenn at home, playing him for a fool, and then come out here and fuck me in the woods. This can't be the kind of life you want to lead. This shit is wrong."

"If it's so fucking wrong, then why are you here, Phil? Huh? Why the fuck are *you* here?"

Phil sighed and threw his hands over his face. "Because I love you, Lydia. A man doesn't have sex with a woman for over a decade without developing feelings. A few weeks, a few months, we probably don't give a damn, but this long? It doesn't go down that way."

I could've tried to reason with Phil about that. I could've tried to convince him that what he thought he was feeling was simply embedded in the power of my vajayjay. But I couldn't; he was in love with me and part of me had always realized that. It felt good to have him love me. It felt good to always have him near whenever I needed someone to talk to, someone to make me feel wanted . . . and needed.

I decided to put a different spin on it and play on his friendship with Glenn. "Glenn doesn't deserve this. He's a good man."

Phil took his hands off his face and stared at me. "I know that he's a good man . . . and he's an even better friend. And no, he doesn't deserve this, but neither do I."

"No, you don't. I dig that. But you're already hurting. What sense would it make to hurt him also?" I shrugged. "If we officially become a couple, we'd never live that shit down in this town. Everyone in Kannapolis would hate us."

I thought I had him . . . for a second.

"People cheat in Kannapolis all the time. Hell, having sex is about the only thing to do around here to kill time; either that or getting high or drunk."

"I could sure use a joint right about now," I said, mad at myself for not rolling at least one joint before I left the house.

"Who you telling? Me too, and some Jack Daniel's. You always have that primo shit. I can't believe you won't share your hookup with me."

Now I could get with some weed in the morning to smooth out my thoughts, but the fact that Phil wanted to hit the bottle was a bit much; yet not a surprise. That was typical Phil.

"I don't tell anybody where I get my weed, Phil. That's between my supplier and me."

"What? You his only customer or something? What kind of drug dealer only has one customer?"

"I'm not saying all that," I replied, thinking that I wasn't dealing shit, simply growing my own stash. "I'll ask him if I can bring you around, but I'm not giving you his number, or taking you past his crib without permission. Dealers don't be playing that, and he's a huge, brawny motherfucker with an arsenal sitting close by."

"Shit, is it safe for you to roll through there?"

"Yes, it's all copacetic between us. Plus, I've become a chat buddy of his chick."

"That's cool. That's cool."

I was a bit upset that Phil had gone from professing his love for me in one breath to worrying about where I bought my ciggaweed the next. How significant could I really have been?

"I need to get to church," I said, getting up and starting to get dressed.

"You're a trip. Fucking me out in the woods and then going to church."

"Hey, I'm not the only sinner that'll be packing the pews this morning. Except I've never professed to be a saint. There are plenty of sluts up in church every Sunday."

"You're not a slut, Lydia. You're special." Phil got up and pulled his pants up.

"Yes, I am special. One of these days I'm going to get out of this town. Maybe go to Hollywood and become a movie star." I twirled in my dress and heels. "You think I'm pretty enough to be a movie star? Or a model?"

"I think you're pretty enough to be whatever you want to be. Look how wide open you've got my nose. I'm not an easy man to catch, but you've got me; hook, line, and sinker."

"Are you seriously telling me that you don't fuck around with any other women?"

"I have in the past. I won't lie. But lately, it hasn't felt right . . . being with someone else. They don't do anything for me, so there's no point in bothering with it. If I know I can get a broad, that's the thrilling part. These women around here are easy. No challenge. No challenge at all."

Phil started folding up the blanket as I stared at his ass through his jeans.

"Is that what it is with me? Am I a challenge, Phil?"

"That you are." He must've realized what I was thinking. "But that's not why I want you. I love you; always have."

"I bet that if I was ever foolish enough to leave Glenn for you, we'd be all lovey dovey for a few months and then you'd leave me for the next piece of ass."

Phil finished folding up the blanket, lodged it under his right arm, and wrapped his left arm around my waist. He gazed into my eyes. "Never. I would never leave you. In fact, I'm never going to leave you now. I'll always be with you, for as long as you want to be with me."

Phil sounded so sincere; it frightened me.

I pulled away from his embrace. "We need to get out of here." I lifted one of my heels. "Look at all of this mud on my shoes."

"Yeah, that rain last night was no joke."

I laughed. "That wasn't rain. That was a kick-ass storm. For a minute it looked like the lightning was coming in through the front door, doing the electric slide across the carpet, and break-dancing out the back door."

"Yeah, that storm was deep. Must've been because it was so hot yesterday."

"Well, it was hot out here in these woods today." I kissed Phil gently on the lips. "Thanks for breakfast."

"Thanks for letting me dick feed you for breakfast."

"You're so nasty . . . but I like it."

Phil and I walked back toward our cars, hand in hand. It was too late for me to make the eight o'clock church service, even entering late. I decided to take my chances, kill about thirty minutes at the local Target, head on home, and pretend like I'd been there all along. I planned to take a shower, get my Sunday dinner started, and then head over to Milena's to get the 4-1-1 on Yosef.

# Milena

I HEARD a loud crash in my kitchen, which startled me awake. I glanced at the clock on my nightstand. It was 9:34 a.m. I had only been asleep about two hours. Gently, I got down off my bed and tiptoed toward my closed bedroom door. Then I heard another noise.

"Shit!" I whispered a little too loudly to myself.

*Calm down, Milena! There's a simple explanation for this!*

*Yeah, it's simple. There's someone in your kitchen!*

*But it could be you know who!*

*No, it's not you know who! He can't even get in the house!*

*You're right! Call the police!*

*They only do that shit in the movies! By the time the police get here, you could be dead!*

*Then hide until whoever it is leaves!*

Okay, yes, I talked to myself an awful lot, but my theory was that most people have inner conflicts, whether they voice them or not. None of that mattered at the moment. Someone was in my house and my spot was not close enough to anyone else for them to hear shit.

I grabbed the golf club that my dad had given me when I'd

flat-out refused to purchase a gun. I should've listened to him. I cracked the bedroom door and slipped out, inching my way down the hallway until I could see the main living area of my house, including the kitchen. Then I froze in place.

"Good morning, beautiful! I'd hoped to surprise you with breakfast in bed. You must've heard me drop the frying pan. Sorry about that; I don't know my way around here *yet*."

I dropped the golf club to my side. "And you never will. What are you doing here, Jacour?"

"I told you. Cooking you breakfast, and if you go back to bed, I'll serve you in bed."

*This man is so damn arrogant!*

Jacour was standing in my kitchen, wearing shorts and a Yankees jersey with his number and last name on it, acting like he lived there as he busied himself with cooking bacon, grits, and eggs.

"I hope you're hungry." He stopped and grinned at me, eyeing me like he wanted to eat me for breakfast instead. "I'm starving. I remember how you always like a big, hearty breakfast." He reached into a paper grocery bag and pulled out two loaves of bread. "You want wheat or white toast?"

"How did you get in here?" I asked, padding across the floor to get closer to him. I was still trying to decide whether or not to clock him with the golf club. "You can't barge into my home like this!"

"I didn't barge into anywhere. I used a key."

I tossed the golf club onto my sofa. "Dammit!"

Jacour laughed. "You're a creature of habit, baby. This may be a different house, but you still keep a spare key underneath the flower pot on the porch."

He was right; I was a creature of habit.

"Well, it won't be underneath there anymore. You need to leave."

"Oh, come on, Milena." Jacour held up a glass of orange juice. "Freshly squeezed; your favorite."

"It's not my favorite . . . anymore. The acid makes my stomach hurt."

"Sure. That's why you have two half-gallons of Minute Maid in the fridge."

I was stunned. "You've been groping through my refrigerator?"

"No, not groping. I was searching for the jelly. That's the only thing that I forgot at the store."

"You must've also forgotten your mind there," I stated sarcastically. "You have to leave."

"Not until you join me for breakfast. My cooking has improved *tremendously* over the years." Jacour chuckled and rubbed his hands together like he was a top chef about to present a feast. "I can't wait for you to taste it."

I stood there, looking at him like he was crazy; he was.

"You don't have to let me feed you in bed," he added.

"Oh, that would *definitely* be uncomfortable," I said.

"I'll set the table for us."

Jacour opened up a couple of cabinets until he located where I kept the dishes. He pulled out two plates and headed toward the kitchen table.

"Um, you need three."

He turned and stared at me. "Huh?"

"You need to set the table for three."

Jacour's eyes became slits as he set the plates down on the counter and crossed his arms defiantly in front of him. "He's here?"

"Of course he's here. Randolph's my man; the light of my life."
I giggled. "What? You thought he left town last night after the
party? That's ridiculous."

I was enjoying this. I sat down on the sofa and propped my left
leg underneath my ass and started moving my right leg back and
forth on purpose. Jacour was talking about me being such a creature of habit. That's what I did when I wanted to cause friction on
my clit when I was horny.

I started twirling my hair with my fingers, another sign that I
was in a sexy mood. "Your party was very nice. They really gave
you a hometown hero's welcome."

Jacour didn't say a word.

"Did you have an after-party? Randolph and I couldn't have
made it anyway. We wanted to spend some quality time together.
We hadn't seen each other in a few weeks, and since he flew in late
yesterday afternoon, we didn't have much time before the party."

Jacour still stood there, dumbfounded. The bacon started burning in the frying pan.

"You might want to check that bacon, Wolfgang Puck." I sighed
and started moving my leg back and forth again, slightly moaning
for effect. "Yeah, we didn't even get to sleep until the sun was up,
but it was worth it."

Jacour was taking the bacon out of the pan; more like *slamming*
it out of the pan. "I get the picture, Milena." He turned the grits off
on the stove. "Look, I'm going to cut out."

"So soon? What about breakfast?"

"You and Randolph can enjoy it." He glanced at his watch. "I
promised Momma that I'd come to church this morning anyway. I
need to get dressed so I can make the eleven o'clock service."

I stood up. "Okay, cool."

Jacour was halfway out the front door when he paused. "I'd like to have a word with Randolph before I leave."

"A word? A word about what?"

"A private word." Jacour looked like he wanted to attack somebody. "Man to man."

"Jacour, now you're really tripping. You don't need to have a word with him about anything."

We stood there, staring into each other's eyes for what seemed like an eternity. Jacour was trying to read me, and I didn't like it. Then he grinned mischievously.

"What?" I asked nervously.

"Maybe you don't want me to speak to him because he's not even here." Jacour moved closer to me. "Come clean, Milena. You and I both know you're not dating that dude. He's probably some local flake doing you a solid to make me jealous." He touched my arm and licked his lips seductively. "Well, it worked. Okay? I was jealous. Now you need to cut out all of this foolishness and make our relationship official again"—he glanced down my hallway—"in your bedroom."

For a second, a very brief second, part of me wanted to succumb to Jacour and wrap him in my arms. But that part of me was my heart, and he had long since damaged it beyond repair.

"I'm not lying. Randolph is in my bedroom . . . in my bed." I hesitated and realized that he wasn't buying into it. I stepped back from him. "Fine. Wait here. I'll go get him."

Jacour chuckled and closed the front door. "I'll be right here."

I backed away from him and then slowly turned around, walking through the living room and down the hallway toward my bedroom. "Randolph!" I yelled. "We have company!"

I opened my bedroom door slightly, slid in like I was trying to prevent Jacour from seeing my bed—which I was—and then shut and locked the door.

"Shit!" I whispered, right back to where I'd started from when I'd first heard the noise in the kitchen.

*What are you going to do now, Slickster?*

*Maybe he'll leave in a few minutes!*

*Not a chance! He knows that man isn't in your bedroom!*

*Shit!*

I felt a bona fide panic attack coming on. Up until then, I hadn't even paid attention to the fact that I'd gone out there with an oversized pair of pajamas on. Not a damn thing sexy about them. I had been sleeping in tees for the majority of the summer, but the rain the night before had cooled things down so I'd put them on to keep warm.

I took them off real quick, pulled on a pair of baggy shorts and a tee. Damn, all of a sudden I wished that all of my clothes weren't so damn loose. If I was really in a relationship, no man would've wanted to see me dressed more like him than a woman. I grabbed a pair of dingy sneakers and sat on the bed to put them on. Then I sat there, panting.

For a second, I thought that Jacour might've actually left. Then I heard my television come on and the channels start flicking.

*Shit!*

Desperate times called for desperate measures. There was no way that I would've been able to sneak past Jacour to get out the front door. The window in my bedroom was nailed shut to keep out intruders.

*Smart move, Milena! It keeps people out and it also keeps your ass in!*

There was no window in my master bathroom. I went to the door and listened intently. When I heard Jacour laughing at something humorous on the television, I inched the door open, slipped back out, and dashed into the guest bathroom.

After I shut and locked that door, I climbed into the tub and unlocked the window on the wall.

*So you were worried about people coming in your bedroom window but not the bathroom window!*

*Shut the hell up!* I told myself.

In retrospect, I realized the *only* window that was nailed shut was in my bedroom. That was rather stupid, considering that I lived in a rancher and a burglar/murderer/sex freak could've easily gained access through any of the others.

*Or used the key your stupid ass left under the plant like Jacour did!*

Because of the slick surface in the tub, it took me a minute to heave myself out of the window and topple onto the ground outside. It was muddy from the rain. *Great!*

My sneakers squished through the mud as I made my way the hundred feet or so toward my kennel. The animals started stirring as I grew closer. People can say what they want about animals, but you can't sneak up on their asses. They're so used to being in protect mode; if they slip up, that's their asses. Literally.

Bessie, Mr. Slater's pig, was still there. I had to make sure that I called him to come pick her up later that day. Bessie had osteochondrosis, an orthopedic disease that was hindering the blood supply to her bones. Most laymen don't realize that animals have many of the same ailments as humans. And some of them seem a whole lot smarter than the idiots running rampant around the earth. I'd diagnosed it as a dietary problem, had given Bessie a muscle relaxant, and she'd seemed to be resting comfortably when I'd last seen her once I'd returned from Concord.

Well . . . once *we'd* returned from Concord. Yosef was resting peacefully in the small bedroom in the kennel. Sometimes, when animals were really sick, I'd sleep back there so that I could keep an eye on them. Right then, I had Bessie, another pig, a few dogs, and a couple of cats in-house. The cats were really temporary residents; there was nothing wrong with them. Mrs. Stallone, an elderly woman in her eighties, had gone to stay with her daughter, son-in-law, and grandchildren in Michigan for the summer. Since I rarely, if ever, went anywhere, I didn't mind keeping her cats for a minimal fee. It had kind of become a tradition.

Yosef was snoring lightly, and I hated to disturb him. He looked so beautiful—if that term can be relevant to men—lying on the quilt that my grandmother had made for me before she'd transitioned a few years earlier. I missed Honey Bear so much. Papa Bear was now living with my parents, and I tried to spend as much time with him as humanly possible.

Part of me yearned to lie beside Yosef in the bed, but that wouldn't have been cool. A, I didn't know the man like that, and B, Jacour was in my house.

*Shit!*

I snapped back to reality and started shaking Yosef. "Yosef, please wake up! I need your help!"

Yosef woke up quickly; surely a reflex from staying in shelters and out in the woods. At any given moment, someone crazy could've snuck up on him.

"What's wrong?" He sat up straight. Even the drool on the side of his mouth was sexy to me.

*You've been too long without a man!*

*Don't I know it!*

"Jacour's in the house. Can you believe he came in without my permission and started cooking breakfast?"

"What? How'd he get in?" Yosef asked, putting on his dress

shoes from the night before. He'd slept in his undershirt and dress pants.

I really needed something else for him to put on so Jacour wouldn't think that Yosef didn't have a suitcase with him. The tattered clothing was certainly not an option, so we'd simply have to make it look like he'd thrown his dress pants back on after a night of serious lovemaking.

"I'll tell you about that later," I said. "I told him that you were in my bedroom, sleeping."

"You did what?" Yosef exclaimed.

"Yes, and I snuck out the bathroom window."

Yosef laughed so hard that he had to hold his belly. "Milena, are you serious?"

"We'll discuss all of this later." I tugged on his arm and started pulling him toward the door. "We have to hurry."

I wish that I could describe how comical it truly was to see a six-foot-five man trying to get through my bathroom window. I climbed in first, then Yosef. A bar of soap had fallen out of the holder. He slipped on it and almost busted his ass, but I caught him . . . and didn't want to let him go.

Before we could sneak out of the bathroom, I heard Jacour calling from the living room. "Milena, are you two coming?" Then he laughed. *Asshole!*

"We'll be right out!" I yelled back. "Give us a second!"

"You go out first," Yosef said. "Give me a couple of minutes to freshen up."

I hadn't even bothered to brush my teeth. "Could you turn your back for a second?" I asked Yosef.

"For what?"

"So I can brush my teeth."

"You want me to turn my back so you can brush your teeth?"

"Yes, I'm not used to brushing my teeth. I mean, not in front of a man."

Yosef chuckled and turned his back. I hurriedly squeezed some toothpaste on my electric brush and did a quick-fix job. Normally, I brushed for a full three minutes, but time was of the essence.

When I was done brushing, I gargled real quick, and it must have sounded crazy, because Yosef started laughing, then covered his mouth to hide his amusement.

I wiped my mouth with a cloth, along with the rest of my face, and realized that both Jacour and Yosef had seen me with dried-up saliva on the corners of my lips.

*Yuck! Milena, you nasty!*

*Don't I know it!*

"Okay, all done," I said. "There's some extra toothbrushes and towels in the linen closet, if you need them."

"Thanks. I still have the toothbrush you gave me yesterday," Yosef said. "But I will use some clean towels. I was kind of grungy the first time I showered here."

That was an understatement, but he looked—and smelled—entirely different now.

"Sorry to put you through this."

"No problem. It's fun," he said.

I left the bathroom and headed down the hallway toward the living room. Jacour was pacing the floor.

"Took you long enough. Where's Randolph?"

"He's coming. Geesh, you did pop up here out of the blue. Plus, like I already told you, we had a long night." I bit my bottom lip like I was reminiscing about some hellified dick action. "A very, *very* long night."

Jacour smirked. "So you keep saying. The breakfast is getting cold. I hope that *the light of your life* won't be too much longer."

"He won't."

I went and sat down at the kitchen table. Jacour made a show of getting an additional plate out of the cabinet and setting the table for three. I could tell that he still didn't think Randolph was there. Truth be told, he wasn't supposed to be there.

The night before, when Yosef and I were sitting in my truck during the storm, something within me simply would not allow him to leave me. Not like that. The man had gone out of his way for me, and then had refused to take any money when it was painfully obvious that he needed it. While I really couldn't have been considered an expert when it came to judging men, since I had technically only ever been with one in my entire life, my gut instinct told me that Yosef was a good-quality man. A good-quality man in a bad situation. There was a reason why our paths had crossed, and while I did not necessarily envision myself becoming an item with him, I wanted to be considered his friend. I had become a veterinarian to show kindness toward animals. That same kindness needed to be shown toward humans as well.

In less than twenty-four hours, my entire perspective on the psyche of a homeless person had changed. Around Kannapolis, the only people that I knew running the streets were either drug addicts or emotionally unstable people, some of them members of my own family that my relatives had given up on—either out of fear or pure disgust.

I had pleaded with Yosef to come back home with me. There was no way that I was going to watch him walk off into the woods to some "village" that he was too ashamed of for me to see. It took some fast talk about how I still needed to have him underfoot. Surely, people would come sniffing around to find out more information. However, when I was utilizing my gift of gab on Yosef, I never imagined that Jacour would be the first one to show up early Sunday morning—in my kitchen, no less.

Jacour was sitting across the table from me, smirking.

"You need to wipe that grimace off your face," I told him. "It doesn't complement you."

"The expression on my face is the last thing you need to be worried about."

"Worried? Why would I be worried about anything? I don't have anything to prove to you."

*Yes, you do!*

*No, I don't!*

*Liar!*

Jacour shrugged and drank some more of the orange juice he'd freshly prepared. "True, you don't have to prove anything to me. I wish you'd stop playing this silly game so we can eat breakfast. It's getting—"

"Sorry about that," Yosef said, coming around the corner from the hallway. He had on the same raggedy bathrobe that I'd given him the night before, and his hair was wet. Beads of water were dripping off his chiseled chest. "I decided to take a quick shower before breakfast. I didn't want to come to the table smelling like . . . well, you know what I'm saying. Right, brother?"

Oh, how I wished that I could've frozen that second in time and taken a mental snapshot to place in my memory book. The look on Jacour's face was indescribable. Stunned, no. Shocked, no. Shamed, no. It was something that combined all three of those S words. Maybe *Stunshockshamed*.

"Why don't you sit beside me, baby?" I patted the pad on the chair next to me. "Jacour has cooked us a fabulous breakfast. Wasn't that nice of him?"

"That's a great gesture, man." Yosef sat down and gulped down an entire glass of orange juice. "Wow, this is incredible. Is it freshly squeezed?"

"Yes, it is," I replied. "Jacour made it himself."

Jacour still didn't say a word. He was floored.

"Jacour, would you like for me to serve the plates?" I asked, getting up from the table but not before Yosef had taken my hand and kissed it. "If anything's cold, I can heat it up in the microwave."

Jacour stood up abruptly, almost knocking over the chair that he'd been sitting in. "I have to go."

"So soon?" Yosef stood up and held out his hand, but Jacour refused to shake it. "You should stay and enjoy the fruits of your labor."

"The fruits of my labor. Humph." Jacour crossed his arms in front of him again; an old habit that hadn't died. "What did you say you do again, man?"

"I'm a veterinarian, like Milena."

"Oh yeah, what veterinary school did you go to?"

"Randolph attended UC Davis," I interjected, realizing that as smart as Yosef seemed, the odds were slim of him being able to name a veterinary school in California. He caught on quickly.

"I went to the University of California Davis School of Veterinary Medicine," Yosef said like he had a diploma from the school hanging up somewhere in a plush office.

Jacour looked skeptical. "I've heard of Davis, California. What county is that in again?"

"Why are you playing twenty questions, Jacour?" I asked. "There's no need to do an inquisition."

"I've asked a couple of questions, Milena. *Two*, and he hasn't answered either one of them."

"Yes, he did." I was getting pissed.

*How dare he?*

*How dare you! Jacour might be a whore, but he's never been a dummy!*

"Shut up!" I screamed, talking to the voice in my head but yelling it out loud.

"It's okay, Milena." Yosef sat back down beside me as I buried my face in my hands. "Calm down."

"Yeah, Milena, calm down," Jacour said. "It's not that serious. I was only trying to be friendly."

"No, you weren't." I glared up at Jacour. "Why would you want to be friendly with Yo— Randolph? That makes no sense." I was about to slip up and had to get my emotions under control. "I'd like for you to leave now."

Jacour threw his hands up in front of him. "I'm already going."

Yosef and I watched as Jacour left through the front door. A moment later we heard his car starting up and then roaring down my driveway to the road.

"So what county?" Yosef asked.

"Huh?"

"What county is Davis, California, in? I need to be prepared, if anyone else brings that up."

"I don't know." Yosef and I looked at each other and fell out laughing. "I'm not altogether sure that there's a veterinary school in Davis. I *kind of* recall hearing that someplace."

Yosef got up and went over to the stove. He looked over the spread that Jacour had prepared. "I have to admit, it looks like the brother can cook. You want me to hook you up with a plate?"

I shook my head. "I don't have an appetite. I still can't believe that Jacour had the audacity to enter my house without permission and make himself at home."

Yosef picked up a piece of bacon and bit off of it. "Milena, might I make a suggestion?"

"What's that?"

"Maybe it would be best for you to come clean about all of this now."

I was speechless.

"Look at it this way." Yosef came back over to the table and sat across from me, pulling the chair back up that Jacour had almost knocked over. "You can't pull this charade off forever; surely you recognize that. I can't remain here in your home, and the more lies you tell, the more difficult it will become to keep them straight. Jacour already senses that something's not on the up-and-up. Surely, he's not the only one who's on to you. From what I'm gathering, you've been unattached for many years and—"

"I've been *unattached* because none of the men around here are any good."

"Oh, come on, you can't judge every man by the actions of one. How many serious relationships have you ever had? In your entire life?"

I stared at Yosef. "What are you now? My therapist?"

"No, that's not where I'm coming from." He grinned. "I'd like to be considered your friend."

"Okay, friend, I'll tell you what. I'll make you a deal. You show me yours and I'll show you mine."

Yosef raised an eyebrow. "Come again?"

"I'll tell you all about my miserable, lonely existence if you tell me about yours. I want to know everything. Who you really are, where you came from, and why you're homeless. And I don't want to hear that abbreviated version that you laid on me last night."

Yosef sat there, looking uneasy, then diverted his eyes from mine.

"Therapy's not so easy when the script is flipped, huh?"

"Look, Milena, it's complicated. I—"

Suddenly there was a knock at the door. We'd been so caught up in the conversation that neither one of us had heard someone drive up.

"Hold that thought," I said, getting up from the table.

The knocking came again, only louder.

"I'm coming!"

I opened the door to find Mr. Slater there, in a panic. "Milena, how's Bessie?"

"She's fine, Mr. Slater." I sighed. "Her bones are a little weak because of her age, and I need to talk to you about her diet."

"Oh, thank the Lord." Mr. Slater smiled; his teeth were yellow and few and far between. "The missus will be so relieved." He glanced inside and spotted Yosef in my bathrobe. "Hmm, I see you have company." He winked. "Good for you."

*It's a damn shame that even the old white people in this town know you're going through a dick drought!*

*Don't I know it!*

Yosef waved at him. "Top of the morning to you."

"Yeah, you too, fella," Mr. Slater replied.

"Why don't I meet you around back," I said. "Bessie's eager to see you."

Mr. Slater removed his cap and swatted at a fly on the porch. His entire head was red, as was his neck, and I held back a laugh, remembering Lydia's theory of the difference between a redneck and a hillbilly from the night before. I was surprised she hadn't beaten a path to my door yet.

"Hurry up, please," he said. "I still need to stop by the market and get some collards for the missus to cook for dinner."

I shut the door gently and turned to Yosef. "We'll continue this conversation later. Cool?"

He shrugged, clearly not wanting to. "That man must really love his dog."

"Dog." I giggled. "Bessie's a pig. A *prize-winning* pig."

Yosef chuckled. "Wow, he talks about her like she's a member of the family."

"To him and his wife, she is family."

"Life is like that." Yosef shook his head. "You learn something new every day. I never knew people cherished pigs like that. I thought they bred them and killed them to make food."

"Like that piece of bacon you're holding."

We both laughed.

"It doesn't bother you? Taking care of animals and also eating them?"

"Please, I grew up sucking on pigs' feet, watching men rip the intestines straight out of a pig and making chitterlings, and taking the skin off of pigs at pig pickings and putting it in the oven to make homemade pork rinds."

Yosef dropped the piece of bacon on the nearest plate. "Now I think that I've lost my appetite."

I giggled and opened the door. "Be back in a few."

"I'll be right here."

As I shut the front door and headed down the porch steps, I started talking to myself again . . . as usual.

*You need to get that man out of here before you do something you'll regret!*

*Shut the hell up!*

# Lydia

## Two Weeks Later

I HATED my life. There had to be a better place . . . somewhere over the rainbow. Shit, I'd never even seen a rainbow!

Saturdays were by far the worst days to work at Food Lion, but no one got a pass from being on the Saturday schedule. Only being maimed, dismembered, or dead were acceptable excuses to call in on Saturdays. It didn't even matter that my uncle Joe was my supervisor. He was in the same damn boat. It was all hands on deck, or your ass would be thrown off the boat.

I was working the express lane—ten items or fewer—and people had been working my last nerve all day. I was sick of folks coming through there with too many items and playing dumb, like they hadn't noticed the lighted sign stating the limit. The lines were too long for that nonsense, and like Helen Slater professed in that trailer-park-trash movie *The Legend of Billie Jean*, fair is fair!

My hair was itching and needed to be washed, the tips on my nails needed to be filled in, and my lower back was hurting from standing in the same spot for so long. I was so busy rolling my eyes at these two young tramps that were in my line with twenty two-liter sodas that I didn't notice Phil walk up behind me and tap me on the shoulder.

"Hey, Lydia, you got a minute?"

I glanced at him and winced. "Can't you see that I'm working?"

"Do you have a break coming up?"

"Do you see a break in my line?" I asked sarcastically.

"No, but they've still got to give you a break. It's the law."

"Thanks for the 4-1-1, Johnnie Cochran."

The two girls laughed, but I didn't see a damn thing funny. When I sneered at them, they both looked away.

"That'll be twenty-four fifty," I said, then had to wait patiently for them to pool their funds to purchase their bounty of empty calories. If they kept drinking soda like that, they wouldn't have ten teeth between the two of them before they were thirty. Phil was standing there looking desperate. "What's the emergency, Phil? You showing up at my job and all that." I glanced around the store. "That's not cool."

"Promise me you'll call me when you get off."

"I don't make promises." One of the girls handed me the money, exact change. "Thanks. Have a nice day," I said, forcing the pleasantries out. I didn't give a shit how their day went, as long as they got out of my line.

"I sent you some text messages. You didn't respond," Phil said.

"Does it look like I have time to sit up in this register texting people back and forth?"

"Oh, come off it, Lydia. You always text me from work"—he rubbed my elbow—"when you want something." I yanked my arm away. "Besides," he continued, "your uncle's your boss. It's not like he's going to fire you."

"That's not the point. I take pride in my work."

Phil laughed. "Whatever, Lydia. Make sure you call me later."

Once Phil walked off, the two girls pushed their cart out of the way and were replaced by some bucktoothed dude from Rose Hill that I recognized. He'd tried to holler at me one night at the BP gas station. He'd spilled some ill lines that had made me want to vomit.

I looked down at the belt. Clearly, he had more than ten items. *Fair is fair!*

"Um, did you not realize what line you were getting in?" I asked, full of disdain.

He was talking to someone on his cell phone, all loud and ghetto-like. "Yeah, you heard me, fool. Imma be through there in a minute. Make sho you got that Cristal flowing."

Cristal? There was no fucking way he was rolling like that. Plus he was buying tortilla chips and off-brand cheese sauce. Nobody mixed that shit with Cristal. More like Mad Dog 20/20 or Thunderbird. He must've been trying to impress somebody, but it wasn't working on me.

He disconnected his call. "What was you saying, sweetness?"

"I said, you're in the wrong line."

He looked around, playing dumb like everyone else that day. "Oh, my bad. I didn't see the sign. Go 'head and hook me up. You know how we do."

"I'm sorry, sir, but you'll need to gather your items and take them to another cashier."

The middle-aged woman behind him snickered. She only had a jar of peanut butter so she would get no beef from me.

"Aw, I get it now," Bucktooth said. "Isn't you that bitch from BP the other night?" He looked me up and down. "Yeah, you'se that *same* bitch. I recognize that raggedy-ass uniform. You still look good as shit tho'. I'd do you in a hot minute."

Now, if that motherfucker had called me a bitch in any other place outside of my place of employment, I would've cut his ass; real talk. But I was determined not to put myself out there as a stereotype and stoop to the level of an imbecile.

I turned on the "assistance needed" light on my register so that Uncle Joe would come over.

"What you puttin' that light on for?" Bucktooth asked. "I ain't going to another line, shortie. You can forget that shit."

"And I'm not ringing you up."

"Oh, yes, the hell you are."

"Oh, no, I'm most certainly not."

He leaned closer to me, and his breath almost knocked me the fuck out. It smelled like a mixture of decaying flesh and feces. I reared back in disgust.

"Come on, now. People waitin' and shit. You coulda had me all ranged up by now."

"Your ebonics is killing me . . . along with your breath."

"Ebon what?" He stepped back, thank goodness. He put his palm in front of his face, blew on it, and then smelled it. "Ain't nothin' wrong wit' my breath. You'se trippin'."

Uncle Joe, who weighed every bit of three hundred and fifty pounds, came waddling over to my register. "What's wrong, Lydia? You need an override?" He had his bypass card at the ready to scan it over the reader. "Your line's getting longer and longer."

"I need to take a smoke break. Can you have someone relieve me?"

"Smoke break? Since when do you smoke?"

I clamped my eyes shut at my blunder. "I don't smoke. I just need a break . . . now."

"Yo, Fat Albert, you needta get ol' girl straight. She tryin'ta not ring up my shit."

My uncle looked at Bucktooth and then back at me. He knew

about my temper and propensity for violence all too well. "I already know what's going to happen if I don't let you out for a few. Go ahead. I'll take over until Sheila gets back from her break."

I was livid. "How is Sheila already on a break and she came in an hour after me?"

"Sheila's a chain-smoker. You've seen her. Three straight hours without a cigarette and she turns into a monster."

I didn't even respond. I stormed away from my register and headed toward the back loading dock. It was amazing how a bad fucking habit got people a lot of extra favoritism at work.

"I'll catch you at BP, shortie, wit' yo' fine ass!" I could hear Bucktooth yelling behind me.


I was standing out back, by the edge of the wooded area, when I heard some footsteps approaching. I stomped out the joint that I'd been smoking, hoping that it wasn't my uncle. That's all I needed—him telling my parents about my weed habit. I reached into the pocket of my uniform, pulled out the small aerosol bottle of body mist that I always kept on me, sprayed some on my clothing and into the surrounding air, then popped a breath mint into my mouth. Covering up my ciggaweed habit was almost as difficult as planting and growing it.

"Hey there, Lydia."

I turned to find Andy standing there. Andy was a truck driver for Food Lion. He and I would talk from time to time; I lived my life outside of Kannapolis vicariously through him. Even though Food Lion was headquartered in nearby Salisbury, they had stores in eleven states. Andy got to make deliveries from Florida to Delaware. That was exciting to me.

"Hey, Andy. How's it going?"

"I'm cool. I saw you walk out here a little while ago. Why you always out here in the woods? You aren't scared of snakes?"

"Andy, I grew up here. If a snake was going to take me out, it would've done that a long time ago." I eyed Andy up and down. He had at least fifteen years on me, but he wasn't a bad-looking man. He was about five-ten with deep-set hazel eyes, light-skinned, and his auburn hair was balding. "Besides, we really only have black snakes around here."

"Humph, it's true that North Carolina has a lot of black snakes, but there are a lot of other things running around here. Did you hear about the coyote problem in Durham?"

I giggled. "Andy, stop trying to scare me. Ain't no coyotes in North Carolina."

He gazed at me seductively. "I'm serious, Lydia. It was on the news last week. They've been having trouble at the Raleigh-Durham airport; planes not able to take off because packs of coyotes were lollygagging on the runway."

I quickly scanned the woods. I wasn't afraid of snakes or deer, but the thought of coyotes scared the shit out of me. Phil and I wouldn't be fucking out in the woods anymore. Getting bit on the ass by a mosquito was one thing; having my neck ripped out by a motherfucking beast was another.

"Shit! That's deep," I finally replied, after I'd imagined a pack of coyotes running up on Phil and me while we were getting it in. "So, where all have you been this week?"

"I did a run to Maryland and one to Kentucky. Tomorrow, I'm headed down to Georgia and then I've got to come back, load up, and go to Tennessee. That's where I'm really from."

"That's so exciting." I pouted. "I'm going to get away from here one day, travel and see the world."

Andy touched my cheek gently. "Let me know if you ever want to take a ride with me whenever you have a couple of days off."

I was so elated that I was ready to tap dance. "Are you serious, Andy?"

He shrugged. "Sure. Why not?"

I took a peek at Andy's left hand. No ring. "Are you married?"

"No." He held up his hand. "You don't see a ring, do you?"

I smirked and patted him playfully on the chest. "That doesn't mean anything these days. Most of the married men that I know don't wear their rings after year one . . . the honeymoon phase. They either lose them, claim they need to keep them off so they don't scratch them up when they're working, or just say fuck it altogether and stuff them in a drawer."

Andy laughed. "Now that I think about my buddies, you have a point."

"Damn skippy, I do. Heck, it's so bad out here that a lot of women don't wear theirs either. They blame it on gaining baby weight, or the stone being smaller than somebody else's or—"

"Let me get this straight. Women compete about the size of the ring? Isn't it supposed to be all about the thought that counts?"

"What rock have you been hiding under?"

Andy chuckled and looked at his watch. "Well, I better get going." He glanced toward the loading dock. "Looks like they've finished unloading. What time is your break over?"

"When I say it's over."

"Oh, so you've got it like that."

I smiled at Andy. "Joe's my uncle, on my mother's side."

"Joe's a cool cat."

"He's a fat cat," I said, referencing my uncle's weight. I had to admit: Bucktooth got a good one in when he called him Fat Albert.

I giggled, thinking about the expression on Unc's face after he said it. "I don't see how my aunt Brittany finds that shit attractive. He's destined to have one of those widow-maker heart attacks any second now."

Andy came closer to me. "Everyone needs love, Lydia." He lifted my left hand and intertwined his fingers with mine. "Where's your ring, young lady?"

I gazed into his eyes, our faces mere inches from one another. "I'm one of those women who desires that *bling*. Until I find a man who can provide me with all that I yearn for, I'm staying single. I'm not settling for any less. I can see it now. I marry the wrong one, and the better man might be right around the corner."

"Or right in front of your face."

Andy placed his free hand on my breast. That shit felt so good.

"You like that, Lydia? You enjoy the way that feels?"

"Uh-huh, I do."

I pushed my tits out farther toward him, and he was about to unbutton my uniform top and kiss me when I heard my name.

"Lydia! Lydia, you out here?"

Andy gave me a peck on the lips and backed away. "Saved by the bell."

"Those damn bells are constantly getting in my fucking way," I said.

"They must need you back in there. Saturdays are a trip at grocery stores."

"True that." I glanced toward the dock. Milena was walking toward the woods. "But that's my ex–best friend."

"Ex–best friend?" Andy grinned. "Well, I better get out of here before the drama starts."

Andy walked away and passed Milena. He must've said hello.

She paused and stared at his back as he walked back to his truck. Then she came over to join me.

I sat down on a tree stump. "I must be hallucinating out in these woods. Maybe Jim Jones spiked my juice this morning."

"Don't start, Lydia." Milena sat down beside me. "I've been busy."

"Too busy for your ex–best friend? Humph."

"You're not ex-nothing." Milena slapped me on the knee. "I have so much to tell you."

I glared at her. "Milena, in our entire lives, we've never gone two weeks without talking. What's good with that?" I stood up and started pacing. "You show up at Jacour's party with some fine-ass man named Yosef, and then you start ignoring a sister like you're Mariah Carey or some shit."

"I haven't been ignoring you. My life is a mess . . . but a good kind of mess . . . sort of."

"That has nothing to do with the fact that I've been calling you, texting you, coming by your crib day and night searching for your ass." I was pissed. "Shit, Milena, I even emailed you and you know I don't even fuck with email. Shit, I barely know how to turn on my fucking computer."

Milena rolled her eyes. "It's not that serious, Lydia."

"The hell it isn't. Milena, people in this town could've set their watches by you until two weeks ago. You were a hermit who went grocery shopping twice a week, bought medical supplies once a week, feed for the animals once a month, and came to church every Sunday. You took care of those funky animals, watched television and DVDs, surfed the internet night and day, and barely spoke to anyone outside of me and your parents."

Milena stood up and placed her hand on my shoulder, preventing me from pacing. "I get it; I didn't have a life. And you're right; I didn't." She smiled from ear to ear and let go of me. "But now I do."

Suddenly, I wasn't mad anymore. I was too concerned with being nosy. "It's that Yosef dude, right? Don't tell me you're fucking him? Hold up. Rewind that. Please tell me you're fucking that Sasquatch-sized piece of meat." I put my hands on my hips. "Never mind. I can tell you're fucking him. I haven't seen that grin in a long-ass time, and I can always tell when you're getting sexed right."

Milena giggled. "If I tell you something, you have to promise not to tell anyone."

I shrugged. "Who I look like? Paul Revere?"

"Now, Lydia, I get most of my town gossip"—she poked me lightly in the chest—"from you."

"Just because I tell you all the dirt that I'm privy to doesn't mean that I'm going to spread yours, or my own!"

Andy's truck revved up and pulled off from the loading dock. Milena and I watched him disappear out of the parking lot.

"Who's that man?" Milena asked. "And what were the two of you doing out here in the woods?"

"Dang, Momma, I promise that I'll be home before curfew from now on," I said sarcastically.

"For real, Lydia." Milena looked around the woods, like she was searching for evidence of some freaky shit. She needed to be looking through the woods at Baker's Creek for that. "You're not fucking around on Glenn, are you?"

I avoided saying no because I hated lying to her, so I covered my ass another way.

"With Andy?" I said, waving toward the dock where he had been seconds earlier. "No way. He's cute and all. I enjoy kicking it with him. At least he gets to travel to other states. But, no, I'm not fucking Andy."

*But I was about to let him suck on my ta-tas before you showed up!*

"Stop trying to divert the attention from you, Milena. What's going on with you and Satch?"

"Okay, I'm going to tell you something and you better not tell anyone. Not Glenn, not Jacour, and for damn sure not my parents, whether you're concerned for my safety or not."

"Hold up!" I threw my palms in the air. "Red flag alert! Red flag alert! What the fuck you mean, concerned for your safety?"

Milena sighed. "It's complicated, but Yosef's a good man. People might get the wrong impression of him if they knew his situation, that's all."

"What situation?" I asked, growing extremely concerned. "Is he a drug dealer?"

"No, he's not a dealer."

"A felon?"

"No."

"Then what? Shit! Come on with it already!"

Milena looked me in the eyes and hesitated for a few seconds. I folded my arms in front of me and started tapping my foot.

"When I met Yosef, he was . . . He was . . ."

"He was what?" I prodded.

Milena looked away from me. "He was panhandling down by the speedway."

It took a few seconds for her statement to sink in. "Panhandling! What for?"

"Because . . . he was homeless."

I stared at her; I had come undone.

"Did you hear what I said, Lydia? Yosef's homeless."

I waved my index finger in her face. "Wait here."

I started walking away.

"Wait here for what?" Milena asked.

I stopped walking and turned to her. "On second thought, go home. I'll be there in less than thirty minutes."

"But weren't you only on break? When I asked about you, your uncle said you don't get off for another six hours."

"I'm getting off right now. I'll tell his roly-poly ass that you sprained your ankle or something when you came looking for me, and that I have to take you to the emergency room."

"He won't believe that. What if he asks to look at my ankle?"

"You and your ankle won't be here."

I hurried back to the store. There was no way that I was waiting six hours to get to the bottom of Milena's shit.

# Milena

I DECIDED to cut up the leftover rotisserie chicken from dinner the night before and make some salad for Lydia and me. This was going to be a difficult talk for me to have, but I desperately needed someone to confide in. Lydia thought that I was beaming because of Yosef and, in many ways, I was, but that wasn't who I'd been fooling around with.

Life is funny. One day I'm going on my ninth year of celibacy; the next I'm torn between the affection of two men.

Yosef had been staying with me for those two weeks. I still didn't let him stay in the house at night. The bedroom in the kennel wasn't half-bad, and he had no problem dealing with the noisy animals. He was used to a lot more noise than that out on the streets. Whenever someone would come over, we'd pretend like he was keeping my sheets warm at night, often putting on enticing performances for the benefit of others. But we had yet to kiss.

Jacour was the problem . . . my weakness.

*How could you do something so stupid, Milena!*

*It felt good!*

*It felt good before, but a canine's a canine! Jacour's ass belongs in one of those pens out in your kennel!*

*I needed it!*

*You need a psychoanalyst!*

*Don't I know it!*

It happened the week after Jacour's welcome home party. Yosef was at the house, cooking dinner for us. The man was quite a good cook. Plus, I think that he wanted to impress me, since Jacour had cooked breakfast that day. I'd gone into town to get some feed. When I was getting into my truck to go back home, Jacour pulled up beside me in his Rolls.

"Hey, Milena," he said through the open window.

I hadn't seen him since the day he'd pulled that breaking-and-entering job at my house.

"Hello, Jacour," I replied.

He cut his engine, got out of his car, and walked over to my window. "Your friend grow wings and fly back to California yet?"

"No, not yet. He's on vacation from his practice," I said, lying my ass off.

"Is that right?"

"Yes, that's right." I paused. "Is that all? You finished playing twenty questions?"

"You and that twenty questions nonsense. I only asked one."

A group of skeezers walked by, smiling and waving at Jacour. He ignored them altogether.

"Aren't you going to address your groupies?" I pointed to them as they walked off down the sidewalk. "I'm sure they'd all like to get busy with the famous, wealthy Jacour Bryant."

"They probably would," he admitted, "but that's their problem."

"Too bad you didn't have that attitude about those floozies the night before our wedding."

"Too damn bad." He paused and touched my hand that was lying on the door. "That was the worst mistake of my life."

"And agreeing to marry you in the first place was the worst mistake I've ever made."

Jacour looked like I'd punched him in the stomach and knocked the air out of him. "I only want a chance to explain myself. You've never given me that."

"You sent me those letters and cards and stuff. I get the picture."

"No, I don't think you do." The sidewalk was getting crowded, and people were looking at us like we were celebrities. Well, in Kannapolis, Jacour definitely was, but not me. "Can we go someplace and talk?"

"Jacour, I don't have time for this. I have to get back. Randolph's cooking dinner."

Jacour stepped back from my truck. "Fine then. Go hurry back to Randolph and his recipe-of-the-week. If you can't give me ten or fifteen minutes of your time when I once meant so much to you, forget it."

He walked away and got back into his car. He had his engine started and was about to back out of the parking space when I yelled, "Where do you want to go?"

He smiled. "You'll come?"

"I can only stay a few minutes. Tell me you understand that beforehand."

Jacour nodded. "I understand."

"Fine then. Where to?"

"Follow me."

He backed his car out and waited while I did the same. I followed him toward 29-South.

•  •  •  •  •

We ended up at an old colonial on the outskirts of town. The outside looked historic, but it had been freshly painted.

"Isn't this the old Watson house?" I asked, pausing on the steps. I had parked my truck behind Jacour's car in the driveway.

"Yes, but it's my house now," he replied, unlocking and opening the front door. When he realized that I wasn't moving, he said, "Come on in. I won't bite."

"You're not the one that I'm worried about. Isn't this place haunted?"

"If it is, I haven't seen any ghosts around here . . . yet."

I stood in place.

"Milena, the house is *not* haunted. That's an urban legend. Well, actually a rural legend in this case. Someone started that rumor when we were kids." He shook his head and laughed. "I can't believe you still buy into that . . . at our age."

He made me feel so ridiculed that I finished walking up the steps and went inside, halfway expecting Casper the Friendly Ghost to leap from behind the front door and tickle me to death.

Jacour had transformed the house into a masterpiece—not that I had a clue what the inside had looked like before. The rooms were painted in various earth tones, the furniture was modern leather, and he had the biggest entertainment center that I'd ever seen. It wasn't a center; it was a wall. Four flat-screen televisions were mounted on the wall side by side; he had two or three DVD players, a Blu-ray player, a massive stereo system, and every video game console on the market, from the Xbox and PlayStation to the Wii and Game Cube. All state-of-the-art; all top-of-the-line.

"You like?" he asked, closing the door behind us. "Have a seat."

"You've done a lot in such a short period of time." I cleared my throat and pointed at the game systems. "Weren't you just making a comment about us being up in age? What's up with all of the video games?"

"Those games aren't for kids." I sat on the sofa and he sat beside me. "That's man gear."

"Man gear?" I giggled. "And I suppose this is your man cave?"

"Something like that, but a man cave is usually the basement of a house, where the man goes to get away from the wife and kids. But since I don't have either, I guess my entire house is my cave."

"I'm surprised you didn't buy one of those new mansions down by the lake. Surely you could afford them."

"I like old school. The architecture's not the same with newer developers. I've owned a lot of homes; still do, but I wanted this one. It's in the cut, it's big, and it's less than five minutes from you."

I looked at him. "And what does that have to do with anything?"

"This house seems like it's more your style, like the places we'd picked out near Cornell and in New York. You wanted to be able to renovate them; I remember that. You were so excited. Once you come to your senses, marry me, and have about three or four kids, you won't have far to go to check on your veterinary clinic."

The entire scenario felt strange, but it appeared that he was sincere . . . or at least making an attempt at being so.

"Jacour, we could've had all of that . . . eight years ago. You made a choice and I governed myself accordingly."

"Have you ever regretted not marrying me? Honestly?"

I looked away from him, out the window. There was a beautiful red maple tree in the yard.

"Please answer me, Milena."

I pretended to be picking some lint off my dress. Over the past two weeks, I had actually gone shopping and purchased some clothing that would fit—mostly dresses and summer sandals. I had begun to care about my appearance once again. It had been a long time.

Jacour grabbed my hand to still me. I gazed into his eyes; his alluring eyes. "I'd like to think that we can at least still communicate. That's one of the things that made us so close; being able to talk about anything . . . everything."

"I've *thought* about you over the years," I admitted. "Wondered how you were, if you were happy. Then I'd see you splashed all over the news, the internet, with gorgeous woman after gorgeous woman. No one can ever say that you've been deprived of your fair share of pussy."

"Milena, I—"

"No, listen. You wanted to address what happened between us, so let's address it." I pulled my hand away. "I want you to know exactly how I felt that day, when I saw that tape, and how I've felt ever since."

Jacour moved closer to me on the sofa and took my hand again. "I'm listening. Tell me whatever you need to get off your chest."

My lips started quivering as I fought back tears.

*You shouldn't have come here, Milena!*

*Well, you're here now! Tell this cheating bastard what he did to you!*

*It won't change anything!*

*No, but it'll give you the closure you need to move on!*

"I'm listening," Jacour repeated. "Please, tell me how you feel."

"Like I'm not good enough for you; like I was never good enough for you."

"What do you mean? You were everything to me. You still are. Are you forgetting that I was at the church, ready to commit to our future? I gave you a ring as a reminder of how much I loved you; eight carats. I made plans with you. You, Milena. Not anyone else."

"So why did you have to fuck those girls?"

*He fucked them because he's a man!*

*There had to be something else!*

*No, there didn't! All men cheat!*

*I don't believe that!*

*Yes, you do! That's why you've kept your legs clamped shut for eight years!*

"It was stupid," Jacour said, looking much ashamed. "You probably won't believe this, but I need to get it off my chest. Before my bachelor party, I'd never cheated on you before . . . in all those years. I wish that I could blame it on being drunk, but that would be a lie, and I don't want to lie to you. I was toasted, but I realized what was happening."

Being drunk wouldn't have been a legitimate excuse, but the fact that he'd been coherent, in my mind, made his actions even worse.

"So why, then?"

"The fellas brought those girls up in there to strip. It was supposed to be a perfectly innocent thing. I'm sure you and your girls hung out that night. I bet you had some dicks swinging in your face and all that."

Jacour had a lot of fucking nerve.

"You have a lot of fucking nerve, Jacour."

"Tell me you didn't."

I sighed. There was no point in harboring secrets; after all, it wasn't like we were together.

"Okay, I'll admit that we went to a male strip show and that things were wild, but the night didn't culminate with my drawers leaving my ass. I didn't suck any dicks, or even touch one, and other than some bumping and grinding up against me, *with my clothes on*, nothing happened."

"I feel you, and I believe you."

"You still haven't answered my question, Jacour. Why did you cheat?"

He shrugged. "I guess that I felt like I had something to prove. I couldn't let my boys think something was wrong with me. I'm nobody's punk and I'm certainly not a faggot."

"So you placed your friends' feelings above mine? Above our commitment to one another?"

I pulled my hand away and stood up. Jacour tried to pull me back down.

I slapped his hand away from me. "Naw! Naw! Let me get this straight. You did that shit to please your fucking friends? Your friends aren't shit, Jacour. Why the hell would you need to impress them? Your eighty-five-million-dollar baseball contract didn't make you feel like your balls were big enough?"

"I realize it was stupid, Milena. I've regretted that night, and if there was one moment that I could take back in time, that would be it."

"Phil and Glenn are working in a truck factory, Jacour! Your brother's strung out on some shit. Half of the time, he's off someplace acting crazy. Hell, he didn't even come to your party, and the rest of these idiots around here are merely hanging on; wasting time until they die. But you had to impress them?"

Jacour stood up and came at me. I pushed his chest with my palm. "Don't you touch me!"

"Baby, we can still make this work. We can."

"Do you have any idea how much you embarrassed me?"

"Oh, so now you care about what other people think. Your friends aren't any better off than mine. Who are you so concerned about impressing, Milena? Lydia? Donita and Kayla? All of your so-called friends would lie down with me if they could. And all of them have tried, except for Lydia, because she knows better."

"Lydia has never tried to sleep with you because she would never do that to me."

"I wouldn't put *shit* past Lydia. Glenn's always talking about how materialistic she is. That girl wants to get the hell out of Kannapolis and she'll fuck her way out of here if she has to."

"You don't even know Lydia like that!" I exclaimed, putting my hands on my hips. "You haven't seen her any more recently than you've seen me."

"I recognize her game. I've been dealing with gold diggers for the past eight years. Women who'll do whatever, whenever, to get paid."

"If Lydia was a gold digger, she wouldn't be with Glenn. That's for damn sure."

"Lydia's with Glenn because around here, being with him is equivalent to hitting the lottery. He might work in a factory, but her ass is at Food Lion, part-time at that. She's not contributing shit to their household."

"Who died and made you the expert on my best friend?"

Jacour sat back down and shook his head. "Like I said, Glenn's been confiding in me, and not just over the past two weeks. He and I have stayed in touch; Phil, too." He stared at me. "You can't honestly say that Lydia didn't have plans to ride your coattails out of this town if we'd gone through with the wedding. She would've waited six months, tops, before devising a scheme to get to New York to be with you."

Jacour did have a valid point. I was sure that he was right about that. Lydia hated Kannapolis and there was no way that she would've watched me traipse off to New York without her. But she was also the one who had shown me that videotape. I appreciated the fact that, in the heat of the moment, she had chosen my emotional well-being over her own.

Jacour was still flapping his gums. "By the way, I don't appreciate that comment you made about Jante."

Jacour's brother, Jante, had moved to New York City with him in the beginning, after I'd backed out of the marriage. I'd heard the rumors of how hard they had partied with Jacour's unlimited funds. Then Jante had started turning up in all the tabloids; speculation about him being strung out on cocaine had surfaced. Apparently, while Jacour had been in training and away at games, Jante had nearly turned his place—that was supposed to have been *our place*—into a drug haven.

Their parents had confided in mine that Jacour had paid for Jante to go through three separate rehabilitation programs, only for him to return to using within days of getting out. It was a vicious cycle that had ended with Jante returning to Kannapolis in shame. The Bryants had allowed him to stay with them at first, but after he'd started stealing items out of their home and heading to pawnshops, they'd been forced to kick him out. Now he was going from house to house, staying with any relative or friend who would let him lay his head on their sheets, but only until he also ripped them off.

Jacour had purchased his parents a mansion around the man-made lake, which is why I was surprised he hadn't followed suit. He was correct about me. My preference was older homes, but not haunted ones.

"You sure this house isn't haunted?" I asked, trying to change the subject. "I could've sworn I heard something right now."

"The house isn't haunted, Milena. Stop trying to change the subject. You shouldn't have said that about my brother."

"What I said about Jante is the truth. If it isn't, why'd you send him packing, and why isn't he staying here now?"

That's when everything changed. I'd come there to talk; only talk. But Jacour looked so sad, so needy. There is something incredibly sensual about a man who's on the brink of tears.

"Do you realize how bad it feels to supposedly have everything that money can buy and having the two things that you really want out of your reach?" he asked, wiping his left eye.

I suspected what his answer would be, but I asked anyway. "What two things?"

"My brother drug-free and your love."

I walked over to the sofa, stood in front of Jacour, and drew his head gently into my chest.

"I'm sorry about Jante. I love him, too. I was devastated when I heard what was going on with him." I paused and ran my fingers through Jacour's hair. "I saw him . . . a few times in town. He looked so sick, and frail. I did a U-turn once but he must've spotted me. By the time I turned completely around, he'd taken off."

"There's nothing you can do when someone's strung out on that shit, Milena. I realize that now, but it's hard. I don't understand it. I don't understand how Jante can do the things he's done. To our parents . . . to me." Jacour pushed me away and stood up. He walked toward the window. "I don't need to lay all of this on you. It's not your problem."

"My feelings for you didn't dissipate when we broke up. Just because we couldn't get married doesn't mean that I don't care about what happens to you, or your family."

I walked up behind him and put my arms around his waist, laying my head on his back. He smelled exactly like I'd remembered him; manly and sexy. All of the memories that I'd attempted to suppress came flooding back into my mind. The way that Jacour used to make slow and passionate love to me. The way that we used to lay in each other's arms for hours, gazing into our souls, and talking about everything of any significance in our lives.

"I have missed you, Jacour. You don't realize that what you did hurt me so badly that my life practically came to a halt once you left for New York. It was so painful . . . watching you with all of those glamorous women that I could never compete with, seeing you jet skiing in the islands with some supermodel clinging onto you and posing for the paparazzi."

Jacour took my hand off his waist, lifted it to his mouth, and kissed my fingers. "I thought that I'd be able to forget about you, baby. I assumed that if I played the odds enough, if I shot craps with my dick enough, a woman would eventually come along that would make me get over you." He turned to me and looked down into my eyes. "But that never happened. It never happened because it was impossible. What I feel for you is as real as it gets, and I fucked up that night . . . for no good reason. I'm not going to try to make up a legitimate excuse; there isn't one. You deserved better than that, and you still do."

Jacour gave me a strong embrace and held on to me for several seconds. Then he let go.

"If that guy Randolph makes you happy, then that's all that matters. Time waits for no one, and I shouldn't have ever expected you to put your life on hold for me."

"Randolph and I . . . we . . ."

"Yes?"

*Don't you dare tell him the truth, Milena!*

*But he thinks that I've been with someone else!*

*And you need to keep letting him think it! He just admitted to shooting craps with his dick and now you're concerned about his feelings!*

*I still care about him!*

*So what! Eight years! Eight years he's been gone and now you're thinking of falling back into bed with him!*

*He needs me!*

*It's a competition for him! A conquest! Jacour's a man! A typical man!*

"What about you and Randolph?" Jacour asked.

"We . . . uh . . . we have dinner plans. He's cooking and I need to get back."

Jacour looked away from me. "Fine. I hope you have a good dinner."

I walked toward the door, paused, and turned to look at Jacour. "Thanks for the talk."

"Did it help you any?"

"I'm not sure yet," I replied. "But I'm glad we had it."

"I am, too."

We gazed at each other from across the room, in complete silence.

"You don't want to leave me, baby," Jacour said, moving toward me. "Don't let one mistake ruin another day of our lives . . . the life that we're supposed to be living together. How is it that a man can be a good man for years, be a provider, be honest, be affectionate, and then get rejected for one mistake?"

I didn't reply.

"There's no greener grass, Milena. The other side of grass is always dirt. Nobody's perfect. Even if a man is faithful, there'll be something else wrong with him."

*Yeah, like being homeless!*

"Trust me, I've been out here, searching and thinking that I could find a woman better than you. She doesn't exist; not for me. You don't care about my money; I get that. That's one of the traits that I admire about you the most. You didn't surrender your morals and self-esteem to live on Park Avenue. Most women would. Hell, a friend of mine on the Yankees built his mistress a fifteen-thousand-square-foot home, and get this, his wife knows about the shit."

"Damn, really?"

I realized that some women were hard up, but that blew me away.

"Yes, really. Hell, there's even a mistress section at Yankee Stadium, and the wives know about that shit, too."

"Is that what you would've subjected me to, Jacour? Would you have had me sitting on one side and your mistress staring at me through binoculars from the other? Would I have been sitting at home with our children while you were taking whores with you to away games?"

"No, and that's what you obviously don't get. I came back here for you. I could've moved my parents to New York, or set them up on an exotic island someplace. I encouraged them to stay here. This is their home, but I also wanted to have some anchor to Kannapolis. It was always my intention to one day come back here and fight for your heart."

I stopped breathing for a moment, then forced myself to exhale.

"Then what took you so long?"

Jacour shrugged. "Months turned into years, you wouldn't respond to any of my efforts to get in touch with you, and time slipped away. I kept myself busy with playing and—"

"You kept yourself busy with fucking other women!" I exclaimed, lashing out at him. "Don't try to make yourself out to be some victim! You've led a good life while I've been here all alone."

Jacour raised an eyebrow.

*Girl, start lying your ass off NOW!*

"That is, until I met Randolph. Going to that convention in California was the best thing I ever did. At first, I only planned to make it a vacationship, but he touched my soul."

Jacour waved me off. "I'm not trying to hear that."

"Why? Because you expected me to spend the rest of my life yearning and crying over you?"

"I never really expected anything, Milena. But I hoped; I hoped and prayed that one day you'd give me another chance. Now I see that you've given yourself to another man and I'll accept it. I don't have any choice."

*Leave, Milena! Leave right fucking now!*

"Tell me one more thing before you leave," Jacour said.

"What's that?"

He started taking off his clothes, and I didn't move. He kicked off his shoes and pulled his shirt over his head at the same time. Then he unzipped his shorts and dropped them to the floor, stepping out of them. All that remained were his blue cotton boxers.

"What are you doing, Jacour?" I asked, even though it was obvious.

Jacour pulled his boxers down and kicked them across the room. There it was, his long, smooth, juicy dick.

He grabbed his dick and started moving his hand up and down the shaft. It was rock hard within seconds. "Tell me that you don't miss this . . . inside of you."

"You think whipping out your dick is going to do what? Make me incoherent?"

*It did!*

*Don't I know it!*

"This was made for you, baby. I was made for you. If you don't want me to touch you, walk out that door. But if you're still here thirty seconds from now, I'm taking you straight to my bed."

*Your ass needs to be out of the driveway in the next thirty seconds!*

*Or riding his dick!*

*He thinks you're fucking Yosef! What are you now, a slut?*

*Then I should tell him the truth!*

*Do it and you'll look like the most desperate, immature sister on the planet!*

*Don't I know it!*

"Time's almost up, Milena," Jacour said. "Either walk out, or I'm coming over there to get you."

"One thing's for sure. You've gotten bolder over the years."

"I'm not bold. I'm brazen. That's it. Time's up."

I'll admit that I could've left, but I didn't want to. I wanted Jacour to make love to me, even if I still didn't intend to take him back. Eight years was a long time to go without sex. Jacour was the only man I'd ever spread my legs for, and, at that moment, I needed him. I needed to feel like a complete woman again.

Jacour was on me, kissing me with my back pressed against the front door. His dick was pressing into my belly button and I could feel it throbbing. I grabbed onto it and it felt so good . . . to touch an actual dick. Not a vibrator, not a dildo, but a dick.

He lifted my dress, picked me up, and I wrapped my legs around his back as he carried me upstairs to the master bedroom and laid me on the bed.

We stopped kissing so that he could pull my dress over my head.

"You're so fucking beautiful," he said.

I was a bit self-conscious about the weight that I'd gained and vowed at that very second that, if I was going to be fucking again, it had to come off.

"I have a little pouch," I said. "Been eating too much."

"Milena, I love your pouch." He gazed over every inch of me and then kissed my stomach. "I love your pouch, this little bit of cellulite on your thighs . . ." He kissed my left thigh. ". . . and the bruises on your knee." He then kissed my knees, one at a time. "You're perfect."

He lifted his leg so I could see it and pointed at the scar from the injury that had abruptly ended his professional baseball career. "Look at my knee. We match."

I giggled as he lowered his leg and kissed the bruises on my knee again. It tickled.

"We shouldn't be doing this," I whispered.

"If you want me to stop, I will."

When I didn't respond, Jacour reached behind me and unclasped my bra. I let him slip it off of me without hesitation. He licked my left nipple and rubbed my right one between his thumb and index finger. My breasts had always been my weak spot, and he knew it. Jacour could play my body like a guitar; he was the only man who had ever played it.

*Someone's moaning!*

*That's you, dummy!*

Jacour stuck his hands down in my panties and started fingering me. I was embarrassed. It must've been like a geyser down there. For a second, I started to panic. Would he be able to tell that I hadn't fucked in years if I was too tight?

*What kind of fool worries about her pussy being too tight!*

*But he thinks that I'm fucking Yosef! Have you seen the size of that man's feet!*

*Yes, I've seen his feet! His pretty feet!*

*Stop thinking about Yosef!*

Jacour kept sucking on my breasts and fingering me for a few minutes. Other than moaning, I wasn't saying anything. I couldn't believe that it was happening. It was.

"You been letting that man taste my pussy?" Jacour asked.

"Huh?"

"Never mind. I don't want to know. It's still mine. It's always been mine."

Jacour removed his hand from my pussy and gazed into my eyes as he licked his fingers. "Still sweet. I've missed you."

He started kissing me again and it turned me on to taste myself on his tongue. I pulled him between my legs so that he could tease me with his dick between my panties.

"Make love to me," I whispered after coming up for air. "Make love to me, Jacour."

"Not yet."

He got down on his knees beside the bed and pulled my panties down over my thighs and calves. He kissed the soles of my feet as he slipped the panties off of each foot. Then he sucked on my toes.

I moaned and squirmed uncontrollably. I was in complete ecstasy.

Jacour lifted my legs over my shoulders and I clasped them behind his neck as he elevated my ass and buried his entire face in my pussy. He bobbed my hardened clit with his tongue and reached around to play with my nipples. Because I was elevated, that allowed me access to reach down and fondle his dick while he ate me out.

I clasped his head between my thighs and locked my feet so that I could move my pussy in rhythm with his tongue. He certainly hadn't lost that touch. Jacour had always been such a gifted lover. Even though I had never been with anyone else, when I was with him, I didn't need anyone else. And I didn't think he did either. I'd done whatever I could to please him . . . yet he'd cheated.

I tried to put all of that out of my head and enjoy the moment. We'd gone past the point of no return. It wouldn't have mattered if I'd made him stop right then. The damage was done. We'd been intimate and I needed some dick.

"Damn, Milena, I've missed you so much."

"I've missed you, too," I heard myself say.

I continued to give him a hand job while he went to town on my pussy.

I grabbed hold of the comforter with my free hand. At that moment, I was angry with myself for allowing eight years to elapse without sex in my life. I was one of those women who believed that celibacy was the key to happiness. That it was more important to stand on principles than to do what came naturally. Right then, I realized that I had missed out on so much. While most of the world was relieving stress and experiencing such incredible feelings, I was playing in my own pussy, convinced that it was a viable solution. I don't give a damn what anyone says: there is no substitution for great sex. No matter what ended up happening between Jacour and me, one thing was for sure: I wasn't going to deprive myself from feeling the touch of a man for any extended period of time ever again.

My thighs started shivering, signifying that I was on the verge of a massive orgasm. Now, that I did recognize; vibrators never fail. They are simply not the same as a human touch. Jacour's tongue had worked its magic, and now he was about to be rewarded with what he wanted.

I let out one last moan, groan, scream, whatever you want to call it, and squirted all over his face. Jacour made sure that he got it all and then gently laid my ass back down on the bed as I loosened my ankles around his neck and spread my thighs to free his head.

I released his dick, but only for a second. By the time he could stand up from beside the bed, I was sitting up and drawing the head into my mouth. Some things are like riding a bike; you never forget them.

"Umm, you want to taste me, huh?" Jacour asked. I licked the head of his dick with my tongue and gazed up into his eyes. Then I stopped. "What's wrong?"

"Nothing." I flipped my body around and lay back on the bed, but now my head was facing him. I reached up and tugged on his dick. "Now give it to me."

Jacour squatted lightly and lowered his dick into my mouth, being careful not to choke me. Then he slowly increased the force of his in and out movement until we had a smooth motion going. I relaxed my throat and could feel the head of his dick tickling my tonsils.

I wanted to suck Jacour's dick until he came, but after a few minutes, he pulled out. "I don't want to miss out on making love to you," he said.

I sat up and giggled. "Oh, in your old age, you can't get it up but once," I teased.

"No," Jacour responded defensively and then laughed himself. "Come here." He pulled me around by my ankles and was about to enter me. "I'm going to show you about old age."

I pressed both of my palms against his chest. "Not without a condom."

"Milena, we never used condoms before," Jacour protested.

"That's because we were in a monogamous relationship . . . or so I thought." Jacour stared down at me and sighed. "Jacour, I don't know where your dick has been, and I'm not trying to get pregnant either."

"Well, we both know where your pussy has been lately, don't we?"

*Tell the man the truth and put him out of his misery!*

*Jacour can never know that my relationship with Randolph is a fairy tale!*

"Let me get this straight," I said. "I'm with one man and you get upset, but you've been with half the famous chicks under the sun?"

Jacour climbed from between my thighs and sat beside me on the bed. "I realized what it looked like, but half of that shit the press made up."

"Like the pictures and videos of all of them hanging all over you?"

"They were all publicity whores."

"And what were you?"

"A man who enjoyed the attention." Jacour lifted my hand and kissed it. "But I didn't sleep with all of those women, baby. I swear to you, I didn't. You know me better than that."

"I thought that I knew you until I saw that tape from your bachelor party."

"If I'm so prone to fuck a lot of women, why am I back here, sweating you? The women in this town are like vultures, swooping around me, trying to be a jump-off, a wifey, whatever they can. I haven't paid any of them any mind. If I needed sex all the time, I would've had to break someone off by now." He sat up on his elbows and looked down at me. "And trust me, you would've been the first one to hear about it because they'd be bragging."

"It's only been a little over a week, Jacour. You act like that makes you a saint, and that doesn't mean you haven't been pulling pussy from Charlotte."

"I can't believe you have such a low opinion of me."

"It's the way that you've put yourself out there."

Jacour grew angry. "Look at you. You've got dude at your house cooking dinner and you're over here feeding me mine. What's up with that?"

I sat up and searched for my clothes. I was getting the hell out of there. When I started pulling on my panties and Jacour realized that he wasn't going to get any, he really got upset then.

"What does that make you, Milena? What do you call a woman

who has one man at home and another one in the cut? A slut? A whore?"

By that time, I already had my bra on and was pulling my dress over my head. I had to get down on my knees to retrieve one of my sandals that had slid underneath the bed. I refused to respond to his comments.

"Oh, so now what?" Jacour watched me slip on my sandals. "Fine. Go run home to *Randolph* and eat dinner like this shit never happened." He lay back and put his hands over his face. "You've changed, and I can't believe that I thought we could pick up where we left off and be a couple again."

"I can't believe you thought that shit either."

I rushed out of his bedroom, down the steps, and out of the house, with sticky thighs and dick breath.

---

Chicken salad was hanging out the side of Lydia's mouth as I finished telling her what had happened between Jacour and me.

"Close your mouth, Lydia. I'm not trying to see your half-eaten food."

She finished chewing and then wiped her face with a napkin. "You little slut!"

"Oh, brother, not you, too."

"Seriously, I'm so proud of you. *Fucking two men.* For some women, that's an everyday occurrence, but for you, that's legendary."

I had yet to tell Lydia that Yosef and I were not lovers, but I planned to.

"You're a one-man woman," I said. "You've been with Glenn for three years and you've never cheated on him." Lydia looked away from me. "Have you?"

Lydia guzzled down half a bottle of a Bacardi Mojito. "I need a joint after that bomb-ass salad. You mind if I light up?"

"No, go ahead," I replied. "I might even take a hit or two."

"What? Whoring and now smoking ciggaweed again? You're really coming out of your shell."

"Shut up, Lydia." I laughed. "It's not like that. I was never in a shell."

"Please, you were like a fucking turtle, just letting your arms and legs out so you could scurry about."

We both fell out laughing as Lydia searched through her over-sized purse and pulled out a quart-sized bag of marijuana and some rolling papers. She collapsed on the sofa and went to work rolling a couple of joints on the coffee table.

"Damn, Lydia, that's a lot of weed. You bought that on the way over here, or you carry that kind of weight around all the time?"

"Neither. I'm going to give this to a friend. He keeps pressing me about my connect, but I'll never tell."

I got my long candle lighter out of the pitcher on the kitchen window ledge and joined her on the sofa.

"You better be careful. The police around here are bored. They'll lock you up for that and everyone will know about it."

"I'm not stupid, sis." She licked the edge of a piece of paper to complete a joint; a fat one. "But you're right. This entire town is boring. They're still listing people who write bad checks in the *Independent Tribune*."

"Did you see it that day when they had the report about Ms. Bart claiming someone stole her apple cobbler off the back porch?"

"Girl, yes. Harriet Tubman probably ate that thing and shitted it out in the toilet and forgot that she did." Lydia lit the joint, took a drag, and then handed it to me. "You're the only woman that I'll trade spit with."

"In today's age, I better be."

"But now that you're sucking dick again, I don't know," Lydia said jokingly.

I held up my middle finger. "Fuck you."

"Naw, I'm not getting in that long-ass line."

We both laughed.

"I'm not sleeping with Yosef," I blurted out.

Lydia looked down the hallway. My bedroom door was closed. "Is he here?" she whispered.

"Do you think I would've told you that long-ass story about Jacour if he was?"

Lydia shrugged. "Guess not. So where is he? You laid that freaky-deaky shit you did in that haunted house on me so fast that you still haven't told me the deal about this homeless situation."

"That house is haunted, isn't it?"

"You won't catch my ass anywhere near it."

"Let me hit that again." I grabbed the joint from Lydia, took a long, hard drag, and then blew it out. I coughed. "This is strong. I haven't smoked weed in a while, but I can see why everyone's trying to get your hook-up. This is some good stuff."

"Thank you." If I didn't know better, it almost looked like Lydia was blushing. "It is some major shit. So where's Yosef? Panhandling?"

"No, he's not panhandling," I answered sarcastically. "He's out applying for jobs."

"Why didn't he have a job before?"

"Most people won't hire someone who doesn't have a physical address or phone number."

"Hell, half the people that I know don't even have landlines anymore, including me. Glenn and I use our cellies."

"Yosef didn't have a cell phone either. Now he does and he can also use my address to apply. I use my cell most of the time, too, but I keep my business phone because I don't want all my clients to have my cell number. Most of them treat their animals better than they treat their children and they'll panic in a second. Good thing that my answering service—"

"Ahem!"

"What?"

Lydia took another drag and then blew it out. "How did Yosef get a cell phone if he doesn't have a job?"

I really didn't want to tell her, but like a bad public defender, I'd opened up that door. "I can have up to six phones with Sprint, so I got him one. It's no big deal; he's on my plan and we're sharing minutes. Plus, the phone was free. So none of it cost me a dime. It makes it more convenient."

"I'm a cell phone plan pro, and while it might not have cost you something upfront, you definitely had to extend your contract."

"I'm not planning on changing my number anyway."

Lydia smirked. "And how is he out searching for a job? He certainly isn't walking out in these boonies. He has a ride? Was he sleeping in his car?"

I sighed. "I let him borrow my old Chevy."

"That thing still runs?"

"Yeah, it runs."

"I didn't realize you still had it."

"It's been buried in my garage. My truck is more practical for my practice. I'd planned on selling it, or donating it, but never got around to it. Now at least it's being put to good use."

"And who's paying for gas in the old clunker?"

"Roll another joint," I said, realizing that we'd killed the first one. As Lydia went to work, I admitted, "Look, I'm helping the brother out *temporarily*. He did me a favor and I'm returning it.

A few bucks here and there isn't going to kill me. I make good money, especially for Kannapolis, and you know my spending habits are minimal. I donate to nonprofits all the time, and if I can do that, then—"

"Milena, I get it. I don't want you to think you have to justify shit to me. I'm concerned about you. Be honest. If the shoe was on the other foot and I told you that I had a vagrant shacking with me, a dude that popped up out of nowhere, you wouldn't be worried?"

"I'd be petrified." I giggled. "Don't think that I didn't have my reservations at first. It was kind of scary, and thrilling at the same time. Having this big, massive stranger around me."

"A Mandingo. That motherfucker is a *Man-din-go*. And you're a fool for not riding that dick every night. I bet he's hung like a fucking horse."

The weed was getting to us and we both fell out on the sofa laughing.

"Have you ever seen a horse dick?" I asked Lydia. "Women always use that analogy, but horses, and mules, are nobody's idea of a joke. Their dicks are not measured in inches; they're measured in feet."

"Ew, you so nasty, looking at mule and horse dick!"

"I'm not nasty. I'm a veterinarian, and animals have issues with their genitals, too."

"So you touch them?" Lydia asked, astounded.

"If they need to be touched." She scrunched up her face and moved away from me. "I wear gloves, heifer, and it's my job. I don't get turned on by that shit."

"Some people are into fucking horses."

"That only happens in Europe."

"Hell no, it doesn't. You didn't read that story in the paper last month about the brother from South Carolina?"

"What story?" I was hoping she was joking.

"I kid you not."

Guess she wasn't joking.

"His name was Ronald Victor. I'll never forget that name, because if I ever meet him, I'm running the other way."

We were crying laughing by that point; weed never fails to make an impact.

"And what did Ronald do?"

Lydia lit the next joint. "He got caught fucking this woman's horse *twice* in Columbia!"

"Get the fuck out of here!"

"He was already on probation from hitting it last year, but he went back, and homegirl was lying in wait for him with a surveillance camera and a shotgun."

"Are you serious?"

"Yep! He went back to get some ass from the same exact horse!"

I fell off the sofa onto the floor as Lydia handed me the joint.

"They even made his ass register as a sex offender!"

"You've got to be making this shit up!"

"No, I swear!" Lydia held up her hand. "Don't take my word for it! You're always on the internet! Look his ass up on Google, Yahoo, or what the fuck ever you use! Ronald Victor!"

Lydia and I were so busy laughing that neither one of us heard the key in the lock. When Yosef walked in, we were both sprawled out on the floor laughing, higher than kites.

Lydia sat up and looked at him. "Hey, Yosef! Oops, I mean *Randolph*!" She lay back down on the carpet and took another drag of the joint.

I was suddenly embarrassed. It wasn't like me to be getting high in the middle of the day—or any other part of the day. Yet, there we were, with a big-ass bag of weed on the table in my smoke-filled living room.

"Hello, Lydia," Yosef said in a low voice, closing the door. He looked at me. "Should I come back later?"

"No, it's okay," I replied. "Lydia knows the deal."

"I kind of figured that since she called me Yosef." He frowned. "What all does she know?"

That's when all the laughter ceased. Even Lydia realized that Yosef was uncomfortable with her knowing his real predicament. She got up off the floor and started gathering her weed, papers, and purse.

"I'm going to bounce," she said. By that time, I was also up off the floor. She gave me a hug and kissed me on the cheek. "I'll call you later."

Lydia walked past Yosef in silence and left. He held the door open for her.

He came and sat on the sofa while I picked up the toss pillows that had been strewn about and propped them back into their appropriate spots.

"She knows everything, doesn't she?" he asked solemnly.

I stood there, staring down on him. "Yes, she does. Well, not *everything*, but she knows how we really met and that you're staying here until you get on your feet."

He looked so hurt. "Why did you tell her?"

"She's my best friend, Yosef. She's not going to tell anyone." I sat beside him. "She was mad at me for ignoring her for the past two weeks. I stopped by her job and I told her. I couldn't keep avoiding her, or preventing her from coming by. That's not my normal behavior."

He pointed at the coffee table, where the pouch of weed had been a moment earlier. "And is this your normal behavior?"

*He has a lot of fucking nerve! This is your crib!*

*Don't I know it!*

"If you're asking me whether or not I get high on a regular basis, no, I don't. I haven't gotten high in years, but I'm not going to lie about it. I enjoyed it. It's been a long time since I've done the things that I truly enjoy in life." I touched his hand. "You're partially responsible for that."

He looked at me and grinned. "Really?"

"Yes, really." I gripped his hand tighter. "How'd your job-hunting go today?"

"I have a few possible hits, but I have to wait to hear from them. I hate waiting. That's the worst part."

"It hasn't been that long."

"Not since I've been here with you, but I've been in this situation for half a year and I need to get back on my feet."

"And you will." I released his hand, got up, and walked over to the kitchen counter to pick up several pieces of paper. Then I walked back over to the sofa and handed them to him. "This is for you."

"What is it?"

"I was on my computer earlier today, looking up some medicine for the Yorkie that's out in the kennel coughing up his lungs. I decided to do a web search for celebrities that were once homeless." Yosef started looking over the list. "It's amazing. Some of the most famous people in the world were once in the same situation as you." I pointed at the paper. "Look, everyone from Charlie Chaplin and Cary Grant to Eartha Kitt and Tyler Perry went through it. Bad things can happen to anyone, Yosef. You shouldn't feel inferior because of it."

"I don't feel inferior," he protested.

"Yes, you do, and we both know it. There's no difference between you and the next man who's living high on the hog."

"You don't even know what happened to me," he said. "How do you know that I'm not some lazy bum who did this to himself?"

"My gut instincts tell me that isn't so. I don't know how you got here. One day, I hope that you'll trust me enough to open up to me. But I'm glad that you're here. You're like a beacon in the middle of a storm. I might have a roof over my head, and money to live off of, but until you came into my life, I was living a bleak existence . . . in a dismal place."

Yosef gazed lovingly into my eyes. "Thanks for saying that. It means a lot."

"I'm saying it because it's the truth. You've changed me . . . for the better. You've shown me attention, you care about what I have to say, and . . ."

"And what?"

"And you're not too bad on the eyes."

He blushed. "Neither are you."

"Do you really think I'm pretty?"

"You're beautiful, Milena." He paused, and then sighed. "This may not be any of my business, but . . . if you're still pining over Jacour Bryant, he doesn't deserve you." He redirected his eyes to the floor. "Neither do I, but there's someone out there who can give you all that you need. Don't fall back into his trap. Whatever happened between you, you called off your wedding for a reason."

*Yes, Milena, you did! He fucked those other chicks!*

*You think I need you to remind me!*

I had never told Yosef about Jacour cheating on me at his bachelor party, but I'm sure he assumed that infidelity had something to do with our breakup. After all, Jacour was a multimillionaire baseball star, so there couldn't have been many reasons. Either he had to have cheated or he had to have been beating my ass. I don't think I gave off any indication that I was the type who would tolerate that; I wasn't.

"Jacour cheated on me the night before our wedding," I blurted out suddenly.

"Jacour is a fool."

"Maybe . . . maybe I was lacking something."

"You're not lacking anything, Milena. Any man that's given the chance to be with you should consider that a gift . . . something to be cherished."

"Would you cherish me, Yosef?" I asked.

"Definitely, but . . ."

I took his chin in my hand and forced him to look at me. "Do you cherish me?"

"I'm not in the right place to be your man."

"You're here . . . with me. If this isn't the right place, then where is?"

"You know what I mean."

"I know what I feel . . . what I'm feeling right now . . . at this very moment in time."

I could feel his cool breath on my skin as I straddled his lap.

"And what are you feeling, Milena?"

"Like I want to do this."

I ran my fingertips over the bridge of Yosef's nose, and then his lips, and then I kissed him, long and hard.

He put his strong hands around my waist and pulled me deeper onto him. I could feel his dick harden beneath me. It was massive. I ground my pussy onto him through our clothing. I was so wet, so horny.

I broke the kiss and started licking and sucking on his neck.

That's when he tried to push me away. "We shouldn't be doing this. A man's supposed to be a provider for his woman."

I stopped licking his neck and gazed at him. "Please, don't push me away."

Yosef hesitated, but only for a second. He grabbed the back of my neck and kissed me with a passion that I had never known. It was different from with Jacour. Tender, yet a little bit forceful at the same time.

We were on our way to the bedroom, with me leading him by the hand, when a loud knock came at my front door.

"You want me to get that?" Yosef asked.

"No." I pouted and let his hand go. "I'll see who it is."

It turned out to be Farmer John. He had nearly a hundred acres on the other side of town where he had enough livestock to give Old MacDonald a run for his money. One of his cows had become ill and he feared that it might have bovine spongiform encephalopathy, otherwise known as mad cow disease. While that was a farmer's worst nightmare—it could lead to all of his cattle having to be destroyed and a massive amount of money lost—I seriously doubted that was the case. Mad cow rarely happened in the United States, but that didn't prevent cow owners from panicking at the first sight of a sneeze.

I asked Yosef if he wanted to ride with me. I hated to be apart from him, and even though we couldn't make love right then, I wanted him near me.

The summer was turning out to be the hottest one of my life, but I had to admit the truth to myself. When it came to Jacour and Yosef, I was torn with emotion. And I was also horny!

# Lydia

WHEN I left Milena's, I was floating too much to head home and deal with Glenn's boring ass. He thought that I'd be at work until that night anyway, so I had an alibi; I needed to use it.

I called Phil on his cell. He'd had a sexy demeanor about him when he'd dropped by Food Lion earlier that day, even though he shouldn't have been there.

"Hello," he answered.

"You got cash for a hotel?"

"Huh?"

"I'm not at work and Glenn's at home so we can't go there. You have any money so we can get a room?"

Phil cleared his throat. "Yes, I'm with Glenn now. We're hunting deer."

I was livid. "Deer-hunting season doesn't start until the middle of September! You fools are going to get locked up!"

"Only if we get caught," he whispered.

I could hear Glenn saying something in the background.

*Shit!*

"Make up an excuse and leave his ass out in the woods! I need some dick!"

"I can't do that. Not right now."

*No, this motherfucker is not turning me down!*

"Phil, meet me at the Days Inn in *one hour* or you'll never even get a whiff of this pussy again!"

I disconnected the call and pulled up to one of the drive-up speakers at Whataburger. I had the munchies something terrible. When Diane—I recognized the heifer's irritating voice—asked me what I wanted, I ordered a Whataburger Jr. with onions, tomato, and mayonnaise, an order of onion rings, and a large chocolate shake. That was a lot of heavy food to put on my stomach before a fuckfest, but weed had that effect on me.

Plus, I was an emotional eater. That shit that Milena had laid on me that day had me stressed. While Yosef seemed innocent enough, most maniacs probably did at first. That's how they were able to walk the earth and kill people without being noticed. Usually, they were capable of blending right in.

But he'd been over there for two weeks and everyone knew he was there. Mrs. Clark had questioned me when she'd come through my line a few days earlier. I'd pretended like I was up on everything in regards to "Randolph" and assured her that Milena was happy. Mrs. Clark was concerned because Milena had been avoiding her parents, as she had been with me. Milena had never been a very good liar, and there was no way that she was going to be able to do it successfully time and time again. But he was still there, and it was only a matter of time before everyone figured out that his ass wasn't returning to California.

Then there was that entire convoluted situation with Jacour. Milena really needed to let bygones be bygones and give the brother another chance. Instead, she was setting herself up to be in some love triangle and she wouldn't be able to handle it. Shit, I could barely navigate mine. She was going to give up those drawers to

Yosef if he kept staying there. Milena was far from a whore, and that was the problem. Any man who managed to get close enough to her to be drooling on her guest room sheets was in there.

"A love triangle," I said aloud as Diane took her sweet time bringing my food out to my car on a tray.

"What's going on, Lydia?" she asked as she propped the tray up on the holder.

"Nothing much, Diane. You?"

"Trying to keep out of this heat. This summer's been a scorcher."

I wanted her to get away from me so I could get my grub on. "How much I owe you?"

"Seven fifty-two." I reached into my bra to get some money out. "I'm surprised you ain't at Food Lion. They let you have a Saturday off?"

"Can't you see that I'm wearing my uniform?" I asked the dummy as I handed her a ten.

She squinted and kneeled down. "Oh, now I see. I keep saying that I need to go see old Doc McLemore at Wally World and get some new contacts. At least you had an early day. I don't get off 'til midnight."

"Well, good luck with that. Saturday nights around here are probably a trip."

"You ain't never lied. All the wild-ass teenagers come through in their souped-up hot rods. I can't stand it."

Diane was digging for some change.

"No, I'm good. Keep the change."

"Wow, thanks, Lydia. Most people are cheapskates. Half of them don't tip at all."

"Well, times are tough for everyone," I said. "We've got to scratch each other's backs every now and then."

"Thanks again. You've always been so cool, Lydia," she said and walked off.

There were many other customers waiting, and with the recession, a lot of places had dwindled down their staff, which led to horrible customer service. I didn't mind giving Diane a tip, even though she was stupid. She wasn't that much different from me though: stuck.

I dug into my food and looked at the clock on my dash. Phil had forty-five minutes to get his ass to the Days Inn or no more pussy privileges for him. I was dying to roll a joint and light it up right there at Whataburger, but the police were some of the best customers. They spent half of their shifts eating or hanging around local businesses, killing time.

That seemed like what most people were doing in Kannapolis; killing time. No true goals or expectations. No proactivity. Watching each other waste away. If they weren't sitting on their porches watching the traffic go by, they were at Walmart or Target, buying shit that they didn't want or need.

I sucked some of my shake up through the straw. "I've got to get the fuck out of here."

I looked around the Whataburger parking lot. Mostly teenagers, laughing and loitering. Now, they were the lucky ones. They still had dreams of becoming successful, but soon enough their bubbles would be busted, unless they were lucky enough to go to college. I should've gone to college, like Milena and Jacour, but I'd been too busy thinking that I was cute. My parents couldn't tell me anything. I had it all figured out. I was going to start my own business—a designer dress shop—and make millions by the time I was forty. But I didn't truly have a game plan—much less a business plan—and I certainly lacked the knowledge to pull it off.

That's what hurt the most—realizing that my failure was

based on my own arrogance and refusal to listen to people who were much older and wiser. My parents loved me, and I should've known that they would've never suggested anything that would harm me. They must've been so disappointed in me. They'd spoiled me as a child and had given me whatever they'd been able to afford, within reason. But my parents weren't wealthy. Like everyone else, they struggled to make ends meet.

During one particularly difficult period, when I was young, I used to think that my father was never hungry. My parents believed that we should always dine as a family, to discuss the day and read a scripture from the Bible. My father would sit there and watch us eat. When I'd ask him why he wasn't eating, he would insist that he'd had a big lunch at his janitorial job. Now I realized that he was lying and going without food because he couldn't afford enough food for the three of us; only Momma and me.

That saddened me as I sat there, contemplating throwing away my onion rings. The burger and shake had filled me up. I got out of my car and walked over to a group of teenagers. I recognized one or two of them from around the way but didn't know their names.

"Excuse me, would anyone like my onion rings?" I asked, holding the container out to them.

One male teenager had no shame in his game. "Sure, shortie, I'll take them. Lucas don't be turning down no food."

His friends laughed as I handed him the onion rings. He started pouring them in his mouth, forgoing lifting them out of the small box one at a time.

I walked back to my car and got in. Then I pulled out of the Whataburger parking lot and headed to Concord to the Days Inn. It was doubtful that anyone would catch Phil and me there. No one around there stayed in hotels unless they were either experiencing domestic problems at home or were up to no good their damn selves.

• • •

Phil showed up, of course, swearing and griping about having to make up a lie to get rid of Glenn.

He was still fussing after we'd checked in to room 412.

"Stop whining," I said as he plopped down on the bed and turned on the television. "So what, you had to lie to Glenn. We lie to his ass every day."

"But we were out in the middle of the woods, with shotguns and shit, and then I had to roll out, looking all crazy."

"First of all, you didn't have to do anything. You wanted this pussy and that's why you're here. Secondly, you didn't have no business out there in the first place. If someone had caught you, you'd be chilling in a cell instead of getting ready to have your dick waxed."

Phil looked at me and licked his lips. "You look kind of sexy in that uniform. Why'd you brush me off when I came through earlier?"

"You came to my job, Phil. That's not keeping shit on the low." I reached into my purse and pulled out the weed that was left over from when Milena and I had gotten high. I tossed it to him. "This is for you."

"That's what I'm talking about. One of these days, I'm going to follow you; see where you get this shit."

"Hmm, good luck with that," I said, and then giggled. I started taking off my uniform. "I'm dying for a shower. I started to go by the house and take one, but once Glenn got home, he would've realized I'd been there."

Phil was already rolling a joint. He had his own rolling papers. "Why don't you come over here and suck on this dick while I get high? From the looks of your pupils, it seems like you started the party before me."

"There's no way I'm sucking an unclean dick, Phil. You've been out hunting deer. Get real." I got completely naked and headed into the bathroom. "You can join me, or shower after me, but you *will* wash that ass before you tap this one; real talk."

Phil joined me in the shower a few minutes later. Hotel showers were like heaven. The house Glenn and I rented had well water, and the water pressure was pitiful. I felt like a princess as the hot water cascaded down my body. I wanted to stay in there for as long as possible. Our water heater was still on the blink—Glenn kept swearing he was going to fix it—but there was no chance of running out of hot water in the Days Inn.

While the Days Inn would serve its purpose, one day I wanted to take a shower or, better yet, a luxurious bath in a marbled bathroom with gold-plated spigots like they showed in movies. I'd only been outside of North Carolina once, and that was when I'd taken a day trip with my parents to see one of Daddy's old friends in South Carolina. South Carolina was only on the other side of Charlotte, but I never had a legitimate reason to venture there. Milena was my only true friend—Donita and Kayla could kiss my ass to the red—and she never went anywhere. Glenn always cried broke after covering the household bills. Yet he had money to waste on ammunition and shit to go hunt some damn deer.

"It's nice and steamy in here," Phil said as he climbed into the shower stall behind me. He started palming my tits. "Like your pussy."

"You going to wash this pussy for me, Daddy? Lather it up and get it all fresh and ready for you?"

"That pussy's always ready for me."

I looked up over my shoulder at him. "What about fresh?"

"It's always fresh, sweet, and smooth."

I kept my pussy shaved bare. At first, I used to experiment

with different cuts, from heart-shaped to oval, but I felt the sexiest when it was as smooth as a baby's ass.

"You like the way I shave my pussy, baby?"

"Uh-huh, makes it easier for me to get a good lick in."

He had a washcloth between my legs, soaping up my pussy and scrubbing it good.

"How many licks does it take to get to the middle of my Tootsie Pop?" I asked seductively.

"Let's find out."

Phil got down on his knees as I rinsed the soap off of my pussy right quick. Then he lifted my right foot onto the side of the tub and started licking and sucking all over my clit.

"Umm, see, this is much better than running around in the woods, chasing Bambi."

"There's no competition," Phil whispered.

"I'm sorry that I was so mean to you earlier. Food Lion stresses me out. I hate my job."

"I hate my job, too." Phil maneuvered his head so he could get at me better. "But I love putting in this kind of work."

"Work it, baby."

I grabbed ahold of the pole coming out of the wall where the showerhead was attached and started rotating my hips to meet the movements of his tongue.

"Ooh, shit. You eat a mean pussy, Phil. You don't front when it comes to pleasing a woman."

He kept eating me until I couldn't take it anymore and climaxed. I washed Phil's dick and ass—no beads in the bed for me—and then we hit the bedroom.

Instead of getting on the bed, I straddled a chair with my feet but continued standing. "I want to try something different, baby," I said.

He came up behind me. "You want me to fuck you right here? I'll fuck you right here."

"I want you to put your feet up on the chair, right here"—I pointed to the seat—"behind me."

Phil did like any good little puppy would and stood on the chair. His dick was poking me in the back of my head.

"Now crouch down," I told him.

He did and I reached around and helped to guide his dick into me. "Umm, that's it."

The chair was about to topple over, so I used both hands to stabilize it. Then I started moving my ass to meet Phil's thrusts.

"You come up with some wild shit, woman," Phil said, moaning. "You don't just give me the pussy. You give it to me right."

Phil held on to my hips to balance himself, and then we fucked like two wild animals. Phil was breathing and kissing all over my neck, but all that I could really think about was the pain going away. The pain that I felt from being such a failure in life. As Phil continued to ravage me from behind, I stared out the window at all of the cars traveling along the interstate. All of those people, headed someplace exciting, someplace full of possibilities. As Phil climaxed some ten minutes later, a single tear cascaded down my left cheek.

PART THREE

# THE SWEET SPOT

# Milena

### One Month Later

I T was after midnight and Yosef wasn't back yet from work. He'd landed a job at a car wash in Concord three weeks earlier. It wasn't much money—minimum wage plus tips—but I could see the positive difference that it had had on him spiritually.

My parents had been asking a lot of questions, but I was always very vague with my responses. I'd go over to their house for Sunday dinner to visit with them and Papa Bear, and when they would bring Randolph up, I'd lie and say that he was tending to the animals in my kennel so I could come over there. It didn't make any sense; I realized that. I hadn't had anyone to cover for me over all the years that I'd been having the traditional dinner with them. Yosef had been there for over a month and a half, and I could no longer use the excuse that he was on vacation from his practice in California . . . so I did the stupidest thing.

I told my parents that Randolph and I were getting serious and doing a trial run to see what it would be like to make a formal commitment and live together after marriage. My dad thought that was the most foolish thing that he'd ever heard. He didn't believe in "shacking up" and had thrown a fit when Jacour and I had mentioned it during our engagement. When we'd been away at college, we'd stayed over his place or mine all the time. What our parents hadn't known couldn't have hurt them. Once we moved back to make wedding preparations, neither my parents nor his were feeling it.

My parents had known Jacour my entire life, and they'd been against my living with him. Yet, here I was, telling them that I was sharing space with a man that they hadn't even known existed before Jacour's party. I had to say *something* to make it sound good. The truth was out of the question.

Even though Yosef and I were not in a relationship, much less a committed one, I was acting like it as I paced the floor of my living room waiting for him to get home. I kept glancing out into the darkness at my dark driveway, the only light emitting from a pole that I paid eight dollars a month to Duke Power for so that I wouldn't feel like I might end up starring in a sequel to *Scream* when I came home after sundown. He was nowhere in sight.

*Calm down, Milena! This is Kannapolis! Nothing could've happened to him here!*

*He might've been in a car accident!*

*The tags are registered to you! You'd be the first to know if he had an accident!*

*He might've been car-jacked!*

*Nobody wants your rusty-ass Chevy!*

I couldn't take it any longer. I grabbed my keys and headed out to my truck. When I turned on my headlights, they were directed right on my garage, and I couldn't believe what I was seeing through the window. My Chevy was in my garage!

I cut the engine, got out of the truck, and went inside the garage. The keys, both to the car and the house, were laying on top of the Chevy. There was a handwritten note underneath them. I picked it up and unfolded the paper.

*Milena,*

*I have to leave. I wish that I could explain, but I'm too ashamed to even face you right now. Please understand that my departure has nothing to do with anything that you have done. You've been a gracious host and an even better friend.*

*I hope that life gives you everything that you deserve . . . a man that you deserve. A real man! For a minute, I thought that I could be that man, but something happened earlier today that made me realize it is never to be . . . we are never to be. You will forever have a place in my heart, Milena Clark. Please keep smiling. You're so beautiful when you smile.*

*Love,*

*Yosef*

I was floored. I couldn't breathe. What could possibly have happened to make him up and leave like that? I hadn't even seen him bring the car home. It must've happened while I'd been working with the animals in the kennel earlier that evening.

I went back into the house and sat there for a good hour, staring into space. No television; no radio; only the sound of my heart beating rapidly in my chest. I tried to call the cell phone that I'd given him, but it went straight to voice mail. Yosef had deleted his custom greeting and it was now back to the default, stating the phone number followed by a beep.

I turned off all of the lights and was headed to bed when I stopped dead in my tracks.

Part of me thought that Yosef leaving was probably for the best. He was a kind and gentle man, but I didn't really know that much about him. It wasn't like I had had a lot of experience in that field, so my judgment of his character was based on my heart, and not common sense. I'd led such a sheltered existence, fending men off for eight years. Now I regretted that. And even though I'd come to the conclusion that I never wanted to go without sex for long periods of time, I still technically hadn't had sex in eight years. Jacour had copped an attitude, and Yosef and I had been interrupted.

After that day when that stupid cow had taken ill—it had turned out to be a classic case of diarrhea and not mad cow, of course—Yosef and I had experienced a couple of close calls and had even kissed once more. But he'd never taken it any further than that. It seemed like he didn't feel like he was worthy of me. Part of me wondered the same.

Jacour was pissed. I'd run into him a few times in town. He was always with one of his parents or hanging out with Glenn or Phil. We'd exchange basic pleasantries but then he'd walk off; more like stomp off. I had mixed feelings about him, too. He had come back there for me when he could've afforded to be anyplace in the world. Lydia told me that Glenn said Jacour was waiting me out; waiting for me to get sick of Randolph and come back to him. That sounded like him. He was arrogant, but could he have been right?

My mind was clouded with confusion, but there was no way that I could go to sleep. Yosef had no one else around here; if he had, he wouldn't have been living out in those woods, or staying at shelters when he could obtain a cot assignment.

*Maybe he met someone at work and he's staying with them!*

*Maybe he met another woman and wrote you that bullshit letter instead of coming clean!*

*No, he'd never do that!*

*And you know this because you know the man so well!*

*He'd never do that!*

I turned the hallway light back on, went into the living room, slipped my sandals back on, and headed out the front door.

Thirty minutes later I was parking my truck near the campground where Yosef had asked me to drop him off that night in the rain. The weather was clear that night, and there were no RVs. It was a weeknight and no races were scheduled.

I sat there, squinting to see if I could make out anything in the wooded area beyond the campground. I saw nothing until I saw a man walking toward the woods. He'd seemingly appeared from nowhere, and he was carrying a plastic bag.

Hurriedly, I got out of my truck, walked to the bed, and pulled out a flashlight that I kept there. As a veterinarian, I kept my flashlight cocked and ready. I could easily end up in some barn or pig trough late at night with limited lighting.

I was more nervous than I'd probably ever been, but I walked across the campground and into the woods, shining my flashlight from side to side. Anything . . . or anyone . . . could've pounced on me at any second. Being brave had never been one of my strong suits, but I was that night. I was out there, searching for a homeless village, trying to locate Yosef.

About two hundred feet into the woods, I almost tripped over a log, but I managed to catch my balance. I was scraping some dirt off my lower calf when I heard voices; lots of voices.

*You need to turn your ass around right now and go back to Kannapolis!*

I ignored my inner voice and kept going, determined to find Yosef and make sure that he was okay. I reached a clearing, and what sat before me was like something out of a constructed movie set. Dozens, maybe hundreds, of people were out there. Some had tents. Some had boxes. Some only had blankets. All of them stared at me: the stranger.

"Hello," I whispered, walking past a family of four with two small children.

The kids looked miserable, as I'm sure they were. Since I'd met Yosef, I'd been doing quite a bit of internet research on homelessness. I was devastated when I discovered that anywhere from five hundred thousand to two million children could be homeless on any given day. The United States was supposed to be such a rich and flourishing country. Yet so many were forsaken, like Yosef.

I kept walking, and as I passed each tent, blanket, or box, I felt tears welling up in my eyes. What struck me the most was that all of the people looked normal, not the vision that I would've expected. The images that were splattered across newspapers and television and movie screens were mostly those of crackheads, winos, and crazy people.

I spotted a group of men standing around a fire. Even though it was still running in the seventies during the daytime, the September weather was chilly at night. As I walked closer, I saw someone stir nervously. One man walked away, and then I couldn't miss him. Yosef was taller than everyone else.

Yosef stared at me and then came walking slowly toward me.

"Yosef, I was so worried about you," I said as soon as he was within earshot.

"What are you doing here, Milena?"

I laughed uneasily, cutting off my flashlight, which I'd pointed directly into his eyes. "I came out here looking for a missing pig."

"This isn't a time for jokes."

That erased the smile from my face. "Okay, fine. I read your note and I wanted to talk to you about it, so I came out here looking for you."

"You shouldn't have come here. This isn't the place for you."

"It's not a big deal." I looked around the village. There were some eyes still on me, but the people realized that Yosef was familiar with me so they didn't seem to be worried any longer. "Everyone seems so nice."

"Nice?" Yosef shook his head. "Milena, the people out here are desperate. They're cold and starving, and some of them are even dying."

"Who's dying?" I scanned the immediate area again. "Maybe I can help."

"I don't mean that they're dying right this second, but a lot of people out here are ill, and without medical care, they will eventually die."

"Why don't they go to the doctor?"

Yosef grabbed my elbow. "Come with me."

We started walking back toward the exit to the woods. Yosef stopped suddenly when an older man spoke to him. "Yosef, are you coming back?"

"Yes, Aaron, I'll be back in a few minutes. You need anything?"

The man coughed, loudly, like he was about to cough up a lung. "No, I'm all right. Was just wondering."

Yosef knelt down and patted the man, who was crawled up halfway inside an old big-screen television box, on the shoulder. "You try to get some sleep. Be right back."

I started weeping. I imagined that old man finding that box in the back of a Best Buy or another store and dragging it across streets and down sidewalks and into the woods. Being subjected to such a humiliating moment. All of them being subjected to it. It wasn't right.

When Yosef and I reached the clearing, he finally stopped walking.

"Why doesn't that man . . . Aaron . . . go to the doctor?" I asked.

"And pay for it how?" he replied. "He doesn't have health insurance."

"Then he needs to go to an emergency room. We can take him."

"You don't get it. No one cares about these people out here. No one's going to give them anything for free, and that includes health care." He stared at me as I wiped tears from my eyes. "I told you that you didn't need to see that. You have no business out here. Go home."

"I'm not going anyplace. Not until you tell me why you left. What was that in the note about something happening earlier today?" Yosef turned and tried to walk away from me, but I wouldn't let him. "Tell me what happened, please."

"I was at the car wash when Jacour came through to have his Rolls-Royce washed and detailed. I tried to avoid him, but, as you know, I stick out like a sore thumb because of my height."

"Oh no!"

"Oh yes," Yosef continued. "I was working on another vehicle, but he came right over to me and called me out of my name over and over. He accused me of lying to you about who I was and said that he couldn't wait to tell you all about it."

"He hasn't called me or come by."

"*Yet!* It's only a matter of time. He's going to tell everyone, and I'm so sorry that I've embarrassed you."

"I'm not embarrassed. In fact, I'm kind of relieved."

"Relieved?"

"Yes, all of the lies were getting to me. It's not in my nature to be conniving and deceiving. So what if Jacour knows the truth. He has no right to judge you. No one does. Not my friends, not my parents, no one. All that matters is that you make me happy. You're my friend."

"You and I both know that everyone's going to try to condemn me and encourage you to cut me out of your life."

"So you decided to do the job for them?" I asked. "That's not your decision either." Yosef looked at me like I was crazy. "I'm serious. There are two people involved in this friendship. How dare you make decisions for me?"

"But I—"

"But nothing, Yosef. I've gotten used to you, and it isn't fair for you to walk away from me."

"Are you saying that you want me to come back?"

"That's exactly what I'm saying."

He blushed. "But what about Jacour?"

"Jacour can't tell me what to do either."

Yosef hesitated. "I should probably stay here."

"No, I won't accept that. You're coming with me."

"But I promised Aaron that I'd be right back."

"And you will be."

"Huh?"

"We're both going back and we're taking him to the hospital."

"He doesn't have insurance."

"It's okay. My aunt Meredith is the nighttime head physician at the Northeast Medical Center in the ER. She'll treat him, guaranteed."

"Wow, who aren't you related to?" Yosef chuckled. "You're amazing."

"No, I'm from Kannapolis, where everybody knows everybody else." I took Yosef's hand. "Let's go get Aaron."

• • •

Yosef and I didn't get home from the hospital until after nine in the morning. Aaron was resting comfortably, and Aunt Meredith was treating him for pneumonia. She said that it was a good thing we brought him in. The pneumonia would've killed him within a few days if he hadn't received medical attention. She cut through all kinds of paperwork, and I told her that I would take care of whatever absolutely had to be paid. Yosef wasn't privy to that part of our conversation, and he never needed to be.

"Thanks so much, for everything," Yosef said as we both plopped down on the sofa.

"You're welcome. You want me to cook some breakfast?"

Yosef took my hand. "You've done enough. I need to be cooking you breakfast."

"Can I ask you something?"

"Sure, go ahead."

"It's not that I don't get a kick out of the mystery surrounding you, but we've known each other for a minute now, and I still don't know that much about you."

"What would you like to know?"

"Why were you homeless in the first place, Yosef?"

"Why does that matter?"

"Please don't insult me by answering my question with a question." I gripped his hand tighter. "Those people out there . . . it broke my heart. To think that there are people like that everywhere. I want to know what happened to you. I *need* to know."

Yosef sighed. "It's very difficult for me to talk about this, Milena."

"I get that, and I wouldn't ask if I didn't feel that it would somehow bring us closer together."

"I was married once," he said. "To a beautiful woman named June. Her birthday was in June, hence the name. She was from here, North Carolina. I moved here from Boston to be with her. She was full of life and energy, much like yourself."

"So why aren't you married anymore?" I asked, feeling myself getting jealous. "Did she leave you?"

Yosef's eyes welled up with tears. "You could say that. June died last December."

"I'm so sorry!"

*Look at you! Jealous of a dead woman!*

"It's not your fault. It's no one's fault . . . but mine."

"How could you even think that, Yosef? Whatever happened, it couldn't have been your fault."

"When I moved down here from Boston, I transferred my job. I was working for a large chemical corporation. But late last summer, the company became a victim of the recession and filed for bankruptcy. June only had a part-time job at a dry cleaners; no benefits."

Yosef's hand was shaking, and I tried to steady it.

"June got sick all of a sudden. One day she was fine, and the next, she was bed-ridden and in pain."

"What was wrong with her?"

"Bone cancer. It took June so quick. It was so painful for her, and since we didn't have insurance, the cost of her medicine wasn't covered."

It was all starting to make sense. "So you paid for the medicine yourself?"

"It took all of my savings." Yosef was completely in tears by then. "I wiped out my 401k but it still wasn't enough. Avastin costs about fifty grand a year, and we went right through everything." Yosef paused and wiped his face with his free hand. "It was worth it though. If she had to leave me, I couldn't watch her suffer."

"And you couldn't pay your bills after she was gone?"

He shook his head vigorously. "No, it was all gone. I sold my car to pay a bill for her to stay in a hospice at the end. While she was in there, they foreclosed on our home and—"

"That's enough," I said, stopping him. "You don't need to say another word." I drew his face to mine and looked into his eyes. "The fact that you sacrificed everything for love makes sense to me. *You* make sense to me. *We* make sense."

"We?"

"Yes, we." I kissed Yosef passionately for a few seconds. "I want to be with you. I want you to stay . . . here . . . with me. Please stay."

Yosef kissed me, and this time it was different. There was an energy that hadn't been there before; a yearning; a desire.

I drew my face back from his. "Take me to bed."

"Are you sure?"

"I've never been more sure about anything in my entire life."

Yosef and I started kissing again, and then he lifted me up and carried me to the bedroom.

Yosef was beautiful as we lay there, the sunlight intruding through the window. He was sleeping peacefully and snoring lightly. I had no regrets about what had happened between us over the previous few hours.

I stared at his perfect skin as his eyelashes fluttered. His perfect mouth. His perfect body. His perfect dick.

Yosef had to be at least a foot long. I'd been frightened when I'd first seen it. It wasn't like I was that experienced. Jacour was about eight inches, and I would've sworn he was huge. I wasn't sure if it was his Caribbean heritage or what, but if anyone ever asked me, I would be willing to testify that the Mandingo rumors were true.

Of course, I had trouble performing oral sex on him. He understood, so I treated his dick more like a lollipop than a popsicle. It was going to take me some time to get used to his size.

That also went for when it came to actual intercourse.

"I'll be gentle with you," Yosef had reassured me.

"It's been a long time for me," I said. "Eight years. I might not be able to take it."

"We'll take our time." He started fingering my clit. "You're nice and wet. You want me to taste you some more?"

I giggled. "You're not full yet?"

"Of you, never," he replied. Yosef had spent a good thirty minutes between my legs, licking and sucking and making me scream. "I love the way you taste."

"I love the way you taste, too."

"Do you have some condoms?"

I laughed. "Are you kidding? If I did, they would've been expired long before now."

Yosef and I both grew quiet. It would've been too easy to go for it raw. But we didn't.

He got up off the bed and pulled on his pants. "I'll be right back."

"The keys to the truck are on the kitchen counter."

He winked, pulled on his shirt, and left.

While he was gone, I masturbated. For one thing, I was horny and, for another, I thought that having my pussy nice and loose from a vibrator would make it easier for him to get his elephantine dick inside of me.

I went to my top drawer and pulled out my weapon of choice, a 16-function super rabbit vibrator. It was only seven and a half inches, but it would have to do. I figured that I had about ten minutes or so for Yosef to make it to the BP, grab some condoms, and come back.

I stuck the vibrator in me, turned it on full blast, and moved it around with my left hand and played with my nipples with my right. I closed my eyes and imagined Yosef fucking the living daylights out of me.

I was so into it that I didn't hear him return. By the time I realized it, he was staring down at me, grinning.

"I see you got started without me," he whispered, setting a pack of condoms on the nightstand.

I was pulling the vibrator out of me, but he stopped me. He took hold of it and started moving it around inside of me. "That's so sexy, Milena."

He sucked on my breasts and fucked me into submission with the vibrator until I screamed out his name.

I was blessed with the gift of flexibility, so it ended up being a wild ride when I ended up with my lower back and legs raised all the way over my head, with my ankles crossed behind it. Yosef put on an oversized condom and entered me slowly. We gazed at each other as he managed to get inch after inch inside of me.

"Do you want me to stop?" he asked. "Just say the word."

"No, fuck no!" I screamed out. "Don't stop!"

I came over and over again. We fucked each other like savages until Yosef passed out.

So there I was, staring at him, with a sore pussy and a smile on my face.

"I knew that you were a good man," I whispered to him in his sleep.

I laid my head on his chest and fell into a peaceful slumber.

# Lydia

UNBELIEVABLE! That is the only word that could possibly describe how I felt. Glenn—my Glenn—had actually taken his ass on Ticketmaster.com and ordered some tickets to a play. A *real* play. I realize that for a lot of sisters, that would have been par for the course when it came to dating, but that kind of shit never happened to me.

The only plays that I had ever been to were the ones at South Rowan High School, and I hadn't been to one of those since I'd graduated. But this was a totally different experience. We were in a real theater, not the school cafeteria converted to a theater. People were dressed up and drinking wine and beer. The seats were red velvet and, most important, Glenn had on a suit. He *never* wore suits, except to funerals.

I had on a powerful number. A tight red dress that caused heads to turn. Men were eyeing me like a piece of licorice, but their women were straight-up haters. Their issue; not mine. If they wanted to be as fine as me, they needed to put in the work. To be honest, genetics were good to me. I rarely did any bona fide exercising, but if fucking counted, I was training for the Olympics.

We had seats in the first row on the balcony. To me, that was better than being all the way up front. I was farsighted, so being up front would've been uncomfortable. Where we were was perfect. I could see some of the action in the seats below, something else that would've been missed out on if we'd been all the way up front.

A deep male voice came out of nowhere and announced, "Charlotte, North Carolina! Are you ready? The Ovens Auditorium welcomes you to Bovine Ebonyman Steele's award-winning play *Love in Plain Sight!*"

Everyone applauded and I was thinking, *Why the hell are you all applauding when the curtain hasn't even opened up yet?*

Two sisters walked out on the stage in tight clothes and four-inch heels, talking smack about how brothers were no damn good. Wasn't that the fucking truth! Everyone laughed, including Glenn. I was checking them out and realized that I looked better than both of them.

By the time intermission rolled around, I was convinced that I could seriously be an actress; real talk. So what if one of the chicks starring in the play *used* to be in movies and the other one *used* to be on a television series. If they were all that, they would've still been in movies and on television. Let's keep it real. No chick is going to pick a traveling stage play over being in front of millions. But I would've done anything to trade places with them and get the hell out of North Carolina. At the moment, I was happy as shit to be out of Kannapolis.

The play was about how one woman had the man of her dreams right in front of her face. He was her business partner, but she didn't see him that way until her best friend started trying to get the dick, and then she got jealous. Then, like a neatly wrapped package with a bow, the two of them hooked up, smashed, and he proposed at the end. Whoopty-fucking-do! I could've written something better than that with my eyes closed. Hell, my life in Hicksville had more drama than that.

As we were walking back to Glenn's car, he asked me how I liked the play.

"I loved it," I lied. "Great storyline, and the actresses were fab."

Glenn unlocked the passenger door and held it open so that I could get in. "In other words, you weren't feeling it."

I looked up at him. "No, seriously, it was on point. And did you see those shoes they had on? Smoking!"

Glenn rolled his eyes and closed the door.

We drove home mostly in silence, which was fine by me. I wasn't mad with Glenn. In fact, I was delighted that he would splurge on the tickets. I was upset because seeing that play and all the people walking around, eating outside at the restaurants we passed, laughing, and smiling, made me realize how much I was missing out on.

I went in the house and slipped out of my dress right there in the living room. Glenn headed to the kitchen to get a beer. Everything was copacetic, and I was looking forward to a warm—not hot—shower. Then I planned to put him to sleep like a baby by sucking his dick in appreciation for taking me to the play. That wasn't to happen.

"Why are you being such a bitch?" Glenn asked as he reappeared from the kitchen, twisting the cap off a Corona.

I looked behind me, searching for a bitch.

"I'm talking to you, Lydia."

"No, you can't be talking to me. The reason you're not talking to me is because you're not fucking crazy."

Glenn took a swig of his beer. "Those tickets cost me more than sixty bucks a pop. That was bill money."

"Glenn, I do appreciate you buying the tickets. And I wasn't lying; I had a great time."

"We've been together three years. I can tell when your ass is being sarcastic, and that's exactly what you were doing. Don't patronize me."

*Damn! He's breaking out the big vocabulary! He is pissed!*

"I'm not trying to *patronize* you, but if you don't take back that 'bitch' comment, I will be ramming my foot up your ass. Don't try me, baby. I'm not that chick. I'm not the one that'll wait until you fall asleep to fuck your ass up. I'll come straight at you; real talk."

"I'm sorry that I called you a bitch." He spread his hands beside him. "Cool?"

"That's better, but the shit still ain't cool. You're tripping."

I walked down the hallway and went into the bathroom. I started the shower and then went into the bedroom to roll a joint. This motherfucker was stressing me, and I'd been too scared to ride to Charlotte with weed in my purse. The cops around the way didn't give a damn about all that, but if we'd been stopped on the highway by the state po-po, that would've been a different matter. Racial profiling was a big thing in North Carolina; anyone black was well aware of that. Everyone had a story to tell.

It had been a few days since I'd checked on my plants, but they should've been nice and moist. There had been plenty of rain. I was so tempted to start selling my weed, but, again, I was also scared. Growing my own shit kept me out of the limelight. I'd never be caught purchasing weight, or selling it.

I did crave another kind of limelight. Somehow, some way, I was going to be famous. If George Clinton and Jacour Bryant could grow up in Kannapolis and be famous, then dammit, so could I.

I wasn't getting any younger. My thirtieth birthday was in a few months, and I had to make a move quick. But what did that mean for me and Glenn? I decided to try to reason with him.

I was in the shower after the hot water had finally heated up, missing that high water pressure from the Days Inn, when Glenn came in and sat on the toilet to take a dump. Now, I don't know about other sisters, but when I was in the shower getting all sexy and lovely and scrubbing with my jasmine vanilla shower gel, the last thing I wanted to smell—or hear—was a man taking a shit.

I yanked the shower curtain open. "Glenn, can't that wait a few minutes?"

"No, it can't," he said, picking the latest issue of *Jet* out of the magazine rack. "I've been prairie-dogging it since we left Charlotte."

"Prairie-dogging it?"

"Yes, pulling it back in when it was trying to come out, like a prairie dog does when he pops his head out of the dirt."

I rolled my eyes at him and closed the curtain. "That's some nasty-ass shit!"

He finished and I could hear him stand up and start wiping his ass. "Yes, it is," he said.

A moment later he was gone. I reached out and got the Indian Money off the back of the toilet. I sprayed half the can, yelling, "You could at least spray!"

Glenn was in bed when I got out of the shower and entered the bedroom naked to find a nightie.

"Um, there should still be some warm water left for your shower," I said, giving him a hint.

"I'm too tired. I'll clean up in the morning."

*A hint's not going to work!*

"Glenn, you know how I feel about dirty bodies on clean sheets."

"Yes, and you know how I feel about you trying to act like my mother."

I sat down on the bed and started putting lotion on my arms and legs. "Can you lotion my back?"

Glenn was watching a baseball game but paused the DVR to grab the bottle from me. He squirted a dime-sized drop of lotion on his hand, slapping it more than rubbing it on my back.

I grabbed the lotion back. "What's really good with you? This isn't about my attitude. Like you said, we've been together for a minute and I know you."

Glenn got up off the bed and started stepping into his sneakers. He had changed into some shorts and a white tee.

"Where are you going?" I asked.

"I'm going to crash over at Phil and Briscoe's tonight."

"For what?" I blocked the door in my birthday suit. "Now *this* is really not like you."

Glenn glared at me, and for a second, I thought the mother-fucker might actually hit me. I was mentally preparing myself to have to cut him.

"Lydia, I'm sick of your Miss High and Mighty shit. You think that you're the cream of the crop, and while you're fine, and sexy, and all of that, it doesn't mean you can treat me any way you want."

"You've never complained about the way I treat you."

That was partially true. He had, but not to this extent, and not in a long while.

"Then it's time for me to speak up. I took you out, trying to make you happy, and instead of jumping on my dick, you're talking down to me and ordering me around and shit."

"All that I asked was for you to go take a shower." I kissed him on the lips and then drew his bottom lip into my mouth to suckle on it. When I let it go, I stated seductively, "You go do that for me, Daddy, and I'll not only jump on your dick, I'll twirl on it."

I almost had him, but his determination to prove a point won out in the end. He pushed me away from the door. "I'll be back tomorrow."

I sat down on the bed in disbelief. He was actually leaving. I heard the front door slam, and, thirty seconds later, his car started and roared out of the driveway.

"Humph, I'm not even gonna trip," I told myself.

I put on a nightie and crawled into bed. I unpaused the DVR but changed the channel. That meant that his game would stop taping but I didn't give a fuck. I turned to the Travel Channel, my favorite, and got lost in the exotic places that I would visit one day . . . soon.

Later on, if Glenn really didn't bring his ass home, I planned to call Andy. He'd given me his number when he'd made a delivery earlier that week. I wondered where he was. I needed a man's attention and I couldn't call Phil; Glenn was over there.

I started playing in my pussy with my index finger. Then I tasted myself.

"Damn fool! Missing out on all this good pussy!"

I put my hand back between my legs and brought myself to a tremendous climax.

# Milena

LYDIA and I were having dinner at McCabe's Steakhouse. They were only open from Thursday to Saturday, from five to ten. Needless to say, the place was packed. I was a fan of their buffalo wings, and Lydia loved the calamari. We were cleaning out the appetizer plates and drinking Mind Erasers—a concoction made from vodka, Kahlua, and soda—while we waited for our entrees.

"What did you order again?" Lydia asked me. She'd been fussing with Glenn on her cell phone while I'd been placing my order.

"I ordered the stuffed flounder."

"Ooh, I've been wanting to try that. I might have to dig in your plate."

I giggled. "No problem. I want to taste your baked ziti. My mother said it's good, but I've never had it."

It wasn't even necessary for Lydia and me to have that conversation. We were always each other's garbage disposals when we ate out. No takeout containers while we were on patrol.

"I'm shocked that we're actually spending quality time together."

"Lydia, don't trip. I've been busy getting my life together."

"Your life together with Yosef?" I blushed. "Aw, look at that glow. Now tell me you're not fucking him yet. You're either fucking him, Jacour, or both of them."

"I'd never fuck two men at once," I stated defensively.

Lydia smirked. "Every woman who's ever done that very thing has probably claimed they never would at some point in their lives."

"Well, I'm an apparition then."

We both laughed.

I took a swig of my drink. It was kind of tart. "I *am* sleeping with Yosef," I blurted out casually.

Lydia perked up in her seat. "And?"

"And what?"

"Don't make me pull a Donita and Kayla on you. What's up with the dick?"

"It's good, and that's all I'm going to say."

"How big is it?"

"A good kind of big."

"How wide is it?"

"A good kind of wide."

"Heifer."

"Tramp."

Lydia looked behind me at the entrance and rolled her eyes.

"What's wrong?" I asked.

"See, this is why I hate going out to eat around here. Everyone shows up. You must've conjured those two hookers up."

I turned to see Kayla and Donita talking to the hostess.

"They're going to have a long wait for a table. Why don't we ask them to join us?" I suggested.

"If you do that, I'm outtie."

I sighed. "Okay, cool."

"I'm not trying to be mean or anything, but we never get to spend time together anymore."

"It's cool, really. And you're right. Let them wait."

Lydia laughed. "Wow, all that *good* dick has turned you into a mean one."

I picked up a buffalo wing and tossed it at her. "Whatever, tramp."

Our food came and we dug in. Both entrees were the bomb.


Lydia and I were about to split up in the parking lot when Jacour pulled up with his parents in the car with him.

"Uh-oh, here comes your man," Lydia said, chastising me.

I hadn't seen or heard from Jacour since Yosef had told me about him spotting him at the car wash. It had only been a few days, but I was still surprised that Jacour hadn't confronted me, and I was hoping that he didn't plan to do it in front of his parents.

"Let me hurry up and get out of here." I hugged Lydia, kissed her on the cheek, and rushed off to the space where my truck was parked.

Lydia was quicker than me. She was already out of the parking lot when I was backing out of the space. I heard someone hit the bed of my truck. I glanced in my rearview mirror and saw Jacour standing there.

*Run his ass over!*

*I can't do that!*

He walked up to my driver's-side window and tapped on the glass. I rolled it down.

"Hello, Milena."

"Hey, Jacour. I didn't know you were here."

"That's funny, because you stared right at my parents and me when we pulled in."

"I didn't recognize the car."

"Yeah, there are a lot of Phantoms around here. You saw me and you were trying to avoid me."

"No, I wasn't." I glanced around the lot. "Where are your parents?"

"I told them to go on in."

"Oh, well, tell them I said hello. You better get in there; it's probably a long wait."

"We made reservations."

"Aw, that's cool."

"So, how's Yosef?"

"Yo who?"

"The Yosef that works at the car wash down off 29-South that looks and talks exactly like Randolph William Henderson the third. You know, the veterinarian from Cali."

*Fuck it! You're not ashamed!*

"Yosef is fine. He's back at the house . . . waiting for me."

"Why'd you fabricate that elaborate story, Milena?"

"Honestly, I don't know. It seemed to make a lot of sense at the time. In retrospect, it was kind of stupid, but I don't regret it. If I hadn't come up with that plan, I never would've met him."

"If you'd never met him, you'd be with me."

"You say that like it's a fact."

"It is a fact."

"No, it's your opinion."

We both fell silent for a few seconds.

"I have to leave town for about a week or two to take care of some business back in New York."

I shrugged. "So, why are you telling me that?"

"Just in case you care. In case you need me."

"And why would I need you?"

He reached inside and took my hand off the steering wheel. "We love each other, and you can fight it from now until the end of time, but it's not going to go away, and that car wash dude—whoever the hell he really is—is not going to be able to take my rightful place." Jacour kissed my hand and then let it go. "If you weren't still in love with me, you never would've gone through all of this to keep me at bay."

"I really have to go," I said.

"You do that."

Jacour walked off and I watched him enter the restaurant. I laid my head on the steering wheel and started crying. I did still love him . . . but I also hated his fucking guts.

# Lydia

My parents made me sick. I went over to their house to have a serious talk with them, and instead they made a complete mockery out of my dream. My father was a little bit better than my mother. She thought my idea of moving to New York was hilarious. All I wanted was a little support, and not the financial kind.

"New York is one of the most expensive cities in this country," my father said, taking it more seriously. "You can't even support yourself here; what makes you think you can afford to live in New York?"

"The cost of living is much higher there," I replied, "so the pay is higher as well."

He shook his head and sat down at the kitchen table to read the newspaper.

"Daddy, please don't ignore me. I'm going to move, and I want you to give me some advice."

"His advice is for you to stay put right here," Momma said. "If things aren't going well with Glenn, you can always move back home."

"Your mother's right," Daddy said. "He's been getting free milk for too damn long. He either needs to buy it or let you go."

"I'm not a cow, Daddy, and this has nothing to do with Glenn. It has to do with me." I sat down at the table across from him while Momma washed dishes. "I feel so trapped here. There's nothing to do. There's no hope. Working for Uncle Joe isn't utilizing my talents."

Momma wiped her hands with a dishcloth and then came over and rubbed my shoulders. "I've lived around these parts my entire life and I've never felt trapped." She kissed the top of my head. "It's probably PMS, dear. Why don't you go lie down in your old room and take a nap?"

"I don't need to take a nap. I'm not three." Momma let go of my shoulders. "I'll be thirty soon and look at me. I don't have any money, I don't have any kids, and I only have part of a man."

Daddy put the paper back down on the table. "See, this is about Glenn."

I stood up defiantly. "It's not about Glenn. It's about life. My shitty-ass life."

"Don't curse, dear," Momma said and started stirring her collard greens on the stove. "Your father doesn't allow cursing in his house."

"His house? You see that mentality. This is your house, too, Momma."

My mother sighed and covered the pot back up with a lid. "I'm going to go fold up your uniforms," she said to my father. "Lydia, if you're still here when I come up from the basement, I hope your mood will have improved."

She walked off like Suzy Homemaker and left me there with Daddy. He took a sip of his coffee and started whistling.

"You don't have anything else to say?" I asked.

"No, I don't. If you're foolish enough to run off to New York without a pot to piss in or a window to throw it out of, make sure you keep in touch. Otherwise, you need to either go back to Glenn's and get your stuff to move back in here, or go be with your *part of a man*. I've had enough of this for one day."

He got up and walked toward the family room, where he often barricaded himself with beer and his old-fashioned console television with a rotary dial.

"Daddy, I'm not finished!" I yelled after him.

He kept on walking, went into the family room, and shut the door.

I sat down at the table and pouted. I was going to show them.

Phil and I were in the movies watching *Carriers*, yet another movie about people trying to outrun the end of the world. If the world was fucking ending, no one could outrun shit, but it was entertaining. Four kids were trying to find a safe haven that hadn't been infected by a viral pandemic. Only problem: there was no safe haven so they kept running into zombies and people trying to take them out first. Then they started catching the disease—one by one—until they started whacking each other.

The movie was so-so. I really needed to escape for a couple of hours after dealing with my parents. I had to work later on that evening, and I'd invited Phil so he could pay for my ticket, popcorn, and ICEE.

There were only a few people scattered in the theater. It was a weekday. That was a good thing; I hated it when people talked in the movies. People didn't spend their hard-earned cash to hear somebody talk about their business or be subjected to their predictions about the outcome of the movie.

Even though I despised people talking, Phil was yapping his gums, asking me a lot of questions.

"Are you for real about New York?" he leaned over and whispered.

I'd given him a brief recap of my conversation with my parents while we'd been at the concession stand.

"I'm dead serious. I'm not staying here," I whispered back.

"Then let me go with you." I glared at him through the darkness of the theater. "I'm dead serious, too. Two people working are better than one. I'm not trying to work at Freightliner forever."

"You can't go with me, Phil. It wouldn't make sense. I'm going there to become a star." I pointed at the twenty-foot screen. "One day, that's going to be me up there, except I'm going to be giving an Oscar-winning performance, not running around blowing off people's heads."

Some woman in the front row, who was there with two other old broads, turned around and looked at us. I gave her the finger, but I wasn't sure if she saw it. She turned back around and started munching on her popcorn.

"You need to relax." Phil tickled the inside of my ear with his thick tongue. "Want to sit on my face?"

"In here?"

"Yeah, in here. The place is empty."

That thought turned me on. "Okay, I'll sit on your face."

I stood up and jiggled out of my panties and then handed them to Phil. He put the crotch of them in his mouth and started sucking on it, dirty dog.

"You are so damn nasty," I whispered.

We were on the back row, against the wall, so I put one foot on each chair beside Phil and palmed the wall and started grinding my pussy on his face. The window that the movie was projecting out of was only about five feet above my head and I could hear the whizzing of the machinery, which turned me on even more.

Phil's head was buried under my dress and I turned my head slightly to see if those old broads were looking. They weren't, because it was a loud part of the film where some other old broads were trying to shoot the main characters with shotguns. I bet they loved that shit, as if they'd ever have the nerve to do something like that. If some shit did break out, they probably would've been the first ones quivering underneath their beds or in their closets that smelled like Bengay.

I fed Phil for about another five minutes and then got down. I wanted some dick.

"Give me a condom," I demanded.

He handed me one, I ripped it open, and then rolled it onto his dick. He'd wasted no time getting it out of his pants. I sat on his dick, facing away from him, and gave him the lap dance of all motherfucking lap dances. That horse underneath me was bucking and throbbing as I worked my magic.

Phil played with my nipples and licked my neck and ear while we were fucking. When he came, he came hard and whispered, "I'm for real, Lydia. If you want me to go with you, I will."

He seemed serious, but Phil would've only been dead weight. He didn't have much more going for him than I had going for me. Besides, I figured that if I went to New York alone, I could probably find some other aspiring starlets to room with. Better yet, with my hellified pussy I could easily land a sugar daddy—maybe some famous producer—and fuck my way to stardom. I'd been fucking for free all of those years; it might as well count for something.

Phil was cool, but he wasn't the man for me. He could serve his purpose until I left, but after that, he was destined to become a distant memory, just like Glenn.

# Milena

WANTED to do something very special for Yosef. He'd been through so much suffering, and understanding that he'd ended up homeless over the love of a woman had endeared him to me even more. June must've been a very special woman to have landed such a special husband.

When I shared his history with Lydia, and how he'd spent his last dollar to make June's transition as painless as possible, she and I both broke down in tears. We were in my kennel. I had two sick dogs and a sick raccoon—yes, a sick raccoon. People in the country considered the strangest things to be pets.

"Aren't you worried about living in her shadow?" Lydia asked.

"I've thought about that. Everyone has a past; even me. Yosef's willing to accept my past, and Jacour's right here in the same town, waiting on me to come back. Yosef can't go back to June."

"No, true enough, but it's not like they broke up either."

I sighed and started washing down a vacant pen with a hose.

"You get what I'm saying," Lydia continued. "He didn't *choose* to leave her, and she didn't *choose* to leave him."

"I get what you're saying, Lydia, but what's done is done. She's gone, he's with me, and we've decided to take a shot at real happiness."

"Do your parents know yet?"

"About how I met him? No, they still think his name is Randolph."

"How long do you plan on playing this game with them?"

"I haven't had a chance to tell them, but I will. I'm not ashamed, and if this is a mistake, it's my mistake to make."

"Now that I can feel you on." Lydia opened up a popsicle that she'd gotten out of the small fridge that I kept in the kennel. "I'm moving to New York."

I stopped and cut the hose off. "Say what?"

"I'm moving to New York. You may have given up the opportunity to move there with Jacour, but I'm going."

"What are you going to do there?"

"I don't know. Eventually, I'm going to be a star . . . either on Broadway or in the movies. When I first get there, I'll find something."

I knew Lydia better than she knew herself. She wasn't going to be easily persuaded to change her mind. It would've taken an act of God to convince her that she had no business going there, so I attempted to be helpful.

"Jacour should be able to help you find a good job. He knows enough people there."

"Do you think he'll let me stay in his place?"

I giggled. "Now that, I don't know about. You can ask him. You never know."

Lydia walked over and patted me on my lower back. "That's where you come in. I need you to ask him for me."

"You've been smoking too much primo weed, sis. I'll talk to him at some point about hooking you up with a job, *if you're seri-*

*ous,* but I can't ask him to let you stay in his crib. I'm not even sure he still has it."

"Yes, he does. They had an episode about it on MTV *Cribs* last month. The place is off the motherfucking chain!"

"If it was on last month, it had to be pre-taped a while ago. Jacour was *here* last month, remember? He did tell me that night at McCabe's that he had to leave town on business. I didn't ask for any details; it's none of my business."

"I still can't believe that you're picking Yosef over Jacour."

I turned and looked at her. "Why? Because he's not a millionaire?"

"He's not a millionaire and he hasn't loved you since the beginning of time."

"Jacour and I didn't see each other for eight years. He's not the same man he used to be, and I'm not the same woman."

Lydia put the entire popsicle in her mouth and popped it out. I laughed, imagining her sucking Glenn's dick.

"You can play dumb if you want and talk all that *I'm not the same woman* crap, but deep down inside, you're still feeling Jacour. You need to be honest with yourself before you fuck up your life for good."

"Thanks for the advice, old wise one."

"You're welcome, my infant child."

We both laughed.

"I need to finish up in here. I have to take these dogs home, and the raccoon's owner is coming in an hour."

"You clearing house, huh?"

"Yes. I'm taking Yosef on a vacation this weekend, to the mountains."

"You've never taken me to any fucking mountains."

I rolled my eyes at Lydia. "We're spending the weekend in a romantic cabin. Why the hell would I want to be there with you?"

"Well, you could've invited me someplace else."

"I've been a hermit for nearly a decade. Invite you where?"

"Now that you've come out of that turtle shell, you better take me on the next trip."

"That's a plan," I said.

"Later, you," Lydia said and hugged me. "Have fun and don't fuck so much that you don't get a chance to enjoy the scenery."

"No, that's what you would do."

Lydia looked at me and then winked. "True enough."

I watched her leave and then hurried about to get things done so Yosef and I could leave on time.

Yosef and I were in a secluded cabin in the Blue Ridge Mountains. One bedroom, one bath, a small kitchenette, and a fireplace; all we needed to be nice and cozy.

"This is a great surprise," he said, gazing into my eyes as we chilled by the fireplace. "I'm glad that I was able to take off work."

"Me too." I gave him a peck on the lips. "The owner's cool for letting you off when you haven't been there that long."

"Yes, Carlos is a good guy."

"I'm so proud of you."

"Proud of me! For what?"

I rubbed my fingers up and down his forearm. "For being you. You're wonderful."

"That's deep. I don't think that I've ever been called *wonderful* before."

"Well, you are wonderful, to me."

"No, you're the one who's wonderful."

"Oh, get out of here."

"I'm serious, Milena. How many women do you think would've given a homeless man a chance?"

I cleared my throat.

"I'm waiting," Yosef said. "How many?"

"I can't honestly say that I know anyone. But"—I held up my index finger—"I never would've thought that I would either. There are always exceptions to every rule."

"Then you're definitely an exception."

"Tell me something," I said, taking a sip of wine. "After June died, and before you met me, was there anyone else?"

Yosef diverted his eyes to the fireplace.

"Hmm, I see," I whispered. It was obvious that there had been someone else.

"It's not like that." Yosef looked back at me. "I met this woman who volunteered at a shelter."

"Did this woman have a name?"

"Her name was Theresa. She was very nice and, yes, she was attractive."

"And?"

"We became friends whenever she was there. I really only came through to get a meal. Like I told you before, I was never too keen on staying in those places overnight."

"Let me guess; the two of you broke bread together." I giggled, trying to make light of the situation.

"Yes, we broke bread."

Yosef blushed; I didn't like that.

"Where is she now?" I asked.

He shrugged. "It was the strangest thing. One day, she stopped showing up. I inquired and they said that she'd called and informed them that her schedule no longer permitted her to volunteer."

I could tell by the pained expression on his face that there was more to it. "I take it that you didn't believe that."

"No, I didn't. I think that Theresa was developing feelings for me, genuine feelings, and couldn't bring herself to admit it. It's easy for people to volunteer to be around the needy, but after they've served a few plates and washed a few dishes, they get to go home . . . back to reality." Yosef sighed. "When Theresa would leave, I'd go back to my reality . . . sleeping wherever I could. She didn't need a man like me." He gazed into my eyes. "And if you really think about it, neither do you."

I took Yosef's hand. "Please don't start that again. I do need a man like you."

"You could be with any man you want, including Jacour."

That's when I looked away from him; huge mistake.

"Milena, you still have feelings for him, don't you?"

"Yosef, Jacour's the only man that I'd ever had a relationship with until you. Forget not having a lot of experience; Jacour *is* my experience."

"Answer my question. Do you still have feelings for him?"

"I still care about him, but shouldn't I? That's got to be normal. People kill me when they break up with someone or get divorced and then claim to hate each other. Some of them even have kids together and, once it's over, all of a sudden the woman was a whore all along, or the man was no good. There had to be something special that drew them together in the first place and—" I realized that I was rambling. "Am I right?"

He nodded. "Yes, you're right."

"All I'm saying is that while I don't have any regrets about breaking off my engagement with Jacour, I don't think he's the devil incarnate or anything. If I'd agreed to marry someone that bad, that would speak volumes about my lack of character."

He let go of my hand. "I'm not a dumb man, Milena."

"I never implied that you were." I sighed. "I don't get this. We came up here to have a good time, to relax and get to know each other better. Why are you making a big deal about Jacour?"

"Because I'm trying to get to know you better and I'm getting the impression that Jacour is still significant to you. It's not merely because of this conversation either."

Now I was really lost. I shook my head in confusion. "I've never given you any reason to think that I'm still in love with Jacour."

"Not verbally, no."

"Then what are you talking about?"

"When you don't realize that I'm looking, I've seen you flipping through your scrapbook, looking at his cards, photos of the two of you embracing, mementos of your time together, and I've seen the expression on your face when you do it."

*Damn, Milena, he saw you!*

*Thanks for telling me!*

*You shouldn't have been looking at that shit!*

*I was only looking!*

"Well . . . say something," Yosef said. "Deny it."

"I'm not going to deny that I've been straightening up some clutter around the house and came across some things. It's not a crime, that I'm aware of, to have fond memories. I also reminisce when I look at my school pictures and old photographs of other family members."

"I didn't see you looking at any of those things."

"Maybe that's because you're not looking at me every second of the day."

Yosef moved back on the floor, away from me a few inches. "I see that you're going to refuse to be honest."

"I am being honest!" I was getting upset. I'd planned, and paid

for, this vacation—one that I desperately needed—and now I was
in the middle of an argument. "I'm not still in love with Jacour!"

Yosef stood up, walked in the bedroom, and closed the door.

I threw my wine into the fireplace, shattering the glass. Then I
cried.

I slept out on the sofa that first night at the cabin. I was determined
that I wasn't going to beg Yosef to forgive me for something that
I hadn't done. He couldn't seriously expect me to have no feelings
whatsoever for a person who had once been so significant to me.
If June had still been alive, and they'd simply divorced, I wouldn't
have tripped. Divorced means no longer together, for whatever
the reason. Jacour and I were not a couple anymore; that's all that
should've mattered.

The sunlight beaming in through the window awakened me.
It was shining right on my eyes. Being in the mountains made it
seem like we'd closed half the distance to the sun somehow.

I woke up and shielded my eyes. I was about to turn over and
face the backside of the sofa when I realized that Yosef was standing at the other end, staring down at me.

"Good morning," he said, and then came around the edge to sit
down.

I scrunched my legs up to give him room. He was holding two
steaming mugs of coffee and set one down on the coffee table.

"I made you some coffee. I know how you crave it in the morning."

"I can't make a move without it." I giggled and sat up to retrieve
it. I blew on it and took a sip. "Ooh, this is tasty."

"That's probably why they call it Taster's Choice."

I laughed. "Probably so. Did you sleep well?"

"I didn't sleep a wink."

"Humph, at least you had the bed."

"I feel horrible about last night. You brought me here, and I totally ruined the vacation you'd planned."

Before I'd fallen asleep way over in the morning, I'd made a promise to myself that I wouldn't let the same nonsense reconvene in the morning. I had much to say about the way he'd acted, but instead, I simply said, "We still have today and half of tomorrow to have fun."

Yosef grinned. "The ultimate optimist. You're right. We have plenty of time to alter the course of things."

"Why don't we start by going for a walk through the woods?"

"Sounds great." He stood up. "I'll shower first."

I pulled the blanket off me. I was completely nude underneath. "Or we can shower together."

Yosef chuckled. "Interesting pajamas?"

"That fire was hot last night. I didn't think it would ever fizzle out."

"Looks like I missed out on a great opportunity."

"There's always tonight. We can make love right here on the sofa, or on the floor."

"Or both," Yosef said.

I got up off the sofa and walked toward him. "I like the way you think."

Yosef leaned down and kissed me. Then he picked me up so that I could straddle his waist, and he carried me to the bathroom for a nice, hot, steamy shower.

# Lydia

I WAS in my usual spot behind Food Lion, smoking my weed, when Andy approached me. I was used to it by that point. He was always joining me whenever I was working a shift. It took about an hour for the stockers to unload everything, so it gave us plenty of time to chat.

Uncle Joe was used to me taking long breaks. Honestly, he was so stressed out about all the drama going on at the store that he didn't have the time to dedicate to trying to get me to straighten up my act. I was at the point where I couldn't have cared less if he fired me or not. We both realized that my parents would never let him live it down if he did.

I was going to blow that town soon enough anyway. Getting fired would've simply given me more time to organize my thoughts. My father had called me a few days after my parents had both walked off and ignored me in their own home. He said that he and Momma had discussed it and realized that I was probably "as serious as a heart attack." They wanted me to come over there so they could give me the advice that I had been seeking that day. I told him to "forget it." I already had all of my plans clearly laid out. That was a lie, but I had a skeleton of a plan.

I was going to catch the train to New York City. I was too scared to drive my raggedy car, and I didn't think that I could deal with a Greyhound bus. The train would be more comfortable, hopefully. It's not like I would've known. The train ride was nearly twenty damn hours. Well, more like sixteen, but when I went down to the train station in Kannapolis, my cousin Sally, who worked in the booth, told me that the trains always ran late; hours late. Of course, she was trying to get all up in my business. I told her that I was asking about the train ticket for a friend. I'm sure she thought it was bullshit, but I wasn't going to purchase my ticket when she was anywhere around. I didn't want my parents to know exactly when I was rolling out. Even though my uncle would blab that I hadn't shown up at work, and Glenn would probably show up at their house looking for me and crying like a baby, I didn't want them to have any chance of preventing me from boarding.

There was no telling. I wouldn't have put it past my parents to plan some sort of "intervention" to keep me there. I didn't think that they would go as far as bolting me down to a bed with a ball and chain, but they would make an attempt to do something; real talk.

"Why you always out here in the woods, woman?" Andy asked once he reached me.

I was getting tired of trying to cover up my weed habit with body mist and breath mints. I had a joint down by my side. I lifted it proudly to my lips and took a long drag.

"Aw, the chronic," Andy said. "Now I get it. I thought you were coming out here doing some freaky stuff by yourself."

"No, I do that at home." I giggled and held the joint out. "You said *chronic* like you're down with it. Are you?"

"I dibble and dabble." He took the joint and smoked it. Then he coughed and beat his chest. "This is some good shit."

I giggled. "Everyone says that."

"That's because it is. I don't smoke weed often; only to knock the edge off from time to time, but I recognize something good when I taste it."

"Is that right?" I asked seductively. Weed always made me horny. "You recognize something good when you taste it, huh?"

Andy figured out that I was coming on to him. "We've been teasing each other for months. Why don't we cut to the main festivities?"

"Where are you going after you leave here?"

"Back to Salisbury, to dump my trailer. I have tonight off."

"Oh yeah? What a coincidence. So do I."

"You trying to make something happen or what?"

I looked Andy up and down. He didn't have a six-pack, but he wasn't chubby either. I needed some adventure, and Phil and Glenn simply weren't cutting it anymore.

"Yeah, it's all good with me."

"You want me to pick you back up here?"

"No, not here." I thought about it for a few minutes. "I'm going to go home and take a shower, so I'll be all nice and fresh. Where do you live?"

"Actually, I really live in Tennessee. That's where my house is, but I keep a little place up in Salisbury."

"Why don't you give me that address? I'll come to you."

Andy reached into his shirt pocket and pulled out a pen and small pad. He scribbled an address on a sheet of paper, ripped it off, and handed it to me.

"You know where that is?"

I read the paper. "I'll find it. Salisbury isn't but so big."

"No, but there are a lot of big things in Salisbury."

"I like it when a man talks dirty." I pressed the burning end of the joint that Andy had handed back to me against a tree trunk to put it out. I was going to save the other half for later. I saw the way Andy was looking at me and shrugged. "Waste not, want not."

"Make sure you bring a few joints with you tonight, if you have any extra."

*Extra! This is my homegrown shit! I've got plenty!*

"I'm sure that I can come up with a little something something."

"What time should I expect you?"

"Around ten. Cool?"

"I'll be waiting."

"Be waiting and be clean."

"As clean as a whistle."

"Good, because I like to blow whistles."

*TOOT MOTHERFUCKING TOOT!*

I brushed past Andy and he tapped me on the ass as I made my way back to the store. I was acting kind of whorish, but, truth be told, I had been only one up on Milena for the past several years and now her ass had caught up to me. When I got to New York, I was going to have to fuck other men. Why not go ahead and get started?

Andy's place was a dump, but he tried to explain to me that it wasn't his permanent home. Apparently, he shared it with two other truckers who were rarely there, and he blamed all of the nastiness and clutter on them. The carpet was filthy, dishes were stacked in the sink, and the odor was almost unbearable.

"Let's go in the bedroom," Andy suggested.

"Bedroom, as in one?"

"Yeah, there's only one bedroom."

"And you and the other two nasty-ass men who made this mess share it?"

"We don't sleep in there at the same time, if that's what you mean." He grabbed me around the waist and tried to kiss me, but I turned my head away. "Hey, I changed the sheets, and I cleaned my whistle."

He did smell nice and manly.

"Listen, if you don't want to stay here, we can go to a hotel. My treat."

He said that like I would've paid for it if it hadn't been his treat.

"If we *ever* go to a hotel, it's a given that you're paying for it," I informed him.

He chuckled. "Of course."

"I've got a better idea. Let's go chill in your truck."

"You're too special to be in that truck. You need a man to lie you down on a bed of roses."

"True that, but I like to put in work in unusual places. Your truck would be like an adventure to me; an *escapade*." I tickled Andy's chin with the tip of my index finger. "It might make me feel freaky and slutty, like a hooker, and turn into a *sexcapade*."

"Aw, you want to do a little role-playing and be a lot lizard for the night. I like that."

"A lot lizard? What's that?"

"Hookers that only work at truck stops."

I laughed. "Why do they call them that?"

"Because they hang out in the parking lots and are slimy like lizards; usually very trashy."

"And the trashier the better?"

"For some men. Not me though. I don't do lizards."

"That's refreshing to know."

I pulled Andy to me and buried my tongue in his mouth. Then

I grabbed his dick through his pants. Before we ended up in his truck, I wanted to make sure his nickname wasn't "Pencil Dick."

"Nice," I said as I broke the kiss. "How long is it?"

"I'm only about seven inches."

"Seven's good. It's thick. I can tell. I like them thick."

"Then I'm your man."

"Let's go," I said, pulling him toward the door.


"Oh, fuck yeah!" I screamed out as I rode Andy in the back part of the cab of his truck. There was a little pull-down bed, and we were putting it to good use.

"Get it, baby!" some trucker who had identified himself as Lou yelled through the CB radio.

I had taken freakiness to the next level. I was so turned on by being in his truck that I wanted to put on an audio show for truckers traveling on the lonely highways.

I'd found a channel that was busy, and several men were listening in and making comments. A few of them claimed to have pulled off on the side of the road to jerk off.

"Shit! That's right, you motherfuckers!" I screamed as I held down the talk button on the radio. "Work those dicks like I'm working this dick in this truck!"

There was one female trucker all up in the mix. I could've done without her. "Damn, woman! You sound fine! You ever bump pussies?"

"Hell, no!" I exclaimed. "The only pussy I love to taste is my own!"

"Tell us how your pussy tastes!" some man who sounded old enough to be my grandfather said through the speakers.

"This is insane," Andy said from underneath me.

"You know you like this shit," I said, digging the fingers of my free hand into his chest.

"I fucking love this shit!" he exclaimed.

All kinds of fodder and cum noises and nasty statements were coming in on the CB as I lifted myself off his dick and turned sideways on it so that my feet were on the floor. I started moving my pussy back and forth as we fucked like a cross.

"I'm riding his dick sideways now, motherfuckers! He can't handle all this pussy!"

I reached over, picked up a joint, and lit it. I took a drag and then put it in Andy's mouth. He couldn't even take a drag; his ass was out of breath.

I felt an orgasm coming on and announced it to the world. "I'm coming, motherfuckers! I'm coming!"

"Come, woman, come!"

"Release that shit, woman!"

"I think I'm in love with you, and I've never even seen you! Let me fuck you in my truck!"

"Aw, yes!" I shivered as I came with an ass clap and a roll of thunder.

Andy was right behind me. "Oh, shit! Lydia, dammit!"

I slapped him on the face. "Don't use my name! I told you to call me Sunshine, like that woman in the movie!"

"Right! Sunshine!" he stated breathlessly.

I pushed the button on the handset. "That's all, folks! At least for tonight!"

"Don't go, lover!"

"No, it can't be over! I haven't finished jacking off yet!"

"Too bad," I said and killed the connection.

I climbed off Andy's dick and got into the front passenger seat.

"I think that I really am in love," Andy said, trying to regain some composure.

"Don't go there," I said. "This was cool, but I'm going home to my man."

"He's one lucky bastard."

"Yeah, too bad he doesn't realize it."

I lit another joint, put my bare feet up on the dashboard, found some hip-hop on the radio, and commenced to getting my mind-fuck on.

# Milena

WHAT had started out as the typical Sunday dinner at my parents' house had turned into me lying in Jacour's bed while he tried to fuck me half to death.

"Aw, I've missed you so much, Milena," Jacour whispered as he started sucking on my right breast for dear life. "I've missed you, and this pussy."

I reached around and grabbed hold of an ass cheek, pushing him deeper into me. "Shit, I've missed you!"

Jacour stopped sucking on my breast and kissed me passionately on the mouth, all the while digging my back out like a bulldozer.

"It's about time you came to your senses, baby. I've been waiting on this."

He lifted himself up on the palms of his hands and started pounding against my cervix. "Damn, this is still the best pussy in the world."

I didn't like the idea of him comparing my pussy to others. Then again, the same exact thing was running a track meet through my head; I wasn't voicing it though. I was comparing his dick to Yosef's. It was smaller but that wasn't a revelation. It wasn't as thick either. I hadn't been positive about that aspect until we'd started fucking. I was glad that he was saying my pussy was good. After being with Yosef, I didn't want any man to think that someone had been putting their entire arm up in me. I measured once while Yosef was sleep; his dick was the same length as my arm from my elbow to my wrist.

*Why are you lying here thinking about Yosef's dick and your arm! Enjoy the moment!*

*Yosef's at home waiting for me! I shouldn't be here!*

*You should be here! You love him!*

*I love Yosef!*

"I love you, Milena! It feels so good to be inside of you!"

I looked up into Jacour's eyes. "Right where you belong."

It was jacked up, my being there. It wasn't intentional. It just happened. Now I kind of understood some of those men on talk shows who, once confronted about an affair, would claim: "It just happened."

I was cheating on Yosef and it felt horrible, but . . . it also felt so damn good. Familiar.

Jacour put my legs up on his shoulders and then continued to brace himself on his palms. I pivoted my hips to meet his thrusts and got caught up in the ecstasy. Even though I was concentrating on the sex, I couldn't help but consider how I'd ended up there.

Momma had cooked a roasted turkey breast, mashed potatoes with gravy, mixed vegetables, and rolls for dinner. I'd brought a batch of my infamous brownies. Daddy, Momma, Papa Bear, and I were sitting at the dining room table, talking about life in general, when the doorbell rang.

"I wonder who that could be. I'll get it," Momma said as she got up and left the room.

A moment later she returned with Jacour, and I dropped my fork onto my plate.

"Jacour!" Daddy exclaimed. "Come have a sit-down! Join us!"

"What a surprise," Papa Bear said, grinning. "It's been a while since you've paid us a visit."

Jacour was dressed in his Sunday best. He came and sat next to me, but not before bending over and planting a sloppy kiss on my cheek. "Milena, how are you?"

I sighed. "All of you can stop this poor excuse for a play right now."

"What do you mean, honey?" Momma asked.

"It's obvious that this little *surprise* visit is only a surprise to me."

"They didn't know I was coming over," Jacour said, telling a damn lie. "I saw your truck out front as I was driving past the house and decided to stop over."

"Okay, fine; whatever."

Daddy chuckled uncomfortably. "Since that's all cleared up, how have you been, Jacour?"

"I've been fine, Mr. Clark. Still getting readjusted to Kannapolis. This is nothing like the city."

"I'm sure," Papa Bear said, then took a sip of his iced tea.

I looked from person to person at the table, all of them puppets with fake smiles plastered all over their faces.

"I had to go back to New York for a while to handle some business. It truly is like night and day." Jacour glanced at me. "Where's Yosef?"

"Yosef?" Daddy asked. "Who's that?"

I took the cloth napkin off my lap and tossed it onto my plate loaded with food.

"Oh, you guys know him as Randolph," Jacour replied. "Randolph William Henderson the third." He patted my hand. "It was the third, wasn't it?"

"What is he talking about, dear?" Momma asked.

I sighed and pulled my hand away. "I'm sick of this." I stood up. "Look, Momma, Daddy, Papa Bear, I haven't been very truthful with you lately. Apparently, all of you concocted some plan to have Jacour here for dinner so that we could talk and get back together somehow. But Jacour's not here only for that reason." I stared down at Jacour, who had this evil grin on his face. "He's here to tell you that there is no Randolph."

"What do you mean, there is no Randolph?" Daddy asked in anger. "Then who's the man staying at your house?"

"His name's Yosef Sampson and, until he met me the day of Jacour's party, he was homeless and living in the woods near the speedway."

"Oh my God!" Momma yelled out and covered her heart with her hand. "Please, Lord, tell me it isn't so!"

"It's so, Momma!"

Daddy stood up. "Are you trying to tell me that you have a vagrant sleeping in your bed?"

Jacour crossed his arms in front of him and shook his head. "This is even worse than I thought." He looked at my mother. "She's chosen a wino over me. Can you believe that, Mrs. Clark?"

"Momma, don't respond to that," I said. "He's not a wino, nor is he a bad person. He wasn't homeless for very long, and it was for a very good reason; the best reason."

"What kind of *good reason* could there be to live in the woods?" Daddy asked.

"That doesn't matter right now. Things are what they are, and I'm not changing my mind about him. He's managed to get a job and—"

"At a car wash," Jacour said with disgust. "A car wash when I could go to the bank right now and hand her a million dollars in cash."

"Life isn't about money!" I screamed. "You stupid asshole!"

Jacour stood up abruptly and got up in my face. "No, it's about love! Money makes love, and everything else, a whole lot easier!"

"You've got money and you don't have any fucking love!" I pushed him back down in the chair. "Stay the hell out of my face!"

Papa Bear finally spoke up then. "Milena, you *will not* curse in this house!"

"I'm sorry, Papa Bear. I'm upset and this was unexpected. I realized that I'd have to come clean sometime, but not like this. Not because Jacour decided to orchestrate the entire thing."

"Milena, we need to have a serious talk about this," Momma said. "Come in the kitchen with me."

"So you can try to convince me to make Yosef leave? No, I won't do it."

"Don't defy your mother like that!" Daddy yelled. "I don't care how old you are, she's still your mother!"

"I get that, Daddy. I'll talk to Momma, but I won't do it today. I'm not trying to be disrespectful and I do apologize, but Jacour was wrong for this"—I slapped Jacour on the back of his head—"and he's well aware of that."

Jacour stood back up. "Mr. and Mrs. Clark, Papa Bear, Milena's right. It was her right to tell you about Yosef, in her own time. I was wrong to bring this kind of drama into your peaceful home." Jacour gazed at me. "But love can make a man do unimaginable things. Women aren't the only ones who lash out when they're scorned. I thought that coming here today and exposing Yosef would force Milena to come back to me. Now I realize the error of my ways."

Jacour went and stood in the doorway to the dining room.

"I had no idea that Yosef was homeless. This makes it clear that whatever Milena feels for him must be genuine and real. No woman in her right mind—especially her—would subject themselves to such reprehensible conditions unless it's emotional."

Everybody was silent, including me. All of us were analyzing Jacour's words.

"Milena, I want to wish you and Yosef a long, happy life together. I'm going to take myself, my money, and my parents, and leave this town. I can't stay here and watch you love another man; my heart can't endure that kind of pain." Jacour started crying. "All I've ever wanted was for you to be happy. I wanted to love you, provide for you, adore you, but I'll concede that Yosef is the better man." Jacour wiped his tears with the arm of his jacket. "You all finish up your dinner. Sorry to bother you."

Jacour left the dining room, and then the house. I looked at my parents and my grandfather, trying to read their faces. I couldn't find any words, so I walked out, too.

Jacour was sitting in the driveway in his car, with his head lowered and the engine running.

*Walk right past him and take your ass home to Yosef!*

*But did you hear everything he said!*

*I heard it and I'm not buying it!*

*But it came from the heart!*

*It came from someplace, but it sounded like complete bullshit! Don't fall for it!*

*But he's in his car crying!*

*Let him cry and go home to Yosef!*

*I can't!*

I walked up to Jacour's car and tapped on the window. He rolled it down.

"Jacour, can we talk?"

"About what?"

"What happened inside?"

"I've said all that I have to say. Go home to your man. The light of your life."

"Not until we straighten some things out. I don't want to be the one responsible for you and, heaven forbid, your parents leaving town."

"I was serious about that."

"I can tell, but it's not necessary."

Jacour got out of his car and stood beside me. "There's only one thing that can make me stay."

I stared at him. I realized that he wanted me to proclaim my love for him, but I couldn't.

"Oh, I almost forgot," he said. "I've got something for you in the backseat."

"What?"

"I was going to surprise you with it later, but now's as good a time as any." He opened up the back door and pointed to a black shopping bag on the opposite side of the floor. "It's in the bag. You mind getting it?"

"No, I don't mind."

I climbed into his backseat and scooted over to retrieve the bag. I leaned down and peeked inside. It was a bunch of ties.

"This must be the wrong bag. It's full of—"

I heard the door slam. Jacour hopped in the front seat and put the car into reverse before I could blink twice.

"What the hell are you doing?" I grabbed for the door handle. It wouldn't open. "Let me out."

I kept tugging at the handle as Jacour backed out of my parents' driveway and took off down the street doing twenty miles over the speed limit. I tried the other door and it wouldn't budge either.

"What the fuck are you doing, Jacour?"

"You said you wanted to talk. I'm taking you to my place so we can talk."

"Why won't the doors open?"

"I set the child safety locks."

I hit him on the back of the head. "You bastard!"

"You've been acting like a child, Milena, so I decided to treat you like one. Don't hit me while I'm driving. Be a nice little girl and let Daddy concentrate on the road. You wouldn't want me to wreck. You could get hurt."

I contemplated climbing over the seat, but it would've been too risky. If he'd swerved because of my movement, we really could've ended up wrapped around a tree.

"As soon as we get there, I'm fucking calling the police!"

I'd left my purse and cell phone inside my truck out in front of my parents'. I could've kicked myself for that mistake. Jacour was seriously tripping. I was sick of his shit. Jacour was a lot of things, but I didn't fear for my safety around him. I didn't say another word; it was pointless.


When we arrived at his place and he opened the door, I hopped out of the backseat and held out my hand. "Phone!"

"I don't have my cell phone on me. You'll have to use the one inside."

"Liar!"

I kept holding out my hand, but he only stared at it and then walked up the steps to his house. I watched him unlock the door and hold it open.

"Fine! I can't fucking believe this shit!"

I stormed up the stairs and into the house, searching for the nearest cordless. I spotted one on an end table and headed for it. Jacour came up behind me and pulled me back by the waist.

"I meant everything that I said back there about loving you."

"Get off of me!"

I tried to get loose, but it was useless.

"I'm not going to hurt you, baby. You know that."

I sighed. "I know that, but I can't believe you did that to me!"

"You left me no other choice." He released me. "Now, you can either call the police and have me arrested for kidnapping, ruin my entire life, and have me splattered all over the tabloids, along with yourself, or you can talk to me."

There was no way that I was going to end up in the tabloids. And while Jacour was tripping, he didn't deserve to get locked up.

I plopped down on the sofa. "I'm not going to call the police, but I want you to take me back to my car. *Now!*"

"I will in a few; hear me out."

I glared at him as he sat down beside me.

"It's totally out of character for me to resort to what I just did. Like I told your parents, love can make a man do *unimaginable* things. Staying away from you, not being able to touch you, it's driving me insane."

"That's for damn sure," I concurred. "Jacour, what we had was special. In fact, it was the only thing that I had until recently, but can't you see that sometimes people aren't compatible? Everyone comes into our lives for a reason, but it's not always for the reasons we think."

"I know exactly why you're in my life. I've always known."

"No, you don't know; you *think*."

"I love you, Milena." He tried to reach between my legs, but I kept them shut, and he whispered in my ear. "I need you. You've got me running around town like a desperado from the Wild Wild West. Why do you think that is?"

My body took over and my legs spread. Jacour wasted no time finding my sweet spot, moving my panties aside and digging into his pot of gold with his fingers.

"I feel it," he said. "Your pussy contracting on my fingers, welcoming me home. You can try to fool yourself all you want, but your body can't lie."

I stared into his eyes, which were mere inches from mine. My breathing became labored and my nipples grew prominent in my dress.

I wasn't the only one who noticed it. "Look at that. They're reacting . . . to me . . . to us. What we have is one-of-a-kind, baby. No man, or woman, can ever change what's meant to be."

Jacour used his other hand to unbutton the top of my dress and move my bra out of the way. Then he lowered his head and nibbled on my left nipple; my weak spot.

My body surrendered to him and, eventually, so did my mind. We devoured each other in the sixty-nine position on the floor in front of his sofa for a half hour. Now we were in his bed; *smashing.*

"Damn, Milena, I'm loving this pussy, baby!"

We'd changed positions and now Jacour was fucking me from the back, with one of his knees elevated. I was also on one knee; the opposite one. My other leg was behind his back, knocking on the top of his ass every time he rammed his dick into me.

"Aw! Shit!" I felt a flood of cum squirt out of my pussy for the fourth time since we'd started.

I moaned, bracing myself on my hands and wondering if Jacour would ever come. We'd been going at it for a long-ass time, not that I was complaining. I was amazed! He might have had a bum knee, but all of that professional physical training had paid off big-time.

"Now that you're moving in here," Jacour said, "I'm going to make love to you like this every single night."

*Tell him that you're not moving in!*

*I can't tell him while he's fucking me!*

*Why the hell not!*

*Because he might lose his erection and this is the shit!*

*What about Yosef!*

I stopped moving in rhythm with Jacour.

"Don't give up on me now, baby. I know I'm beating this pussy up, but it's been too long. I need you."

I started moving again, but something within me had changed. I was so confused. I had no idea how I'd managed to go from being a woman whose only sexual partner was a vibrator to a woman with two lovers . . . seemingly overnight.

Jacour finished up and finally came a little while later. Then he immediately passed out. I lay there and watched him sleeping for about twenty minutes, then snuck out of the bed.

After I got dressed and went downstairs, I used the cordless to call Lydia and asked her to come get me.

"I'm not driving over to that haunted house at night!" she exclaimed. "Not motherfucking Lydia!"

"Yes, the hell you are. Hurry your ass up," I whispered.

I eased out of the front door and waited for her on the porch. My lower back was hurting from all of that fucking. I relaxed on the wooden swing, gazing up at the stars and wondering what the hell I was going to do.

# Lydia

PHIL and I were up to our usual routine. I had grown bored with it, but I definitely had some type of sexual addiction; real talk. Glenn didn't get off work for another five hours, so we had plenty of time to blow each other's backs out.

"Ready for round two?" Phil asked, licking a trail down my spine to the crack of my ass. "My dick's hard again."

I could feel his dick poking me in the ass. "Your dick stays hard."

"Yeah, it does. That's a good thing, right?"

"Sometimes."

"What you mean? Sometimes?"

*Judge Judy* was on and he was breaking my concentration. Two sisters were on there arguing over some trifling-ass man. Of course, he was nowhere in sight to testify for either one of them. He was playing the odds; playing it smart. If he'd been stupid enough to show his face in the courtroom, Judge Judy would've read his ass like a book, even if the two women were stuck on stupid. Girlfriend did not play; that's why I tried to never miss an episode, even if I had to DVR it.

"What do you mean by sometimes?" Phil asked again, irritating me.

"Don't you ever want to fuck women other than me, Phil?"

"No."

Lying ass. "Why not?"

"Because I'm fucking you, and you know how to put it down."

"True that," I said, turning over briefly to lay a fat, juicy kiss on him. Then I turned my attention back to the television. "Why don't you take a nap? Rest up while I finish watching this. Then I'll put it down on you hard."

Phil sighed and propped his head up on a pillow. "You still going to New York?"

"Yep. I sure am."

"When?"

"Soon. Very, very soon."

"You taking me with you?"

I didn't respond.

"I'll take that as a no."

"Phil, you couldn't survive a month in New York City."

"Oh, but you can?"

"I *will*."

He started massaging my right shoulder. "Think about it; that's all I'm asking. You're not the only one who's bored around here. Without you, it's going to be even worse."

"There are a lot of sisters around here who'd love to get it in with you. You need to give some of them a shot."

"What kind of woman encourages her man to sleep with other women?"

"That's the point you're obviously missing." I pushed his hand off of me. "You're not *my man,* and soon enough, Glenn won't be either."

He started all the touchy-feely nonsense again. "Did you tell him that you're leaving?"

"You must be smoking crack instead of weed. No, I didn't tell Glenn that I'm leaving. Who do I look like? Boo Boo the Fool?"

Phil tried to place his dick between my ass cheeks. I snickered; he knew that wasn't happening. I moved my butt so that he would get the point.

Phil whispered in my ear, as if whispering would disturb me less when I was trying to watch television. "He's going to find out eventually."

"Yeah, and *eventually* is going to be when my ass is safe and sound on an Amtrak."

"You planning to roll out like that?"

I smacked my lips. "I'll leave a note."

"That's fucking cold, Lydia."

"And fucking me behind his back is what? Warm?"

*Judge Judy* went off.

"Shit, now I'm going to have to play it back later. You made me miss the outcome of the case."

"Ain't I a little more important than Judge Judy?"

I giggled. "You don't really want me to answer that, do you?"

"Since you put it that way, I guess not."

I turned over to face Phil. "Look, I like you. What we've been doing has been exciting, stimulating . . ." I kissed him on the lips. "You're as freaky as I am, my match, and that's saying something."

"So why you leaving me?"

"I have to. I only get one opportunity at this thing called life. We all do. I don't want to waste mine here."

"Then let me—"

I placed two fingers on his lips to stop him from sounding like a broken record. "No, I *won't* let you come with me." I sat up and yawned. I was still sleepy from the pounding Glenn had put on my pussy the night before. Cheating was a lot of work. "That's not to say that you can't come visit me sometime once I get settled."

Phil got excited. "Word?"

"Sure, why not? It's not like Glenn is going to want to come and visit. He's going to be livid once I move away. In his mind, I can't live without him." I stood up and looked at my naked body in the mirror over the dresser. "The fucked-up part is, as long as I live here, he's probably right."

"You haven't even tried to do better around here." Phil got off the bed and stood behind me, his dick hard and throbbing as I eyed it in the reflection. "That Food Lion gig isn't the only game in town. You've got a car. Try to get a job in Charlotte."

"Yeah, right. I don't have gas money to go back and forth to Charlotte. Plus, I only have a high school diploma and most of the city jobs require more than that. I can flip burgers right here in Kannapolis. Even when it comes to those jobs, people are lined up around the building whenever they have one slot open. I went to Walmart the other day to get some shampoo and people were piled up in the back, near layaway; they were having a job fair. But working there isn't any better than where I am. At least my uncle's my boss at Food Lion."

Phil reached around me and ran his hands over my breasts, down over my navel and my hips, and then landed one on my pussy. "You're so beautiful, Lydia. You're special. You can be whatever you want to be."

I was checking myself out, too. "You're preaching to the choir. I realize that I've got it going on."

"You do, and don't get me wrong for asking this question, but—"

"But what?"

"If you've convinced yourself that you can't get a good job in Charlotte, how the hell you going to get one in New York?"

I pushed Phil's hands off of me. "I'll worry about that shit when I get there. I'm prepared for whatever comes my way. I look forward to the excitement." I turned to glare at him. "Look at you; trying to give me advice on how to better my life when you've been stuck in the same factory job forever."

"At least I still have my factory job!"

"Only because the fucking place hasn't closed down yet. What happened to me wasn't my fault. How am I supposed to work at a place that doesn't freaking exist?"

Phil's dick was losing its vigor. "Great, now you're fucking up my erection."

"No, your smart-ass mouth is fucking up your erection."

I lay down on the bed on my stomach and started flipping through *Sister 2 Sister* magazine. "You can leave now."

"We haven't done anything yet."

Phil sounded like a wimp.

"You can't leave me hanging like this."

I reached over on the nightstand and turned on my iPod, which was docked into a stereo system. Prince's "Do Me Baby" started blasting through the speakers.

"Lydia, come on, baby. Talk to me."

" 'Here we are, in this big old empty room . . . ,' " I started singing, ignoring his ass. " '. . . staring each other down.' "

"Oh, so it's like that?"

I turned the volume up to full blast and kept singing and flipping through the magazine. Phil finally took the hint and started picking his clothes off the floor to get dressed. How I longed for a man who took his clothes off and folded them neatly on a chair or something. Glenn and Phil were "tossers," which irritated me.

He was about to put on his underwear when Glenn stormed into the room.

"What the fuck?" he yelled.

I froze, right there on my stomach, my naked ass spread out for the world to see.

"Phil, what the fuck are you doing here?"

*Fuck it! I'm leaving anyway! I'm about to confront this bastard!*

I turned over, sat up, and turned the iPod off. "We didn't hear you come in," I stated casually. "I see you got off of work early."

Phil looked like he was about to faint.

"Didn't hear me come in?" Glenn said. "That's not the fucking point." He turned to Phil. "Answer my fucking question. What are you doing here with her?"

"Uh, Glenn, I can explain," Phil finally managed to get out. "It's not what it looks like."

Glenn was so mad, his cheeks were shaking. "Both of you are naked; it's exactly what it looks like."

Damn, there was something incredibly erotic about two men about to fight over me. I was hoping it would come to blows, like those people on *Jerry Springer*. That what I got for having some incredible punta.

I got up off the bed and reached for one of Glenn's T-shirts that the "tosser" had thrown on the floor. I pulled it over my head as I said, "Glenn, don't be mad at Phil. He couldn't help himself."

"What the fuck are you talking about, Lydia?" Glenn asked. "He damn sure could've helped himself."

Phil had become a quick-change artist and was completely dressed by that point, shoes and all. "I'm sorry about all of this, Glenn."

The next few seconds will remain in my memory forever. It was like being caught in some bad movie.

Glenn walked over to Phil and yanked him up by the collar. "I can't believe you're cheating on me!"

"I'm not cheating! I . . ."

"How could you do this to me, Phil?"

That's when the two of them noticed that I was staring at them. Glenn let Phil go—quick.

I was speechless. I covered my mouth with my hand, holding in a scream. Then I collapsed onto the bed and stared at them. Both of them looked like deer caught in headlights.

I pointed to Glenn, then waved my index finger over to Phil, and back.

I threw my palms up in the air and then let them fall on my lap.

It was so quiet in that bedroom that you could've heard a mouse pissing on a cotton ball. I tried to tell myself that I was imagining things, but there was no confusing what had happened and what had been said.

Glenn looked at Phil. "You should go. We'll talk later."

Phil looked at Glenn and then at me. "Okay. Call me."

He was halfway out the door when I yelled out, "Don't you fucking move!" I stood up. "It seems like I should be the one leaving!"

"Lydia, just let Phil leave," Glenn said, walking toward the bed. "Whatever happened between the two of you, I forgive you. I'm sure there's a reasonable explanation for all of this."

I wasn't even looking at Glenn; I was staring at Phil, reading the expression on his face.

"You forgive me?" I asked incredulously.

"Yes, of course. I love you, baby," Glenn replied.

Phil said, "Glenn and I will work this out. We've been best friends forever. I'm sure there won't be any hard feelings. Shit happens."

"That's right," Glenn concurred. "Shit happens."

*These two rotten bastards are fucking each other!*

"You sick fucks!" I started pulling on a pair of sweatpants. "You're both fucking me and each other!"

"Don't be ridiculous." Glenn chuckled and tried to touch me, but I was too fast for him. "We're not gay."

"No, hell no," Phil said. "Lydia, you know good and damn well that I'm a real man."

"I *know* that I'm a real man," Glenn blurted out, trying to convince himself.

"You've been faggots all along! Those damn hunting trips! I should've known this was some *Brokeback Mountain* shit!" I was putting on my shoes. "I can't fucking believe this!"

"Lydia," Phil said. "You're tripping. What on earth would make you think that we're gay?"

"I may not be the smartest cookie in the jar, but I'm nobody's dummy!" I smirked and pointed at Glenn. "Glenn grabbed you by the collar and accused you of cheating on him. Now, in a normal, *straight* world, he would've been accusing me. You two make me sick!"

Glenn and Phil stared at each other while I threw my baggie of weed, my lighter, and my rolling papers into my purse. I was going to need all of that shit to escape this madness; real talk.

"Glenn, we need to tell her the truth," Phil whispered.

"Shut the fuck up, Phil!" Glenn yelled.

"You know what?" I grabbed my iPod off the dock. "I'm going to leave you two queens to do whatever the hell it is you do together."

As I walked past Phil, he grabbed my arm and begged, "Please, don't tell anyone."

I yanked my arm away. "I'm telling everyone who will listen, beginning with Milena."

"No, you can't tell Milena," Phil pleaded. "She'll tell Jacour."

"Phil, didn't I tell you to shut up!" Glenn exclaimed. "She's only speculating."

I turned to Glenn. "I'm not speculating shit." I shook my head. "It's amazing. The world has truly gone to shit. I wouldn't have ever pegged either one of you as a fruitcake."

"We're not fruitcakes," Phil said. "We're bisexual." He glanced at Glenn. "At least, I am."

I looked at Glenn. "Oh, so you're the homo? Let me guess. You turned Phil out when you were younger and now you're what? Pumping him in the ass?"

Phil let out a groaning noise.

"Oh, did I touch a nerve?" I asked. Then a lightbulb went off. "Aw, if Phil's bi, then that means he's the pumper . . ." I pointed at Glenn, recalling how he'd always enjoyed it when I'd teased his asshole with a fingertip. If I'd gone a little farther in, I would've hit the Grand Canyon. ". . . and you're the pump."

Glenn lowered his head. "We can still make this work, Lydia. I love you."

Phil said, "And I love you, too."

Glenn's head snapped up and he glared at Phil. "How could you?"

Phil smirked. "If you weren't willing to be exclusive with me, why should I have been exclusive with you?"

"Oh, cut the shit!" I punched Phil in the chest. "You've been fucking me for more than a decade; years before I even hooked up with Glenn. Now you want to pretend like you were fucking me to get back at him?"

"What?" Glenn said to Phil. "What the fuck is she talking about?"

I walked over and slapped the hell out of Glenn. "What the fuck are you talking about? We live together! You sleep in the same bed with me *every night*! What was I to you, Glenn?" He rubbed his cheek and stared at me. "Huh? Tell me, motherfucker! What was I to you?"

Glenn wiped some blood from the corner of his mouth and glanced at it, then rubbed it between his fingers. He glared at me. "Cover."

I stared at him for a few seconds, slapped him again, walked past Phil, stopping long enough to knee him in the groin, and then stormed out of the house.

# Milena

A SWARM of honey bees could've flown into my mouth and I still wouldn't have been able to close it. When Lydia came pounding on my door, I was anxious to drop my drama from the night before on her. Even though she'd picked me up at Jacour's house and dropped me off at my parents' to get my truck, I'd been speechless the entire time. I'd told her to come by the following day so that I could fill her in. I'd been too exhausted to get into it right then. Between the confrontation with my parents and grandfather, being kidnapped by Jacour, and then fucked to my wit's end, all I'd wanted to do was go home and take a long, hot bath.

Of course, when I had arrived, Yosef had been waiting up for me. He'd pretended to be watching *True Blood*, but I'd been sure that he'd been wondering where I'd been. I never stayed at my parents' that late on Sundays. Plus, I would always fix him a plate. Surely, he'd already eaten by that time, after eleven, and he'd stared at me when I'd walked in the door, all disheveled and discombobulated.

"I'm sorry that I'm so late," I'd said. "I didn't bring you a plate. I assumed that you'd already eaten."

"What kept you?"

"Momma wasn't feeling that well, so I stayed for a while to keep an eye on her. I'm not a physician, but I am a doctor; I wanted to make sure she was okay."

*Damn shame, lying on your mother like that!*

*What else am I supposed to do!*

Yosef had sat up on the edge of the sofa. "Is she all right?"

"Yes, she's fine now. It's probably a case of acid reflux, but I told her to go get some tests run tomorrow."

"Oh, okay."

I hadn't been sure that Yosef had bought my bullshit, but it was the best excuse that I'd been able to come up with.

I hadn't wanted to walk any closer to him, so I'd headed down the hallway to the master bedroom.

"Why don't you come sit with me for a while?" Yosef had suggested.

I'd called back down the hall. "Sure. Give me a few minutes."

I'd taken a quick, but thorough, shower, and then spent the remainder of the night in his arms watching the *True Blood* marathon.

Now Lydia was sitting on my sofa, in tears. Yosef was still at work, and I'd been on pins and needles all day, anticipating Jacour showing up. Thus far, he hadn't called or come by, but I wasn't foolish enough to believe that a storm wasn't brewing over the horizon. As complicated as my situation was, Lydia had me beat.

"Lydia, are you sure?" I asked.

"Milena, I ran the entire thing down to you. Yes, I'm sure. That Negro walked over to Phil, jacked him up by the collar, and asked why he was cheating on his ass with me."

"Maybe you misunderstood."

"I didn't misunderstand shit. Phil's punk ass ended up confessing, and Glenn had the nerve to tell me that I was his cover. His motherfucking *cover*."

I shook my head. "This doesn't make any sense. When did you start fucking Phil, anyway?"

Lydia looked at me, then lowered her eyes to the floor. "More than ten years ago."

"Get the hell out of here!"

"No, really. And you're right. It doesn't make any sense. Right before Glenn came home early from work, Phil was trying to convince me to let him move to New York with me. He was always professing his undying love to me and all of that bullshit."

"I'm at a loss for words!"

"You? How the fuck you think I feel?" Lydia sighed. She was holding a joint, but she put it out in an ashtray. "Even this shit isn't helping today."

"And you didn't see any of this coming?"

"Sure, Milena, I saw the shit coming," she replied sarcastically. "Of course, I didn't know those two motherfuckers were booty bandits." She waved her index finger in the air. "But you know what? Now that I'm not as high as a kite for the first time in a minute, I'm starting to add some shit up."

"Like?"

"Like Phil drinking all of the time, and smoking weed, because he was trying to escape reality. I was so busy trying to escape my own fucked-up existence that I didn't understand what was bothering him."

"So what do you think was bothering him? His homosexuality?" I asked, wanting to light a joint myself even though I was nowhere near a pothead like Lydia.

Lydia shrugged. "I'm still trying to figure out how Phil was such a fantastic lover if he's gay. You wouldn't believe all of the freaky shit we've done. We've fucked everywhere from the church rectory to the top of the fire station. Shit, just in the last couple of months, we got it in at Baker's Creek out in the bush and in the movie theater."

"Damn, Lydia, it's like that?"

Lydia looked at me solemnly. "I have a serious issue. Sometimes I think that I'm an addict; real talk."

"I don't think you're an addict, but you're damn sure a nymphomaniac."

"Takes one to know one, hooker."

We both laughed.

"What about Glenn? Is he a good lover?"

"He's all right, but not like Phil. I'm telling you, Milena, I've been such a fool. I thought my pussy was so good that men would cut off their right arms for it; all based on the lies of two motherfuckers."

I put my arm around her shoulder. "Well, at least you know. You need some time to heal. You'll be okay."

"Milena, please don't run down any *time to heal* nonsense on me. This is some serious bullshit. It's bad enough for a woman to get caught up with one man on the down low, but I was messing with two of them . . . *for years*. What does that say about my judgment?"

"It doesn't say anything about your judgment. You didn't know."

"Glenn always wanted to be on top. I'm thinking, maybe he wanted to feel dominant with me because he was being Phil's little bitch, taking it up the ass."

Lydia's descriptions were making me nauseous. Not because Phil and Glenn were gay; because I knew them, had known them for years, and I'd been fooled, too. That made me think about Jacour.

"Damn, Jacour's going to hit the roof if he ever finds out about them!"

"If? Sis, I'm telling every fucking body that will listen. There's no way in hell that I'm going to let another chick in this town have that game run on her. No damn way."

"Lydia, I don't know if that's a good idea. Starting rumors means that you're stooping to their level and—"

"Then consider me an oompa loompa, because I'm stooping very low, and it's not a rumor."

I sighed and took my arm off of her.

"I'm serious, Milena. They made the choice to put me through this; both of them. Glenn didn't know that I was doing Phil, but Glenn knew *he* was doing Phil. And Phil's ass takes the cake." Lydia stood up and started pacing the floor. "I need to scar his ass up with my box cutter; real talk."

"Stop talking crazy. You're not cutting anybody. On top of everything else, you don't need to do time behind them."

Lydia's bottom lip was trembling, she was so mad.

"Promise me that you're not going to resort to violence behind this." She didn't respond. "Promise me, Lydia."

She held up her palm, like she was taking an oath. "I promise. They're not worth all of that. Let those two do what it do, but I'm not backing down from telling everyone."

"Okay." I decided to give up that fight, as long as she wasn't going to pull a Lorena Bobbitt. "Do your thing, Phyllis Diller."

Lydia sat down on the edge of my coffee table. "So what happened last night?"

I sunk back into the sofa and laughed. "My drama pales in comparison to yours."

"Tell me anyway. You made me come out to that haunted house in the middle of the night, risking life and limb. You need to come up off the goods."

"You didn't risk a damn thing." I sighed and sat up a little. "You're not the only one in a love triangle. I fucked Jacour last night, and then I fucked Yosef this morning before he left for work."

"Damn! Not Milena 'Saint' Clark!"

I was embarrassed. "It's not anything that I'm proud of."

"What are you going to do?"

"I don't know. I can tell you this much; Jacour's not going to drop it. Before he fell asleep last night, he was under the assumption that I'm moving in with him."

"And did you clear up this *assumption*?"

"Um, no."

"How come?"

"He was fucking me from behind when he said it."

Lydia giggled. "Humph, alrighty then."

"I don't know when the other shoe is going to drop, but it will."

"Then maybe you need to hop off on one foot before it does."

"If only it were that simple."

Lydia sat back down, and I laid my head on her shoulder. She patted my hand. "Look at us. Two beautiful black women, two love triangles. This is some shit right here."

"Don't I fucking know it," I whispered.

Then we both started crying.

# Lydia

THREE suitcases, a backpack, and a purse. My worldly belongings amounted to that. I'd asked Milena to drive me to Andy's place in Salisbury. We were waiting for him outside, to get ready to make a delivery run to Nashville. One of his roommates was there, sleeping in the bedroom. We didn't want to go inside and disturb him. Plus, I didn't want Milena to see the condition of the place; she was already stressing out enough over my predicament.

"Are you sure about this?" Milena asked. "What happened to New York?"

I took a drag of my joint and handed it to her. I was going to miss my marijuana plants, but I couldn't take them with me. No one knew that I'd been growing that shit, and transporting them across state lines could've landed me in prison. I was trying to get out of Kannapolis, but not that way.

"New York was a pipe dream. I was being delusional. I don't know a single soul there, and the cost of living is ridiculous."

"What's in Tennessee?"

"Andy, for starters. He has a house there, so I'll at least have a place to stay. It'll give me time to find a decent job, and there's a lot of entertainment in Nashville. I've never imagined myself as a country singer, but I've done my share of square dancing in my life."

Milena giggled. "Oh, please, I don't need that visual. Make sure that I'm at the premiere of the first show you're in, prancing around the stage in a lace shirt and polka-dot skirt."

"Shit, no polka-dot skirts for me."

Both of us grew quiet as cars and trucks whizzed by on the nearby interstate.

"I'm looking forward to this adventure," I said. "You should be happy for me."

"I am happy for you," Milena said. "That doesn't mean that I won't be worried about you, or miss you."

"I'm going to come back and see you. And you better come see me. Andy's here all of the time. I'll ride with him, maybe even once a month, but I'm going to have to stay with you if I do."

"Mi casa es su casa."

We both laughed.

"I'm so excited!" I jumped up and down. "I get to see other states, what people look like in other states, and I get to see lot lizards."

"Lot lizards?"

"Andy said hookers that hang out at truck stops are lot lizards. Isn't that cool?"

Milena grinned and leaned against the front of her truck. "If you say so."

"I've got my digital camera with me. I'll take some pictures and email them to you."

"You can take some pictures of the scenery, and your new crib, but I'll pass on the lot lizards. I can imagine what's up with them."

"You know, we should be grateful."

"I am grateful," Milena said. "Every day is a gift."

"True that, but what I mean is that, all in all, we've been pretty lucky. Look at Yosef, being homeless like that and losing his wife. That's some serious shit."

"Yes, it is, but that's over for him now. He has me."

I looked at Milena. I didn't think that I'd ever seen her happier. "Look at you. You've got two men pining over your ass."

Milena frowned. "Yes, but I shouldn't be sleeping with both of them."

"You need to cut the guilt trip, Milena. Men do that shit all the time, and we're supposed to accept it." I sighed. "Then you've got motherfuckers like Glenn and Phil, fucking each other and playing games."

Milena shook her head. "I still can't get over that!"

"You can't get over it? How do you think I feel?"

"Are you sure that you're not running away to Tennessee just to get away from them?"

"No, I was planning on leaving before that. Those two can't dictate my moves. They have enough shit to worry about, like everyone in town knowing that they're fruitcakes."

Both of us giggled.

"Goodness, you weren't playing when you decided to tell their business. That phone chain you had going was better than the one the elementary school has for the PTA."

"Did you see the fliers that I handed out?"

"Please tell me you didn't!"

"I sure did." I reached into my purse and pulled one out. "Here," I said, handing it to Milena. "I'm taking a few copies with me; I plan on making a scrapbook, like you."

Milena fell out laughing. "You're crazy!" She looked at the flier, which had photos of both of them on it, and read it. "'Don't date these two men. They won't have quality time for you. They're too busy screwing each other.'"

"I think that about covers it," I said, beaming with pride.

"You're going to run them out of town!"

"That's their issue; not mine. As far as I'm concerned, they might as well shack up and adopt a couple of children. Have their parents over for Sunday dinner and shit."

"Lydia, you are off your rocker." Milena looked and spotted Andy coming out of his place with a duffel bag. "Well, looks like it's time to go."

I felt a crying spell coming on. "Don't you tear up on me," I said.

Milena gazed at me. "You're the one that's about to cry."

"That's because I know you're going to cry, and then I'm going to start, so I figured that I might as well get it over with."

"That makes absolutely no sense." Milena wiped her right eye. "But you're right, I am about to cry."

By the time Andy reached us, we were boo-hooing like crazy.

"Oh wow," he said. "I'm not prepared for all of this." He started getting my bags out of Milena's truck bed to put them in the cab of his eighteen-wheeler. "She's not going to Siberia. Tennessee's a hop, skip, and a jump away."

"Maybe for you," I said, sobbing and wiping my face with the sleeve of my jacket. "But Milena and I aren't used to going places, so it seems like Siberia."

"I better go," Milena said, throwing her arms around me and then kissing me on both cheeks. "You take care of yourself, and I'll see you soon. Don't worry about your car. It'll be fine in my garage. No one wants to steal that clunker any more than they want my Chevy." We shared one last laugh. "Call me as soon as you get there."

"I will. I promise."

Milena backed away from me.

"I love you, sis," I said.

"Love you, too." Milena looked at Andy as she got into the driver's seat of her truck. "You take care of her. If you don't, that's your ass."

"I've got her covered," he replied. "I'm going to make sure that she gets to see new things, and I'm going to make her happy."

"Then that's all that matters," Milena said.

Within seconds, she was gone, and my heart was filled with both joy and fear.

*You always wanted to get the hell away from Kannapolis! Now go!*

Andy had everything loaded in the truck. "You ready?"

I took his hand. "As ready as I'll ever be."

# Milena

SHIT ... hitting ... fan. Shit ... hitting ... fan. Shit ... hitting ... fan. Even though I'd heard that term a thousand times throughout my life, I'd never truly grasped the concept until the shit hit the fan in my own house.

Jacour and I had the strangest thing going on. Jacour Bryant, one of the most sought-after bachelors in the country—the world even—had agreed to be my jump-off. He showed up at my house the day after we fucked in the haunted house, and he confronted me in front of Lydia. He tried to insist that I pack my bags and move in with him, even though Yosef was living with me. His exact words: "Leave that vagrant in here by himself. Let him have the damn house. I'll build you a state-of-the-art kennel someplace else."

Lydia did start smoking weed then, like a chain-smoker.

Jacour and I went at it for a good hour. I tried to explain to him that the night before had been a mistake. He tried to convince me that it hadn't been. After Lydia was fucked-up, she dropped the nuclear bomb and told Jacour about Phil and Glenn being lovers.

Complete silence.

I went and dug through my cabinets to find a bottle of moonshine that Uncle Joe had given me years earlier for Christmas. I had no idea what it tasted like, but I poured a glass for Jacour and handed it to him. "Drink this."

He didn't even examine what was in the glass. He simply guzzled it down and then cringed a bit from the aftertaste.

Then he shocked both Lydia and me by saying, "You'd be surprised how many ballers are gay."

"Ballers?" Lydia asked.

"Yeah, professional ball players. Tons of them."

I didn't think that my heart could take having Jacour run down the list, but there was one that I needed to know about. "Are you? Gay?"

Jacour glared at me and I left it alone. I didn't think he was, and I'm sure that was part of the reason that he was pissed; because of what I'd just asked. Everyone in town was going to think Jacour was guilty by association, even though he hadn't resided there in eight years.

I begged Jacour to leave before Yosef got home from work, and—I don't know if it was the moonshine or not—but he left, demanding that I come see him later that night.

I did, and our official "jump-off" relationship began. I explained to him that Yosef hadn't done anything to deserve being cut out of my life and that I had deep, loving feelings toward both of them. I even cried on Jacour's lap and told him that I was confused. He ran his fingers through my hair, then whipped his dick out so I could suck it. The sad thing is that I wanted to suck it; it calmed my nerves.

We fucked for a couple of hours and then I left. This went on for several weeks. Jacour was convinced that eventually I would come to my senses. He was really big on my *senses*. As it turned out, the decision turned out not to be mine at all.

"Are you fucking him?" Yosef asked me point-blank after storming into the house one day.

"Huh?" I replied, playing dumb.

"Are you fucking Jacour?"

"No, why would you ask me something like that?"

"I heard you've been going over to his house."

"Have you been spying on me?"

Yosef balled his hands into fists and then turned his back to me. "I haven't been spying on you, but this is a small town and people talk. You should know that better than me."

*Just come out with it and tell him the truth!*

*Hell no!*

*He already knows!*

*I see that!*

"Yosef, I'm confused."

He turned back around to face me. "Confused about what?"

I sat down at the kitchen table. "Yes, I'm sleeping with Jacour."

Yosef clamped his eyes shut.

"I never meant to hurt you," I said. "I never meant for any of this to happen."

"But it is . . . happening, Milena. I realize that I could never compete with Jacour when it comes to money, but he can't compete with my heart."

I stared up at him. "I'm so sorry."

"Sorry isn't going to cut it."

"Please . . . forgive me."

"I can't forgive you."

I stood up. "Oh, come on, Yosef. I made one mistake and now you're—"

"So you only slept with him once?"

I lowered my head in shame. "No."

"How many times?" When I didn't respond, he got louder. "How many?"

"I don't know." I shrugged my shoulders. "Too many to count."

"Too many to count?"

Yosef went down the hallway and I heard doors and dresser drawers opening and shutting. I sat there at the table, speechless. I'd broken things off with Jacour because he'd slept with someone else at his bachelor party—once. There was no way that I had the right to expect Yosef to forgive me.

He came back out a little while later, with two garbage bags full of clothing. I didn't say anything as he made his way toward the door. He stopped, paused, and turned to look at me.

"We've come so far in such a small amount of time, Milena. I'm disappointed, but I'll make it through this."

"You can stay," I whispered. "We don't have to be together, but you can still stay. Where will you go?"

"I'll be fine. I've made some friends; they'll let me crash at their place until I rent one. Having a job makes things a lot easier. In fact, I was planning on celebrating with you tonight. I got a new job, making about forty thousand a year."

I perked up and grinned. "Really? Where?"

"I can't tell you. I don't want you showing up there."

I looked down at the table. "I understand."

"I do love you. I always will love you."

"I love you, too, Yosef."

"I know that you do, but it's not enough."

With that, Yosef was gone. He left the car and walked off down the road, never to be seen or heard from again.

# Lydia

NASHVILLE, Tennessee, Music City, home of the Grand Ole Opry. I loved it! I missed North Carolina though, especially my parents and Milena. I wished that I could have combined the two worlds and made them one. I'm sure a lot of people have felt that way before. Imagined that they could lift a house up out of the ground, or relocate their loved ones with them. But it was cool. It was a new life, and I desperately needed that.

Andy was a sweetheart; thank goodness. I'd tried to hide it, but I was a nervous wreck when I pulled off in that truck with him. Sure, we'd been friends for a while, and we'd fucked a time or two, but that didn't mean that he was going to be good to me. Life was about taking chances, and I'd gambled big-time. I figured that since Milena had done it and it had turned out good for her, shit, why not go for it.

I take that back. It had turned out good for her in the beginning. Apparently, no sooner had I left town than the proverbial shit hit the fan in Milena's crib. She called me and told me all about it. I swear, Milena needed to learn how to be a better liar. When Yosef asked her if she was fucking Jacour on the sly, she confessed. He wasn't having it and rolled out. Now, in my opinion, the motherfucker had a lot of nerve. Milena had taken him in when he hadn't had a place to lay his head, and yet he couldn't see it within his heart to forgive her for her transgressions. After that nonsense with Phil and Glenn, I realized that men were even lower and further-down dirty dogs than I'd thought.

Now Andy, I was not going to be delusional about. I planned to enjoy all that life had to offer and protect the hell out of my feelings. He understood that. Our connection wasn't about love, or building a long-term future together; it was a matter of convenience. When he was out of town working, I had "me time" to explore and get to know myself better. It was a strange feeling, but, honestly, I realized that I didn't truly understand who the hell Lydia was. Sure, I could give a quick rundown on my basic stats—age, place of birth, schools attended, family tree—but when it came to my inner workings, there was much confusion.

I had assumed that my pussy was lined with gold, the way that I was giving Phil and Glenn a daily run for their money. I thought that my shit was primo and that no woman could compete with me. But pussy was pussy—I now understood that—and the only thing that a woman could really expect was to enjoy sex when it was happening. Thinking that men wouldn't stray was nonsense. Hell, with Phil and Glenn, I could've been Helen of Troy and had men fighting wars over my coochie and it wouldn't have mattered. When it came right down to it, I simply didn't have everything that they needed.

I did feel bad about putting their business out in the streets of Kannapolis like that—kind of. It was going to be damn near impossible for them to hold their heads up around town, and not because they were gay. That was widely accepted, even in small hick towns. What was unacceptable, as it damn well should've been, was people dragging others into a situation that they weren't privy to. I didn't have anything against homosexuals; I didn't want to fuck them, that's all.

In the end, I got what I deserved. I was playing games as well. It was wrong for me to be living with Glenn and fucking his best friend. Knowing that Phil was even capable of dirt like that should've warned me about his character. My character wasn't much better though, which is why I needed to get to know myself.

I did manage to land a job within a week of moving to Nashville. Yippe-ka-ye, motherfucker! It was my luck that B.B. King's Blues Club needed a cocktail waitress because some chick had quit to move to North Carolina; talk about irony. I loved my job! It was ten times—no—*a million times* more exciting than standing behind a cash register at Food Lion. They had awesome bands performing every night, like the House Rockers, the Soul Brigade, Burning Las Vegas, and the Soul Searchers. Even hearing different types of music was incredible. I'd thought Charlotte had it going on when it came to nightlife, from what I had heard, but in Nashville people were off the fucking chain.

I got to eat free during my dinner breaks but I had to pay for my liquor when I was off the clock. The fried catfish was my favorite. One of the bartenders hooked me up with a weed connect in town. People were serious about their ciggaweed there also; a definite plus.

When Andy was in town, he'd take me around to see the sights. Public transportation was limited so I didn't venture out much without him, other than to work. He'd leave me his car, a kitted-out Ford Mustang, but the engine was super powerful and I was afraid that it might take off on me if I pressed the gas pedal too hard. I'd catch the bus to work. I enjoyed seeing all of the people and, sometimes, even sparking up conversations with them. I would drive the Mustang to the grocery store; a definite exception.

I wasn't trying to lug a bunch of bags on the bus, especially frozen items. It was so hot there, ice cream had become a regular in my diet plan; some diet.

I still planned to become famous, and I often scoured the newspaper ads for possible extra roles for one of the musical shows throughout town. After talking all of that shit, I was now too nervous to actually try. What had happened with Phil and Glenn had fucked up my self-esteem—a little bit.

For now I wanted to concentrate on becoming an adult—really becoming an adult. Even though I was staying with Andy, I only planned on being there temporarily. My pay was shitty but the tips were great; people tipped a lot when they were drunk. They tipped even better when you flirted with them a little and showed some cleavage. A lot of men had tried to fuck me since I'd arrived there, and even though Andy and I had an understanding, I wasn't trying to lie down with anybody. My track record had not been a good one.

Andy had a nice crib. Three bedrooms, two and a half baths, and a nice little patio. I had my own bedroom, but I slept in his room the majority of the time when he was in town. The cool part was that it wasn't mandatory. Andy almost felt like an older brother of sorts. Like so many people, he was trying to survive and have a little fun. Our sex was freaky, interesting, and satisfying, but love was *not* in the cards, and wasn't going to be in the cards.

As I stood out on the patio, watching the cars drive by and killing an hour before I needed to leave for work, I couldn't help but grin.

"You've done it!" I exclaimed. "You've actually done it!"

# Milena

*Five Years Later*

HURRY up, Lydia! Come get into the picture!" I yelled, posing with the group of people at the party.

"I'm coming. Give me a second. I don't walk as fast as I used to." Lydia made her way slowly across the restaurant and joined us.

The photographer yelled out, "Everybody say cheese!"

We all did, and the flash from the camera almost blinded us all.

I felt some hands wrapped around my waist from the back, and a kiss on the curvature of my neck. "You're even more beautiful when you're pregnant."

"Thank you, Hubby." I blushed. "You're not so bad on the eyes yourself."

"Stop it, you two lovebirds," Lydia said. "You've already put one bun in the oven. Pace yourselves."

I laughed. "You have a lot of nerve."

Lydia rubbed her protruding belly and sighed. "This pregnancy nonsense is no joke. Who in this world created this?"

Everyone responded in unison: "God!"

"Well, alrighty then," Lydia said and sat down beside her husband, who was holding their two-year-old daughter, Lydia Jr., on his lap.

Yes, Lydia was so conceited that she'd demanded they use that name. In her opinion, if men could have juniors, so could women.

I went over and sat next to Lydia while my husband went to make sure that my parents didn't need anything. It was a huge double baby shower. Lydia and I were expecting two weeks apart; the second for her, first for me.

Lydia rubbed my belly and leaned over to whisper in my ear, "Looks like we were riding dicks the same night."

"You climb up on that saddle every night. Don't play."

"Yes, you're right, I do." She paused. "You know what the worst part is about having children?"

"What?"

"Having to give up my ciggaweed."

We both laughed.

"Well, you needed to do that anyway. You almost had me caught back up in that nonsense for a minute," I said.

"Milena, that was only for a few months back in 2009. I was hooked for like twenty years." Lydia looked down at her tummy. "But it's all worth it." She glanced up at her husband, who was now showing off Lydia Jr. to the crowd. "Besides, I can't be flying around the globe with weed in my suitcases, and I'm not about to get my head chopped off with a machete on some island trying to cop some weight."

"You still talk like an extra from *New Jack City*," I teased, "but I'm glad you have enough common sense to realize that."

"Can you believe that I'm sitting here talking about flying around the globe?"

"That's amazing. I remember when your biggest goal in life was to get out of Kannapolis." I took her hand. "I'm so proud of you. You've really made something of yourself. The world-famous Lydia Sterling."

"I always told you that I'd be famous. You didn't believe me."

"I believed that you were serious. The difference between you and so many others is that you were determined to make it happen."

"True that."

"You've even stopped cursing, haven't you?"

Lydia laughed. "Well, you know, the kid and all. I can't be setting a bad example for mini-me."

"Don't forget, tomorrow's our day to cook at the shelter," I reminded her.

"I haven't forgotten."

I glanced around the restaurant. "This is amazing! Paparazzi at our baby shower because of your crazy behind."

"Life is full of surprises."

"Don't I know it!"

Lydia had stayed in Tennessee for more than a year before she'd relocated to New York City. She'd saved up her money while she'd been staying with Andy, and then taken the next step in fulfilling her destiny. It is true that what's for you will be for you, no matter what. Finding out that Glenn and Phil had been messing around had been, in my opinion, the best thing that had ever happened to her. She didn't see it that way, but I did. That revelation had served as the catalyst to make her leave, despite what she said. She had kept talking about climbing aboard an Amtrak train and heading north, but saying something and doing it were two different things. Lydia had been afraid to actually do it, but facing the humiliation of everyone in Kannapolis knowing about her mess—even though she'd made fliers in the heat of passion—had been too much. So she'd left with Andy. Then it had become a butterfly effect.

Lydia was actually destined for greatness. Within one month—*one month*—Lydia had been discovered by a producer on Broadway who'd been looking for a "new face" for his upcoming production. It turned out that the producer had won numerous awards. He'd thrown Lydia on the stage, with zero experience, because he'd felt she'd had "the look," and she'd been a natural; like she had always claimed to be.

Jump ahead four years, and Lydia Sterling was an international movie star. Yes, *movie star*. One of the highest-paid female actresses out there, and she had married her costar, another movie star named Donnell Wayford, after they'd fallen in love on the set of *Addicted*. Amazing!

My life had turned out to be pretty amazing as well. Jacour and I had dated for a few months, exclusively, but then I realized that even though he loved me, he still didn't respect me. I'd found out that he was incapable of keeping his dick in his pants. More important, he realized it also and had finally conceded that things simply couldn't work out. He didn't want to subject me to that level of disrespect; I truly appreciated it, because I was finished with allowing it anyway. I'd realized that, at one point, Kannapolis had seemed like a "hot box," a baseball drill where players take turns being fielders and runners and trying to tag one another out. It had seemed like everybody had been fucking everybody, but that hadn't been the game that I'd wanted to play.

I still had my veterinary practice, but after seeing so many people suffering in that homeless village, I had to do something. When Jacour had decided to leave town for good, I asked him if I could purchase the haunted house and turn it into a shelter. He sold it to me for a dollar.

I looked over at my husband. He seemed so happy to be with me. I adored being with him. We'd run into each other at Starbucks. He'd been sitting there working on his laptop when I'd come in to purchase a Venti hot chocolate. I'd stared at him while I'd waited in line, debating about whether or not to approach his table. He'd seemed so peaceful, caught up in his work like a true professional black man.

Thank goodness that I'd found the nerve to walk over to him. That decision had changed everything. *He* had changed everything. But, then again, he had already done that long before that day.

I stood up, walked over to the table where my husband and parents were sitting, and sat down on Yosef's lap.

"Are you all right?" he asked, rubbing my belly, which was carrying his son.

"I'm perfect," I said, burying my tongue in his mouth.

# Commentary by Zane

I HAVE a theory about life. It is my opinion that women are still seriously undervalued in today's society. However, the blame does not reside completely with men—unfortunately. In many ways, a lot of women have still been brainwashed into believing that men are the dominant sex. What does that have to do with *The Hot Box*? A lot, actually. My core audience will read this book and understand where I am coming from with it. They understand that I always have a purpose behind whatever I write. Others—the critics who spend their time reading it when, on any given day, they have thousands of other options in reading material—will say that my books are too sexually graphic and lack substance. Yes, the two women in this novel were both sleeping with two men at a time . . . but is that really a crime?

Low self-esteem translates into several things: subjecting oneself to abuse, both verbal and physical; believing that you cannot accomplish your dreams; and allowing others to dictate how you live your life. It never ceases to amaze me that people feel more comfortable witnessing others go through all of those scenarios, seemingly prefer it even, but take issue when women openly embrace their desires—when it comes to overall life, but *especially* when it comes to their sexuality. They will watch and read about women being raped, tortured, demeaned, or chastised but cringe when women take control of a single situation. That is truly sad but a sign of the double standards that exist.

My goal in life is simple: I want to make as many women feel good about themselves, and embrace their talents, their visions, and their minds, as I possibly can. I use sexuality in my writing for three reasons. First, sexuality is a normal part of life. No matter how much a woman is told that she will go to hell if she does this or that, or how many times her parents try to convince her that she should abstain outside of marriage, she will have natural sexual desires and needs. That is nothing to be ashamed of, and I am certainly not ashamed to be writing about it. Second, sexuality is the area in most women's lives that they feel the least comfortable opening up about. I believe that if I can make them feel liberated in that area, the same liberation and feeling of empowerment will trickle over into other aspects of their lives. Third, I use sexuality in my writing as a segue into much deeper societal issues. Most people would not purchase and read a nonfiction book about sexual addiction, domestic violence, drug addiction, homelessness, health care reform, incest, unwanted pregnancy, mental illness, narcissism, self-esteem development, death, or emotional healing after a failed relationship. What do all of those topics have in common? They belong to the shorter version of a much longer list of subjects that I have covered in my books. Utilizing drama and humor makes the lessons of life much more entertaining. Getting the true point across is what really matters. The amount of sex, or lack thereof, in my writing is not systematic. It is strictly based on the characters and is not intended to be any more descriptive than any of the other topics. I am a very detailed and graphic writer, *period*, so I refuse to tone that aspect of my imagination down when it comes to the sex. Why should I?

So what are the lessons of life that I was trying to get across in this book? That's a deep question, but, as with all of my books, I can easily answer it. Whenever I pen a story, I begin by spending a tremendous amount of time developing the characters. It is all about the characters. Who they are, where they come from, what they desire, and, more important, what their flaws are. No one is perfect, yet a lot of books are written about seemingly perfect people. You will never find that in mine. All of my characters have issues, some of them very serious ones, but that is essential because my readers have issues, too. I want my characters to spark thought, to reignite memories, to inspire hope, and to encourage proactivity. I want my readers to understand that faith makes everything possible, but rarely easy. I adore all of my characters. Throughout the periods of time that I am writing them, they become an integral part of my existence. It is almost like they are walking around with me, eating dinner at the kitchen table with the family, and watching my favorite television shows beside me. That is because they are always on my mind. I am constantly playing out a movie about them in my mind until the last word has been written, whether I am writing a short story, a novel, or a script.

The characters in *The Hot Box* all have a special place in my heart. I am going to spend a little time going over each of them for a couple of reasons. I want you to understand who they are and what makes them tick. I also want to help some of you who might be out there aspiring to become a published writer, or those who often ask me where I come up with my material. So, for those who would like to know those things, read on.

Milena Clark is the protagonist in this story, a.k.a. "the main character." The main character is the one who moves the story forward. She does something, endures something, or says something that causes the other characters to react. The exceptions to that have been few and far between, such as the case with the story

"Cinderella." Cinderella is often referred to by writers as the worst main character in history because she did absolutely nothing to move her own story forward. Her evil stepmother and evil stepsisters, her fairy godmother, and the prince did all of the work.

In this case Milena is a young woman who resides in a small, Southern town; she has limited her existence to taking care of animals and communicating with her best friend, Lydia, and her parents. She is completely embarrassed about Jacour cheating on her and decides that she is never going to be put through that again. So she lets herself go and stops caring about her appearance in the hopes that no men will even attempt to date her. After eight years of this self-imposed solitude, due to the need to save face in front of Jacour, she finds herself actually looking for a man, instead of hiding from them. Her self-esteem is low, and, up until that moment, she had been perfectly content to be miserable. After she meets Yosef, she begins to open up and discover that she is actually capable of feeling feminine and special. She also realizes that her sexual needs have suffered because she decided to punish all men by withholding her sex and her heart. In the end, she is the one who has lost so much valuable time. Time that she can never get back. Know anyone like that? Someone who was so busy proving a point that they harmed themselves instead while the other person was living lovely?

Lydia Sterling hates her life but loves the hell out of herself. In her mind, she is the perfect female—beautiful, sexy, street smart, talented, and intriguing—trapped in an imperfect world. Her only desire in life is to get the hell out of a place where most people have lost hope because of the economy and see the "real world." Since she cannot make that happen immediately, she decides to drown her sorrows in her marijuana and sex life. She believes that she has both Phil and Glenn wrapped around her finger. Even though all she ever talks about is escaping that life, she never does it; never takes a chance. That is, until the shame of finding out that she is not all that she thinks she is hits her in the face. If that had never happened, Lydia never would have stepped outside of her comfort zone. To this day, she would still be working part-time at the grocery store for her uncle Joe and growing her marijuana out in the woods. She would still be defining herself by her sexuality instead of her brains. But once she was "forced" to take a chance, that decision catapulted her to her actual destiny—international stardom. How many people do you know who are so trapped in a comfort zone that, odds are, they will never pursue their real dreams unless they are fired, or forced to move on for some other reason? How many women do you know who believe that they are defined by the men in their lives? Or women who are convinced that their sex is so much better than others but they are actually delusional?

Jacour Bryant has it all—*supposedly*. He is handsome, wealthy, famous, and women are constantly falling at his feet. He has escaped the small-town life by being a gifted ballplayer and has lived a life that most men would cut off their right arms for. But it is not enough to make him happy. He truly loves Milena and regrets cheating on her, but his smaller head overruled his big head. In fact, that happens all the time. He only wants to get her back and prove that he does not want a large quantity of women; only one quality one. He is convinced that Milena still loves him and that her heart belongs to him. But Jacour is also very competitive, and his determination becomes a combination of loving her and wanting to conquer her. Once he does get her back, he still does not have it within him to be monogamous. They both realize his issue, and, instead of continuing to hurt Milena, he resigns himself to playing the field and never settling down, even if settling down would bring him true happiness. How many men do you know who have risked the love of a good woman because they feel that they need to be involved in sexual relationships with several women, or it would mean that they are not real men?

Yosef Sampson believes that manhood is based on the ability to provide. He is depressed that he has become homeless. Yet he has no regrets. If it had to happen, it happened for the best reason possible: love. He willingly sacrificed the roof over his head, and his dignity, to make sure that his wife, June, did not suffer from pain in her last days on earth. Once out on the street, he realized that he had become someone that the world was ashamed of, one of the people that society had tossed away. Stuck because he cannot get a job without an address or a telephone number, too embarrassed to let his relatives in Boston know what has become of him, and too proud to ask them for help, he decides to accept his fate. But then he meets Milena, who is like an injured bird that needs to be mended. He instantly falls for her, and, in order to become the man that she needs, he is willing to pick himself up out of the ashes and try to improve his life. Do you know anyone who has given up on life because their existence seems too bleak to ever improve?

Glenn and Phil are two men totally confused about who they are, but for different reasons. Glenn has always been a homosexual but refuses to admit it. So he has sex with women and even moves Lydia in to "cover up" who he really is. He insists on being in control in the bedroom with her because it helps him avoid the fact that he actually craves being dominated by a man. He does not get into the freaky stuff or dirty talk that Lydia craves; even though he can put on certain pretenses and anatomically perform, he can carry his pretenses only so far. Everyone regards him as the pillar of honesty, but he is anything but. He is a master manipulator. He keeps his real love close by: Phil. Phil does not want to face the fact that he likes to sleep with men. He wants to be completely straight and he does love Lydia, but that does not stop him from doing what Glenn wants. Phil thinks that if he can get away from Glenn by running away with Lydia to New York, everything will change.

I purposefully did not say what Glenn and Phil were up to five years later. I want you, the reader, to ponder that thought. Do you think that Phil left town in shame? Do you think that Phil moved in with Glenn and they transitioned into an open, gay relationship without caring what people thought? Do you think that they are still having their sexual trysts on the down low and both still dating women, even though they were outed? Do you think the women in the town care that they might be homosexual? How many people do you know who have gone through something similar? How many women do you know who suspect their men—even their husbands—might enjoy the company of men more than women?

I want my characters to make you think. I hope that the ones in *The Hot Box* have, as well as their situations. I was shocked to discover many things when I was doing the research for this book. There are some medications that cost as much as $400,000 a year that are not covered by any insurance plan. According to CNN, a study conducted by Family USA in early 2009 found that 86.9 million people in this country were uninsured for their health. Four out of five of them were from working families. According to the National Coalition for the Homeless, a study conducted by the National Law Center on Homelessness & Poverty concluded that 3.5 million people, 1.3 of them being children, are likely to experience homelessness in any given year. Those statistics are sickening when you consider that the wars in Afghanistan and Iraq have cost Americans more than a *trillion* dollars over the past decades, not to mention thousands of lives. I doubt that I am the only one who has a serious problem with this picture. There are millions of people suffering the same plight as Yosef, and, unless there is an overall improvement in the economy *soon*, those numbers are destined to increase. The next time you see someone panhandling or begging for assistance, if you can do something, do it.

So many people feel uneasy when approached, or assume the person asking is pulling a scam. I am not saying that it never happens, but I certainly do not believe that is the norm. I gave a woman ten dollars in the eatery at Union Station one day. She said that she wanted to purchase a meal to take back to her homeless shelter. I was sitting there—reading a book, of course—and noticed her still hitting other people up an hour later. Sure, I could have been angry, but I was not. I did what I felt was right, and if she was doing the wrong thing, she was the one who would suffer from the repercussions. Another time, an older woman approached me in a parking lot and said that she was going to swallow her pride and ask me for gas money. She could not afford gas to get home. I handed her a twenty-dollar bill. If not for the grace of God, that could have been my mother, or grandmother. My giving stems from a life-altering experience that I had more than twenty years ago in New York City. I was visiting with a friend from college and we were in Grand Central Station on one of the coldest nights that I could remember in my life. There were old abandoned tracks, and, as we walked past them, I saw people lying on them for as far as I could see. Men, women, children, babies. It broke my heart, because, until then, I'd had the wrong impression of the homeless. I was wearing a pair of penny loafers—you remember the ones where people actually would put a penny into the slot to be cute—until we arrived at our destination, where I could put on my high heels. I took them off and handed them to someone who needed them a lot more than I did. That experience changed me forever. I do not mean to preach, so I will end by saying, if you can help, do. If you need help, ask.

Now you know what *The Hot Box* is really about. So the next time that someone says, "Zane's not a real writer. Zane only writes about sex. Zane this and Zane that . . . blah, blah, blah," maybe they can explain to you what their own writing is about. There are many who feel that I should "reinvent" myself and be more straightlaced so I can increase my brand potential. I am not concerned with that, nor do I hide the fact that I believe that if women are going to be sexually active in this life—and most of us are—then we should not walk away from the experiences any less satisfied than the men. But don't simply make love; make it count. Please practice safe sex and remember that every time a woman has sex with a new partner, she increases her risk of contracting HPV by 15 percent and that women are the fastest-growing group of people contracting HIV. The women in my books are not meant to serve as role models or to encourage you to be promiscuous; I have stated that from day one. Their purpose is to shed light on how some women think. Many of them are the type of woman that a lot of females would be if they did not fear being judged, if they had no responsibilities, and if sexually transmitted diseases did not exist. While I do not believe that anyone should fear being judged, I do feel it irresponsible to risk your life. So always, always protect yourself and be selective in who you choose to allow inside of your temple. For when they leave, and most will, a part of them will remain inside that temple forever. Remember that, and remember that I love and appreciate you all.

Please check out some of the dozens of other authors that I publish on www.zanestore.com. If you want to read more books similar to mine, please read all of the titles by my protégée, Allison

Hobbs: *Pandora's Box, Insatiable, The Climax, One Taste, A Bona Fide Gold Digger, Pure Paradise, The Enchantress, The Sorceress, Dangerously in Love, Double Dippin', Big Juicy Lips: Double Dippin' 2, Disciplined: An Invitation Erotic Odyssey,* and *Stealing Candy.* Her upcoming titles include *Lipstick Hustla* and *Put a Ring on It.* If you have been sleeping on her, wake up. Allison Hobbs is the only woman on the planet freakier than me, but she is also a phenomenal storyteller.

If you are looking for me on the web, my personal website is www.eroticanoir.com, and my online social network for all of the "Zaniacs" is www.planetzane.org. You can find me on Twitter and MySpace as "PlanetZane," and on Facebook as "Zane Strebor." My online store is www.zanestore.com, and you can find out information about Zane-inspired music at www.zanemusicgroup.com.

*Zane's Sex Chronicles,* my original series on Cinemax, has recently completed its second season. The first season is available on DVD from Zanestore, Amazon, HBO, Netflix, or Blockbuster. I am so pleased that the viewers were so caught up in the characters. Ninety percent of the comments are about the lives of the characters and not the sex scenes, although those are beautiful and natural as well. Thanks for helping me prove that an erotic series can be engaging and thought provoking.

Zane's Boudoir, my new company that will reinvent sensuality and style one body at a time, is proud to present THE HOT BOX COLLECTION, the first in many lines of lingerie to spice up your life. Find out more information at: www.zanesboudoir.com.

Thanks for reading this.

With much love and appreciation,
*Zane*

**Readers Club Guide**

# THE HOT BOX

## by Zane

1. Do you make assumptions about homeless people when you see them, or do you realize that anyone could find themselves in that situation?

2. Do you think that Lydia did the right thing by telling everyone about Phil and Glenn being lovers?

3. Do you think Lydia or Milena was the more intriguing female character? What were the differences and commonalities between them?

4. Would you have picked Jacour over Yosef because of his wealth? Do you think that money can truly ensure happiness?

5. Would you ever become involved with someone who was down on their luck? If you have, do you regret it?

6. If you live in a small town, do you wish that you lived in a big city? If you live in a big city, do you wish that you lived in a small town? Why or why not?

7. Do you feel like the recession has been more distressing for people in rural areas or urban areas?

8. Do you believe that either Phil or Glenn really loved Lydia? Why or why not?

9. Do you think it was wise for Lydia to run off to Tennessee with Andy? Why or why not?

10. Is there something that you have always wanted to do but have refrained from trying because of either fear of failure or fear of success?

11. Who was your overall favorite character in the book? Why?

12. Do you spend any time doing volunteer work? Why or why not?

# ZANE'S
## SEX CHRONICLES

The Cinemax® Original Series
Based on Zane's
Best-Selling Books.

## Available on DVD

**ATRIA BOOKS**
A Division of Simon & Schuster
A CBS COMPANY

4000021878